Max Brod

Jewish Women

Max Brod

Jewish Women

Translated from the German by Julia Rivers

Aspal Vintage

Published in Great Britain in 2020 by Aspal Vintage
an imprint of Aspal Press Limited
1 Quality Court, Chancery Lane, London WC2A 1HR

Originally published in German in 1911 as 'Jüdinnen'
Copyright © The National Library of Israel

This English translation copyright © 2019 Aspal Press Limited by
arrangement with the National Library of Israel

All rights reserved. No part of this publication may be reproduced
stored in a retrieval system, or transmitted, in any form or by any
means, without the prior permission in writing of the publisher or as
expressly permitted by law.

A catalogue record for this book is available from the British Library

ISBN 978-0-9957167-7-3

Printed in Great Britain by Clays Ltd, Elcograf S.p.A

www.aspalpress.uk

Contents

Introduction	1
Irene	7
Hugo	27
The Manor House	39
The Ascent	53
Frau Lucie	63
The Tennis Court	71
The Bowling Game	91
Gretl	109
The Snake Dance	119
Visiting the sick	135
The Public Meeting	159
Olga	187
Little Elsa	205
Eichwald	211
Departure	227
Notes	245

Introduction

by Benjamin Balint

The book you are about to read, besides affording a glimpse of flourishing Central European Jewish life in the early twentieth century, provoked one of the earliest debates of a question that has grown more contentious ever since: what is a 'Jewish' novel?

In March 1911, the unknown writer Franz Kafka reflected at length in his diary about his friend and mentor Max Brod's new novel, *Jewish Women* (*Jüdinnen*), a book set in the pre-First World War untroubled terrain of the resort-town Teplitz (Teplice), not far from the Czech-German border, among respectable assimilated Jewish families on summer holiday.[1] Brod, then 26 years old, and still basking in the success of his first novel, *Schloß Nornepygge* (1908), was already well on his way to literary acclaim. Along with Gustav Meyrink and Rainer Maria Rilke, he would become one of the best-known representatives of Prague's German-language literature.

From now until his death in Tel Aviv in 1968, Brod would prove as prolific (to the point of graphomania) as Kafka was not. His published work would run to almost ninety titles – twenty novels, religious treatises, polemical broadsides, plays (including on the biblical heroes Queen Esther and King Saul), essays, translations, librettos and biographies. Brod was also just then negotiating his Jewish identity, in the wake of encounters in Prague with the Zionist thinkers Hugo Bergmann and Martin Buber. After the First World War, Brod would play a central role in the Czech Zionist movement and as a mediator between the Czech and German cultures.[2]

Jewish Women met with immediate success. It was reprinted four times within five weeks of its publication. A decade after its appearance, Brod ranked it among his best early work, 'because in it I seem to have managed to ascend from the everyday to the heroic sphere'.[3]

In his journal, Kafka dissents from Brod's characteristically contented self-evaluation. He ascribes the novel's main flaw not to the pathos of its style (as did the Viennese satirist Karl Kraus) or the lack of distance between its author and characters (as did the German-Jewish essayist Kurt Hiller) but to its claustral, self-enclosed treatment of 'the Jewish question':

In Western European stories, as soon as they even begin to include any groups of Jews, we are now almost used immediately to hunting for and finding under or over the plot the solution to the Jewish question too. In [Brod's] *Jüdinnen*, however, no such solution is indicated, indeed not even conjectured, for just those characters who busy themselves with such questions stand farthest from the center of the story at a point where events are already revolving more rapidly ... Offhand, we recognize in this a fault in the story, and feel ourselves all the more entitled to such a criticism because today, since Zionism came into being, the possibilities for a solution stand so clearly marshaled about the Jewish problem that the writer would have had to take only a few last steps in order to find the possibility of a solution suitable to his story.

This fault, however, has still another origin. *Jüdinnen* lacks non-Jewish observers, the respectable contrasting persons who in other stories draw out the Jewishness so that it advances toward them in amazement, doubt, envy, fear, and finally, finally is transformed into self-confidence, but in any event can draw itself up to its full height only before them ... In the same way, too, the convulsive starting up of a lizard under our feet on a footpath in Italy delights us greatly, again and again we are moved to bow down, but if we see them at a dealer's by hundreds crawling over one another in confusion in the large bottles in which otherwise pickles are usually packed, then we don't know what to do.[4]

As so often in Kafka's world, metaphor precedes reality. Some five months later, on a trip to Italy with Brod, Kafka records in his travel diary: 'Shivery feeling at the sight of lizards wriggling on a wall.'

Picking up where this strange metaphor leaves off, Nadine Gordimer imagines an accusatory letter from Hermann Kafka to his son Franz:

When your great friend Brod wrote a book called *The Jewesses* you wrote there were too many of them in it. You saw them like lizards. (Animals again, low animals.) ... From where did you get such ideas? Not from your home, that I know.[5]

In the tradition of the 'seaside novel' inaugurated by Jane Austen (as in her unfinished novel *Sanditon*), *Jewish Women*

tells of 'two wounded hearts', Hugo and Irene, who meet on summer holiday 'under the veil of a secret'. His secret: a failed school examination. Hers: a broken engagement.

Hugo, a sensitive and sentimental high-school student, is susceptible to infatuation. His 'soft heart' rises and falls as he feels favoured or rejected by women. Though sometimes pretending to indifference, he rests his self-worth on the acknowledgment of women. 'Yes, yes, I confess that I couldn't live without women. Life seems worthless and dark without them ... Women are better and more perfect than men in every way ... That belief is the very foundation of my life.'

Here as elsewhere, Hugo speaks in his creator's voice. 'For me,' Brod once told Kafka, 'the world takes on meaning only through the medium of a woman.' Brod often hailed the redemptive power of women. 'Of all God's messengers,' Brod wrote, 'Eros speaks to us most forcefully.'[6]

At first, Hugo admires Irene's 'feminine obstinacy' and 'the charm of her feminine illogicality'. Later, fearing his love has been premature, he grows annoyed with her 'caustic, calculated eroticism'. By the end, he sees 'in her faults and weaknesses the sad fate of girls, particularly Jewish ones, who had been brought up with no other purpose in mind than marriage'. (Brod himself would describe this novel as 'a vehement satire against the type of the "educated" average Jewish woman'.[7])

Hugo, like his author, 'felt himself to be strongly Jewish but yet not excluded from the nobler feelings of mankind in general'. Brod sharply contrasts his young protagonist with Irene's brother Alfred, one of the tangential characters who in Kafka's estimation come closest to addressing the 'Jewish question' even as they 'stand farthest from the center of the story'. Alfred, an admirer of Richard Wagner, has read the misogynist and self-hating Austrian Jew Otto Weininger (a convert to Christianity who despised Judaism as feminine and weak) in the worst of ways: superficially but 'with enthusiasm'.[8] Hugo describes Alfred as 'one of those young Jewish men who have a strong leaning towards the Aryan and find everything Jewish to be contemptible'.

Who would prove better braced for the coming cataclysm: Hugo or Alfred?

Brod's experience of the First World War had awakened him not only to the tenuous position of Prague's Jews but also to the realisation that politics cannot be wished away. 'We were an over-indulged generation,' Brod recalled in his memoir. 'Debates about Richard Wagner's music, the foundations of Judaism and Christianity, impressionist painting, etc. seemed far more important. And now this peace had suddenly come to an end, overnight. Never has a generation been so brutally trampled by the facts.'

In March 1939, when Hugo would have been 45 years old, Max Brod, 54, stood at platform 2 of Prague's Wilson Station with British immigration visas to Palestine in his coat pocket and Kafka's unfinished manuscripts in his cracked-leather suitcase. That morning, he had watched columns of Nazi youth marching four abreast down Prague's main avenues chanting '*Sieg Heil!*' Max and his wife Elsa boarded the train not knowing that it would be the last permitted to leave. The train scraped through countryside just occupied by the Wehrmacht, at last pulling into Ostrava on the Czech-Polish frontier. When the train came to a halt, Brod peered out from his compartment and stared at a motionless German soldier guarding the platform. He looked 'like the statue of a Roman legionnaire,' Brod said. 'Truth be told, he was rather beautiful.' Brod noticed that his legionnaire was not alone; the tracks were lined with fully armed Wehrmacht soldiers. 'It's hard to say why this sight caused me no fear,' Brod recalled. 'I think it was because I was so tired, so sleepless, and had thought I was still dreaming. And because the young soldier standing closest to me was such a beautiful specimen. This was always my weakness: beauty, in any form, always aroused my wonderment, and has more than once in my life brought me to the very edge of total disaster.'

'A quiet whistle was followed by the small jolt that almost unnoticed starts the train moving, and yet, like the deepest cut, separates the present from the future.' It is impossible to read this scene from the end of *Jewish Women* without calling Brod's departure to mind, indeed without wondering whether Brod's own life might serve as the ideal epilogue to this valuable novel.

Benjamin Balint, a writer living in Jerusalem, is the author of *Kafka's Last Trial* (Picador, 2019).

Irene

Overcome with a feeling of melancholy, Hugo wandered down the woodland path. As he rounded a bend an unexpected sight brought his footsteps to a halt.

A woman dressed in white lay flat upon the ground. She was face down with her head on her outstretched arms. Another woman, dressed in dark clothes, and a man were apparently attending to her. The woman seemed the more concerned and was vigorously fanning the face of the prostrate figure with her hands, all the while speaking rapidly and unintelligibly. The man was wearing a tailcoat but was bare-headed, and looked like a waiter. On closer inspection he appeared to be just standing there rather than helping, and after a moment started speaking to the prone woman in a way that sounded threatening. Hugo stood there, uncertain whether to intervene or not. Suddenly the elderly lady turned round and called, 'Help, help!' in a faint despairing voice as if appealing to someone far off. In an instant Hugo was at her side.

'What is going on? May I be of assistance?'

Jewish Women

Immediately the woman in white raised her head from the ground. She was young, with blonde locks tumbling around her face like a ruffled garland. 'Save me, protect us!' she sobbed, and put up a trembling hand to her hair.

Hugo looked at her and then turned to the older woman. She seemed relieved by these signs of animation and, without saying anything more to him, took the young woman's face between her hands and covered it with kisses.

Ignored by the two women, who in all the excitement were intent only on one another, Hugo approached the waiter. Perhaps this man could tell him what was going on. 'What has happened?' he asked.

'Oh, nothing. Please ... I only wanted ... the bill came to one Krone more ... I gave the wrong change.'

From her mother's arms, the young woman gave Hugo a pleading look. He had only a moment ago found out what had caused this scene, and found himself at a loss for a suitable response. Once her daughter was back on her feet the mother began to cry, as if she had been suppressing the tears until that moment. Now she was the one in need of help, and was being supported by the young woman. 'Quick, quick!' they both cried. Hugo was taken aback, but reached into his pocket, took a Krone from his purse and handed it to the waiter. With a small formal bow, he took the money and quickly disappeared among the trees.

The young man took off his hat and politely acknowledged the two women for the first time.

'He's gone, Mama. He's gone away. Thank you, sir.'

'But I have no idea ...'

'You have saved me.'

'You are so hysterical,' the girl's mother observed in a

critical tone and immediately stopped crying. 'One never knows with you ... Sir, you have found us in an unusual situation ... This is all your fault, Irene ... I beg you to excuse us, sir.'

'Please, it was the least I could do ...'

Hugo was alarmed. He had been on the point of saying a few modest words of acknowledgement when he was stopped by a strange glance from Irene. The look she gave him was suddenly cool and calculating, with something cunning and maybe even mocking about it. 'Would our knight in shining armour like to walk with us a little?' Suddenly he found himself being measured, assessed and evaluated. He felt the need to say something assertive.

But Irene, by now walking next to him, was deftly pinning on her hat while smiling at him and saying: 'It would be only good manners to introduce ourselves properly, wouldn't it? My name is Irene Popper, and this is my mother ... and you, Sir Knight?'

'Hugo Rosenthal.'

'You're a *Gymnasium*[9] student, aren't you?'

'Yes.' He looked at her in surprise, though he supposed she must have realised that after noticing the schoolbooks he was carrying. But why did her tone seem vaguely reproachful? Or was she perhaps laughing at him? She spoke as though correcting mistakes he had made, though without attaching any particular significance to them. All his self-satisfaction disappeared in an instant. Instead, he wondered if he had been clumsy. Perhaps he should have introduced himself first. Until that moment he believed he had acted chivalrously. Who would ever imagine, seeing this elegant young lady, that only moments before she had been lying prostrate on the grass.

'We have become acquainted in such very special circumstances,' she continued, smiling calmly at him, 'that I feel we can manage without the usual formalities. You seem to be expecting an explanation …'

Hugo said nothing, by now completely intimidated.

'Don't be embarrassed, you have every right to it.' She put her hand into her small bag. 'I believe that you paid something on our behalf. I was so overcome …'

'Believe me, there was nothing to it,' interposed her mother, walking close behind them. 'The waiter followed us to ask for additional payment, nothing more. But Irene had been so nervous the whole afternoon that, as soon as she saw him, she fainted.'

'So the young lady …'

'My mother is ever the diplomat,' the daughter said to him in a confiding manner. 'What you haven't explained, Mama,' she said, turning around to her, 'is *why* I was so nervous the whole afternoon. Perhaps you didn't even notice that the man was continually staring at me while we sat in the clubhouse, and that he tried to press my hand when we paid.'

'Pure imagination.'

'That he followed us and, in this lonely place, suddenly screamed at me.'

'You screamed, not him.'

'That's how mothers are,' said Irene, speaking only to Hugo. Her own seemed to have calmed down by now and, apparently used to being ignored, lagged some distance behind. 'They see nothing, hear nothing, but when it comes to their daughters getting married, there they are, eyes peeled, taking in simply everything. Oh, God!' she sighed and gave a look of resignation.

'We will never really know ...' he said, trying to mediate.

She seemed immediately offended and said: 'If you don't believe me ...' But then she thought better of it. 'Anyway, I have no real reason to be proud of that particular conquest, have I?' She gave a wry smile. One half of her mouth curled upward, while the other seemed to move in the opposite direction. It wasn't exactly an expression of contempt, but nevertheless there was something equivocal, reserved, about it – something that seemed to smile at the act of smiling. Or as if Irene was smiling about something completely different from what one would expect, as if she wished to signal with a certain degree of pride: 'If only you knew what I was really smiling about! That's not so simple, not something I'd share with you.' It was also strange that when she smiled she didn't open her mouth, didn't show her teeth, but kept her lips pressed together so that they seemed thinner and paler than ever. Watching her, Hugo was completely captivated. She continued, 'After listening to my mother, you must think me rather strange.'

'No ... not at all. Please, I assure you ...'

She interrupted him with: 'No, no. That's perfectly all right. I must seem peculiar to everyone. The reason why is quite simple, though: it's because I am. Or rather, because I'm not. Perhaps I am quite ordinary. Or, at least, I would like to be. But my fate is so strange. I live by secrets ... experiences. I must feel something every day. I don't want it to be like that. I have had enough of it. But nothing helps. It just happens, forces itself upon me ...'

Hugo had never heard a girl speak like that before. A plethora of vague, half-formed ideas overcame him then. Previously girls to him were stupid pale creatures, to whom one brought flowers in the dance hall or told jokes on the tennis courts, whose slightest needs one had to accommodate and facilitate. And now ... this one was talking to him just like a clever man would. One could speak to her perfectly sensibly, about anything that one wanted to, it seemed. He was by nature inclined to be emotional, and now he was gripped by a feeling of intense admiration for the woman next to him; it seemed to him impossible to foresee how far this meeting would affect his life. In any event he was sure of one thing: what he had previously found arrogant in her manner, he now found entirely justified. Such an outstanding person ... he would have dearly liked to have said all that to her immediately, but was reluctant to use the word 'arrogant' and in the heat of the moment could not think of anything milder. Gripped by a feeling of excitement, he opened up his heart to her: 'Oh, I understand you when you speak of secrets ... I know what that means, having a secret.'

'In my case there is no longer anything normal in my life,' she continued with a pained turning down of her mouth; and that turning down had something of the previous smile and the previous smile had something of the turning down. 'And the worst of it is that everything is governed by a secret, everything goes back to that ... even if I don't immediately see the connection, I am convinced that there is some connection to the same old thing. My whole life takes its character, its strange outward appearance, from that one thing. So for example, that stupid business with the besotted waiter today, believe me, I wouldn't be surprised for a moment if that also had something to do with my secret ... no, not just surprised, I'm convinced of it.'

'You are so right, Fräulein,' said Hugo in sincere admiration. 'I can sympathise entirely with you ... even if I haven't yet expressed my feelings in words. In fact, I too have a secret.' He hoped that she would ask him for more details.

But instead she turned to him with a peculiar glint in her light grey eyes: 'You too?' She was almost a head taller than him, and he told himself that perhaps the rather unpleasantly arrogant way in which she seemed to look at him was caused only by their difference in height. 'You're still very young, aren't you?'

'In the seventh grade.'

'I could have guessed that.'

'It's not so bad.' He tried to echo her dismissive tone. 'I am not actually at a *Gymnasium*, as you guessed a moment ago, but at a *Realgymnasium*[10] ...'

'Oh. What is that then?' She listened attentively while he explained it to her. Joy rose up in him once more. What a fantastic girl! He had never before been able to speak to one so freely. In order not to bore her, he hurriedly scrambled everything together in three sentences – his upbringing, his ambitions, his ideals.

'That is unusual,' she acknowledged.

'Why unusual? Do you really think so?'

'Well, a *Realgymnasium* is something unusual. At least, it is not as commonplace as a *Realschule* or a *Gymnasium*.' Hugo had always taken a matter-of-fact approach to his own daily life and that thought had never before occurred to him. Even now it seemed superficial and of little importance, but nonetheless interesting. He dared to express a mild reproach. Not from his own inclination, since he would have preferred only to have praised her, but primarily to imitate her direct way of speaking. To his surprise she almost completely ignored what he had said, but responded with, 'So we are well suited. There is something unusual about both of us. And you too have a secret?'

He smiled: 'It's difficult to answer such a question – don't you think? It's another matter if one raises the subject oneself.' He felt a sudden urge, unusual for him, to split hairs and quibble over the slightest detail.

'Everything with you is so complicated and difficult to explain ... you *Realgymnasiast*!'

He quickly glanced into her face. Was she mocking him? But no, she looked at him benignly, and with a certain pleasure it seemed. 'I will call you *Realgymnasiast* ... to myself. That's nice. It expresses everything about you, everything special.'

'But as I have already said, I don't find it particularly special, being a *Realgymnasiast*.' He laughed out loud at the thought and said, 'There are so many other students in my school.'

'That doesn't matter. Don't you understand? It sounds special to me. It's all about my impression of you. I am in the habit of making up my own catchwords. Minting new coins,' she said as if quoting. Then suddenly she stretched out her hand to him, saying: 'I am happy to have found you.'

His face flushed. Confused, he said: 'And in such a special way too!' and put out his own hand. But she pushed it away. '*Pfui*, what an ugly word that is ... special ... how I hate it!' She suddenly and tyrannically demanded a response from him by seizing his hand despite her earlier rejection. 'Must one always have that word in one's mouth ... always be mentioning it? Let's just be happy!' And then she smiled widely and her eyes shone with friendliness. He squeezed her fingers joyfully. She quickly withdrew her hand which was cool and narrow, like a fish.

Now the mother took a few quick steps forward and

intervened, saying: 'So where are we actually going?' The two women stood still and looked down into the valley from the edge of the Königshöhe, which they had reached. 'I don't know where you ladies would like to go?' asked Hugo.

'Back to Teplitz obviously. We are staying in the Manor House. Do you know it?'

'I live in Teplitz.'

'Really? So you're not a spa guest? I thought you were.' The young lady laughed loudly and puffed out her narrow chest as though she were coughing. 'A *Realgymnasiast* who lives in Teplitz ...'

'Is that special too?' he asked anxiously.

'Would you have the goodness,' said the mother earnestly, 'to show us the shortest way down? They will be waiting for us, Irene.'

Hugo turned to the mother. It was a relief to him to be able to speak without feeling under pressure and he did not try to express himself too briefly: 'We are wonderfully lost. We have made a splendid detour. We really can't go down that way. That's entirely the wrong direction – to Prasseditz.'

'To Prasseditz,' said Irene, almost jubilantly. 'Enough, enough ... you have proved that you are a real Teplitzer ... let's go.'

'Is that so terrible?' Hugo said, looking at her in annoyance now.

'What are you talking about now, Irene,' warned her mother, who reluctantly joined in the conversation, perhaps feeling she had a duty to because she was standing there.

Irene didn't hear her. She went on in a joking tone: 'So you will know the Weils and the Kappers. They are my relations, real Teplitzers ...'

'I have some acquaintance with them ...'

'At the end of the day we are possibly related. You know how it goes: "Our cow has grazed in your meadow ..." When two Jews meet, they will find out within ten minutes that they are related to one another.' And she began to imitate one of those conversations: 'So my mother was born a Bondy ...'

Her own mother's attention was immediately caught by the turn the conversation was taking and she said eagerly, 'So your name is Rosenthal? Perhaps the Rosenthal in Laun, who has a big business in hops, is your brother ...'

'My brother died a long time ago.'

'I beg your pardon.'

Irene quickly changed the subject. 'The people who live in Teplitz are insufferable, particularly the women. My cousins, for example. At the moment I don't have anything to say against the men. But the women wear clothes from Vienna, and Paris. Everything must be *à la Grossstadt*[11] – the whole of Teplitz is *à la Grossstadt*. That's the word I hear there all the time. Nice, isn't it? About the splendour of the Theatre Café. Or the telephone connections, the cars, the theatre ... *à la Grossstadt*. So that the women can telephone each other and say what they are cooking for the midday meal. They drive in their cars to take a book from the lending library. But actually things here aren't really the same as in the *Grossstadt*.' She shook her head, an ironic expression on her face.

To his own surprise, Hugo anxiously tried to defend himself saying, 'I am only at home during the holidays. I study in Prague. There is no *Realgymnasium* in Teplitz ...'

'Look, your good nature comes from your being a *Realgymnasiast*. I could tell that straight away.' Hugo noticed that Irene's air of self-confidence served her well. As she spoke she stood up straighter. Her weak spine was otherwise inclined to curve, as if her joints were giving way. As her mother had once again discreetly withdrawn, and the conversation had turned away from ordinary matters, he could observe her from the side without drawing attention to himself. It seemed she was not as young as he'd first thought, probably around twenty-five. Her face was small, and although it did not have any obvious blemishes, did not make a particularly striking impression. It was delicate, unlined, and pink but seemed to be covered with a light brown tone overall, so that there was no clear demarcation of the pink areas, and no visible shadows. Her complexion was almost too even. The setting sun shining through the trees gave a red glow to her hair and its beams made it seem thicker than it otherwise was. 'You have beautiful hair,' he said softly.

She hung her head sadly: 'That's all I needed to hear! When one says of a girl that she is nice ... or that she has beautiful hair ... then she is definitely ugly. You shouldn't have said that, Herr Hugo.'

'But I didn't mean anything like that!' He was startled by her openness.

'It doesn't matter. On evenings like this every word is dangerous. And how the memories come back! There is a painful nostalgia in the air. It whispers that one must control one's own longings, otherwise they will rise up ...'

He was surprised once again. Now she was walking with tiny steps, darting about, jumping over roots, so that he had difficulty in keeping up with her. A pallor appeared at the edges of her cheeks and they instantly looked rounder and more girlish. Even her otherwise prominent long, thin nose seemed to soften slightly under the alleviating influence of the delicate sparkle in her eyes. Her hair floated softly in the breeze and when one looked more closely, her whole being seemed to tremble as if beneath an onslaught of invisible kisses. Blue veins showed at her temples like a pair of lightning flashes. She ran towards someone, embraced a shadow. With an ecstatic pout of her lips she breathed out gentle sighs. She smiled rapturously and peacefully, without a trace of artifice, as if her deepest being had now been laid bare. Hugo felt she had abandoned him. To reclaim her attention he said, 'You are very much in love, aren't you?'

She nodded. His words didn't seem to touch her. She sank more deeply into her self-indulgent mood. She walked even more quickly, flying at his side like an elf.

He knew that it would sound naïve, but could not stop himself from saying: 'Just like me. I am also very much in love ...'

She looked at him with sympathy. There was no trace of an angry response. She stood in the shadow of a pine tree and, breathing heavily, leaned against a bench. 'That's bad, isn't it?' she said, nodding to him.

'Bad and beautiful at the same time.'

'Yes, it's also beautiful ...' A tear came into her eye. 'It's really good that I have found you. We will become friends.'

'We already are,' he said in a noble tone. 'Tell me, don't you think it strange that we already speak so intimately to each other? Half an hour ago we didn't know each other, didn't even know of the other's existence.'

'No, I don't even find it so remarkable,' she said tenderly.

'No, I don't either,' he hurried to say with conviction. 'I didn't mean it like that ... but there are so few people in the world who ...'

'And those few belong together.' He stood in front of her, resting one knee on the bench and listening to her as she continued to speak in her melodious voice. 'There are so few people in this world... so few with whom one can really speak. You are right.' It seemed to him like flattery, that for the first time she agreed with him.

'Life is strange,' he said for reply, and it seemed newly puzzling to him that he should be standing in front of this woman, who was a stranger and yet to whom he felt so close, with his knee up on the seat, while the evening wind sighed high above in the trees. Their swaying seemed to make the narrow strips of sky that appeared over the path at one moment narrower and then wider, depending on the direction in which the trees moved. And as that same evening wind blew against his hot cheeks, it softly lifted a strand of blonde hair above Irene's ear. And there was a view through dark tree trunks, to even further trees, peeling bark, fallen pine cones and earth, and in the distance everything merged into an impenetrable background. 'It's so strange,' he repeated, 'that I should come along exactly that path ... and you experience that incident there. If I had left the house just five minutes earlier or later...'

'Look, talking like that makes no sense. We must wait here for Mother.' She sat down abruptly on the bench.

'Won't you catch a chill?' When he spoke he appeared quite calm and had removed his knee from the bench, but inwardly he was trembling with awe. What had she said? 'That makes no sense'. In those simple words there was something concealed, only half acknowledged, that he too had felt in his most secret thoughts. Oh, how well he understood her! And with a feeling of delight he had never before experienced, he quietly asked, 'What do you mean, it doesn't make sense?' It seemed thoroughly improbable to him that someone could have exactly the same ideas as he did, when his were only at the edge of his perception and he barely aware of them. He was anxious to find out more.

She laughed, but this time there was nothing hurtful in the sound: 'I have a word for it — *antiefen*.[12] One shouldn't go into things too deeply with another person. There are certain things which, in my view, are the last that should be discussed, even in all good faith, because it leads to banalities. Death, fate, humanity, life, God, and similar things ... There is a man staying in the Manor House, whom you will soon meet and whose name is Nussbaum, who always wants to have deep discussions with me, and I find it sickening ... and what's more, he's a comedy writer.'

Hugo had been thinking exactly the same thing. Or at least it seemed like that to him for a moment. But just when he began to voice his agreement the words slipped away. He felt his own thoughts, which previously he had considered crystal clear, turn hazy. 'Perhaps one can have deep discussions between friends,' he ventured.

She looked at him shrewdly. 'That's a new idea. Yes, perhaps.'

'If one does it with feeling, not just with reasoning, it loses all offensiveness.'

'Yes, between friends one can have deep discussions. This is the outcome of our first stroll isn't it? We will do a lot of philosophising.' She straightened up and her mood seemed to lighten. Previously she had been talking in a rather downcast way. Now, she seemed newly happy, confident once more. 'Yes, a friend is not a comedy writer ...'

'One could even say,' Hugo put in quickly, 'that friend and comedy writer are complete opposites.'

'Or that comedy writer and *Realgymnasiast* are complete opposites,' she said happily. 'Or a philosopher and an *Antiefer* using only reason.'

'We already have a shared secret language ... that's wonderful.' He grinned and his boyish spirit came to the fore – he broke off a nearby branch and slashed it through the air like a whip.

'A secret language for secrets – isn't that how it should be?'

'Tell me—' he stopped whipping the air, was filled with enormous joy and the desire immediately to deepen their mutual understanding, to penetrate it further, to enjoy it while he could. 'Do you want to carry on speaking about your secret as a secret ... or would you like to entrust it to me? One day perhaps, if not today.' He gestured with his hand; he could see himself with almost grey hair and her as an old woman and both of them still friends, and only then about to tell each other their respective secrets.

'I would rather ask you about something else.' She smiled at him astutely, and even this air of cunning had something affectionate about it. Her eyes had narrowed to slits as though she were peering deep into her own thoughts through dazzling light. 'May I guess? Your love, your being in love, which you spoke about before, that is your secret.'

He was almost shocked: 'Oh, no ... it's something completely different.'

'And with me too.' She hesitated, embarrassed by her mistake. 'I mean ... it is not something completely different. They are connected. But they are two different things.' He had the impression that her secret did in fact have something to do with love. She didn't want to give herself away, though, until he had confided more in her.

'I would be happy to tell you about it,' he said quickly.

Her mother appeared at the end of the path. He felt that time was pressing and there would be no further revelations that day. So he quickly tried to lighten the atmosphere. 'In my case things are also connected.' And now that he had said this, it even seemed correct. 'In the way that everything is connected to everything else, don't you think?'

Her mother drew level with them. 'How you do run ahead, Irene! Are we nearly there, Herr Rosenthal?'

He looked around. 'Yes, we have nearly reached the steps ... and then we will be at Stephansplatz.'

A few steps later they emerged from the woods onto a railed platform.

'I will remember this walk,' sighed the mother, glancing fondly at Irene and then at the town below. Hugo remained standing there and expected to receive some words of gratitude. They didn't come. But hadn't they already thanked him for his help? He took a step away from the women, and it seemed to him to be a very significant move, like a departure. After that one step he could see, over the railing, the dark mass of the rows of houses and the square, the sky on the other side into which the town rose like a hill, with two or three towers that seemed too small against the immensity of the firmament.

Finally the mother said, 'What a fine view!' and sighed again.

They wound their way down the steps. The lamps there were already lit.

Without any introduction Irene expressed some trivial concerns to her mother ... where would be the best place to buy their evening meal ... should they eat at the Town Hall? Deflated by her lack of interest in him, Hugo walked a few steps ahead, feeling himself to be superfluous, but at the same time indispensable and closely bound to Irene. Nevertheless he felt the need for her to be willing to stay with him in order for the feeling of dependency and togetherness to be shared by her, now and for the future. He deliberately moved in front of her; she could draw him back to her with a call. He waited. Nothing. He turned round; the two women were preoccupied with each other. Higher than him on the steps, Irene towered above him so that his glance only reached as far as her belt.

'Do you already recognise the area?' He reluctantly made small talk. Perhaps he should have kept quiet. 'There is the spa lounge and there is the post office ...'

'Yes, the post office ... how I know it!' Irene sighed, and jumped down the steps to join him.

'The secret?' he whispered to her, burning with curiosity now.

'No, let's leave that. It doesn't interest me. Let's talk about something else.'

'Can one do that to order?' He looked at her reproachfully.

'You won't understand. You can't imagine ... it is too much for you. As I told you, I am completely surrounded by mystery.' He pondered this. Should perhaps have ignored it. But maybe she didn't really mean him to. 'And my cousins are waiting. We are already in the town. Time is too short ... it's very good that you know my cousins. That means we will meet each other more often ... Herr Nussbaum! There you are!'

A group of several men and women were approaching them.

Jewish Women

'A fine thing,' shouted a shrill and not very friendly voice. 'You've come at last! We've been standing here since seven o'clock ...' It was the oldest Fräulein Kapper. Hugo greeted her briefly and stood to one side.

'The public meeting will take place next week!'

With these words a tall man with a forked beard made his way through the throng of chattering girls. Irene suddenly changed her usual dreamy, slow way of speaking to a lively chatter, approaching him with the others. She greeted them and shook hands all round, leaning towards them all eagerly. The other girls responded with great animation, as if they had had the most earth-shattering experiences during her absence. They started to laugh together. Another man shouted above the racket: 'Are we going to the bowling alley today then?' One of the cousins – Hugo recognised her from a distance as Alice Weil – was unfolding a letter. Immediately Irene's laughter froze on her face. She stepped out of the crowd to join the other woman.

Hugo took a few steps away, having decided to go home because no one was bothering with him anymore.

Then he heard Irene behind him, saying: 'Herr Rosenthal!'

He turned around.

'It's my fault – I completely forgot we had arranged to meet our friends.'

He must have looked at her rather wildly, because she quickly continued: 'I hope you're not offended. After what you saw today, I expect you consider us a pair of confidence tricksters, don't you? People who walk off without paying their bill properly ... I would be honoured if you thought of me that way ...'

'There's no hurry ...' he stammered.

'That's true. So, to the *revanche*.' She quickly turned away. 'We shall see each other from time to time, shan't we? Won't you call on me at the Manor House early tomorrow morning?'

Hugo

At home his mother was waiting for him in the front hall with a mild reproach: 'Olga has already arrived. You were not at the station …'

'I made a mistake. It was another train.'

His mother immediately accepted his answer: 'It's not important. I collected her myself. Did you have a good walk? That's the right thing to do. Today you are looking a little better.'

'I was in the forest.'

'Come along now, you will like the food. Are your legs hurting? Poor boy.' She stroked his hair. Although he was small he had to bend down, otherwise she would not have been able to reach him. Then he kissed her cheek and her thin, white, bony hands, and turned around so that he could deftly take the book out of his jacket where he had hidden it when he was at the door and slip it onto a chair. Now his second hand was also free and he embraced the little lady and led her gently into the dining room.

His father, who had been a civil servant in Kolin, had died several years before. The small pension would not have been sufficient to support a widow and her two children, if his mother had not had some money of her own. She had already inherited the house in Teplitz on the death of her parents and she moved into it soon after her husband died. It had been Hugo's idea to rent out that part of the house which gave onto the street to spa guests during the summer. With his natural technical skills (he used to repair watches which had stopped and set up small electric lamps for the children etc.) he had drafted plans to renovate the house and then carried them out with the help of an ordinary builder. Those had been good days. Frau Lucie was very proud of her 'little engineer'. She helped and advised and was very much hands on. She demonstrated as she had in other circumstances, how much feeling and mobility was hidden in her delicate body. However in summer she found it difficult to manage with the many guests in the front house. But even that difficulty was soon overcome. The daughter of a former neighbour in Kolin, Olga Grosslicht, was invited to spend the Season in Teplitz. The very likeable fresh young girl was happy to come and the friendship between the two families made it obvious that Olga should live with the Rosenthals and help in the business. She was very grateful to be able to join in the spa life, everyone loved her and was sorry when she had to leave in the autumn, particularly because the school term began again shortly thereafter and mother and son also had to be separated. These household circumstances (the companionable life when all three worked together in the summer, and the loneliness of the mother in autumn) had developed so naturally and for three years so regularly followed the same pattern, that arranging their life in any other way was hard to imagine.

'There you are Hugo!' called Olga as the two came in and

she interrupted her laying of the table. 'How is everything going?'

'But how you've grown!' Hugo looked at her with astonishment.

'And especially when I stand up.' She came up to him and stood up straight. 'But what did you expect?'

'Yes, Olga,' said his mother, 'now you are a real teenager, last year you were a child.'

'No, last year I was a teenager and today I am already a young lady.'

Hugo laughed: 'Do you know what? Last year you were a child. And today you are a young lady. You completely bypassed being a teenager.'

They sat down at the table. In order to celebrate Olga's arrival, Frau Lucie had brought out the silver cutlery and the decorated porcelain. The pictures of small roses and angels' heads, which were painted on the plates, seemed to float on the surface of the clear soup.

Olga brought greetings from her relatives and other old acquaintances in Kolin. Otherwise not much had changed. The city was growing, new houses had been built with lovely gardens but unfortunately none of them belonged to her. She enquired about their friends in Teplitz. As Hugo said: 'Yes, yes. Herr Klein is very well,' she blushed. She quickly asked about other people. Hugo laughed. 'Now you are not answering?' she said. 'I didn't ask about any particular person.' She gave him a light slap on the arm. He wanted to hit her back. But was unwilling to touch the round gleaming forearm which lay on the table next to him.

'Don't hit each other,' called his mother. 'Everything will be happy again here now that Olga is with us.'

Hugo no longer felt the slight headache which had been bothering him as he came home. That realisation put him in high spirits, and when Olga stood up to fetch the roast meat, he caught her by the hips. The strong girl quickly escaped; but he let her go even more quickly, disturbed by her perfume and the soft feeling under his fingers. No, that wasn't his playmate any more. He looked at her in admiration, as she eagerly sprang to the door, and then back into the room; always laughing in a friendly way, with the shadows changing on her full dark red cheeks, whose rosiness was made up of several red patches. Her dark eyes were large and open, shining and healthy, the only darkness in that unbelievably delicate haze which, in spite of all the strong colours, lay over her face.

'Now everything will be fine,' said Frau Lucie, as she got up and gave everyone a portion on their outstretched plates. Now that she was standing she was almost as tall as Olga sitting. 'In the morning we two will finish our work and in the afternoon we will go walking with Hugo. No more running around young man! Until now, I could never get finished,' she said, turning to Olga, 'and I had to allow him to wander about unprotected.'

'Then what do I do in Prague? You don't watch over me there either.'

'God only knows if that is a good thing,' his mother sighed.

Hugo thought of Gretl. Perhaps his mother was right? He thought of all his unhappiness ... Yes, perhaps it would have been better to have remained at home and to have followed a narrow path, protected from love. He was overcome with emotion. Was it still possible to turn back? Wasn't he already completely lost? He looked around him and was overcome with a feeling of despair. He was even moved by the furniture that had been pushed together, and the brown background colour of the room; by the festiveness of the white tablecloth close to the low hanging chandelier. In that safe environment he felt secure. Could anything possibly take him away from that? He stroked his mother's shoulder and put his arms round her neck and kissed her. Her loose-fitting blue housecoat, her warmth, her trembling hand in his ... all those things seemed honourable, soothing and sacred.

'That's real love,' said Olga, jokingly approving of the scene as she came in. 'The dear God in heaven will be pleased to see that.' Her happy seriousness made her face look even more beautiful.

'You are my second child,' declared his mother,

'Yes, indeed. I'm beginning to feel jealous,' cried Hugo, while Olga cuddled up to the other side of the old lady who was moved and thoughtful and bent down her head. How much she had already experienced! Her cheeks were grey and fallen in, her white hair tied in a small knot on the top of her head. 'Now, children,' she suddenly said. 'I must find out what our Baroness needs for the night. I don't yet know what the Russian customs are.' A new tenant had moved in that day and the conscientious Frau Lucie was always worrying about the well-being of her guests.

She had barely left the room, when Hugo jumped up with sudden resolution: 'You must advise me, Olga ... won't you?' He had always shared his worries with her; there was no one who inspired as much trust as she did. It seemed to flow from her dark hair to his heart and his lips.

She looked at him quietly, expectantly. He seemed to already experience relief, simply from the thought that he could now say everything. 'So, to put it briefly ... I failed this year ...' That was the big secret which continually weighed on him.

'Failed! At school?'

'Yes, that's right. Actually it's not ...'

'Failed!' She wrung her hands. 'You will have to stay down!'

'It isn't yet completely certain, Olga. There will be a retake.'

She looked at him questioningly.

'That means that after the holidays I must take another examination.'

'And if you don't pass that ...'

'But it's only in one subject. If I pass that then everything will be all right.'

'Really ...'

The fact that his situation and his confession seemed so strange to her, hardly troubled him at all. On the contrary, it strengthened him in his trust. It was so clear to him that there was nothing false about Olga, only pure good will. How carefully she listened to him, and how she tried, from her outside position, to take an overview of his affairs and to put them in order! 'Does your mother know?' she asked him immediately.

'Not a word so far,' he continued, struggling to hold back the tears. 'That would be terrible. It mustn't come out. I am so ashamed. And it would make her ill.'

She immediately spoke more quietly, as if to avoid any possibility of betrayal: 'And how did it happen? In which subject? How was it possible?'

He had not made a mistake. It calmed him so much that she took the matter seriously. Anyone else might have attempted to comfort him by making fun of a school matter. That never even occurred to her. She made a shocked face, an honest face, as was her nature: 'In which subject?'

'One day I will tell you everything. It was not my fault. I mean it was. I don't know ... perhaps I was partly to blame. The teacher was against me. But there were other things. I would need hours to tell you about it. But you must promise me one thing – that you will help me. Mother doesn't allow me to look at a book during the holidays. She means well by it. She would be wide-eyed if I wanted to do some revision, and everything would come out. Until now I have smuggled my physics book out in my jacket and gone into the woods. Now, as you know, you will come with me. So, what can I do? ... I am lost.' It did him good to see her looking at him so sadly but constrained him at the same time. He felt the need to say everything, to off-load everything on to her immediately. But the more he said, the more he felt that there was something of his suffering still left over.

'That's terrible.' She shook her head. Caught up in her participation, he sobbed. She had already made a decision. 'I will get candles for you. You will learn at night.'

'Shh!' Steps could be heard on the stairs. She repeated the sound – 'Shh!'

'And to fail in physics,' he whined, quietly and yet sounding full of anger from the pain of it. 'A subject for which I was always thought to have a particular talent ...'

His mother came in, smiling with satisfaction.

'So, everything is all right. These Russians aren't so bad. But's what's going on here with you? Not cleared up yet, Olga. It seems to me that you have forgotten how to be a good housewife over the winter.'

Olga blushed and jumped up, and while she took the plates away and the tablecloth off, Hugo said enthusiastically, 'Oh, Olga is definitely an excellent housewife. I can really see Olga as a housewife!' Her worried face, which she was trying to control by being busy, flattered him to the core. Her cheeks glowed redder than usual and her thick black hair, her strong nose and the large soft mouth were all generously proportioned and lively. They seemed to magnify the troubled look in her eyes. It seemed that her powerful frame, broad shoulders and broad face could mourn more intensely than any more meagre figure.

Hugo felt very confused as he later went up to his room. It was on the third floor of the front part of the house. His mother and Olga slept a long way off in rooms next to the courtyard. The staircase was broad, with wide, low wooden steps and short landings. It went round past broad front rooms and stone covered platforms. A cat jumped out from a projecting wall with a muffled sound like a ball of wool and reached the ground via some washing hung out to dry. The moon shone in with white beams which broke up here and there on the edge of an old wardrobe and then continued over its bulging front. Although the beams were quite narrow because of the curtained and covered windows, they gave off a glimmer which reached even into the smallest corners of the dark rooms. Pots and tubs stood around, there were chests along the walls, and the corners were full of junk. How well Hugo knew the old house! How happy he had once been here as a child! He was particularly aware of the cool night air after sitting in the room for a long time and he was overcome by disconcerting memories. The winter wreaths reminded him of the dancing lessons. He put out the candle which he had

Hugo

brought with him up the staircase, so as to allow those echoes to be undisturbed. Now the moonlight took on more of a bluish tinge. Oh, how much it resembled the arc lamps which had shone out in the snow in front of the dance-hall when he ran out to order their carriage – sweating, and with the collar of his winter coat turned up, his hands hot in the white kid gloves which in his haste he had forgotten to take off. That girl, Gretl Mahler, had driven him mad. During that winter, his whole being had received a shock and he had difficulty in getting back his equilibrium. Previously he had been convinced that he was called to do great things, but now he felt contemptible, already worn out. And those unhappy nights when she danced with others – because she didn't love him; no, not in the least. And then came the summer, the afternoons on the tennis courts of the Hetzinsel; his hopes, his shy and fruitless approaches, which were always rebuffed, when he accompanied her along the dimly lit Karlin streets; the jokes, the parties, her cheerfulness and his disappointment. What did he want from her anyway? But now he had failed his exams because of her, he was sure of that. Without even intending to, she had made such demands on his feelings, that he had nothing left to give to his studies. Oh, one misfortune had followed another, no afternoon without a catastrophe, without despair. 'And I am still only seventeen years old …' he said quietly to himself, as he went into his room. 'They say that it is the best time, the prime of life. But could anyone be more wretched than me? Perhaps I should shoot myself.' He thought about all the coming years which probably lay ahead of him. The prospect was unbearable; he did not see how he could survive so much trouble. He thought of his mother. No, he couldn't do that to her. But, as if it would be a waste of time to think of anything other than Gretl, he immediately forced himself to bring her face to mind again. He opened the window, the white lace curtains billowed out, distant music was borne in on the wind and seemed to come from the dark recesses of the trees which stood in front of his window and cast shadows on him with their branches and leaves. They were black, and only a few leaves which caught the light from the street lamps shone with a metallic green sheen. The half-moon came out from behind a cloud, and the music died away at the same time. White-faced, and almost dazzled in the glare, he looked into the now moving sparkling white trees, and he imagined that the music and the breeze and the ever changing light were trying to make him happy. He felt such pain, that there was nothing more in the world for him, nothing more. If Gretl had only been fond of him, at least as fond as she was of the fat *Couleur*[13] student, or more fond! Oh, God, if she were only with him now and he could show her his apartment, the view over the Allee, behind which one could imagine large parks – he could see it all very clearly and he couldn't believe that on that evening, in that beautiful light, in the echoing sounds of the horns of the spa orchestra, she would have remained unmoved. He would perhaps have kissed her lightly on the cheek. He had never yet, in his whole life, kissed a girl. He would do it very gently; how much love he would put into that very gentle movement. He wouldn't even touch her, only put his lips near her skin, so that she would feel his breath which caressed her cheek. And above all to speak with her, a great deal and warmly; 'Look Gretl' and 'Is that so Gretl, you understand me then' and 'So that's how it was, Gretl, that's how it was meant? I understood it quite differently.' In his mind he showed her his whole room, enjoying the intimate moment. It was dark but to him it was like broad daylight and he could see the particular features of the individual objects in the room. He stood with his back to the open window and leaned out so that his hair was ruffled by the cool breeze. He imagined that he led Gretl by the hand and took her for a walk along the walls. He showed her the crooked walls which appeared carelessly built – but they were thick, she could be sure of that – and the three windows with white painted frames ... three, for a small room, but they were also quite small and low. In fact the whole room was low – it was an old house. There were glass fronted cupboards full of crockery and small ornaments including the wreath of silver wheat ears with long stiff awns which his parents had received for their silver wedding. But the most important was the second glass-fronted cupboard close to his bed which contained his laboratory – the electrifying machine, the camera, the Leiden jars, the batteries, the steam machine and all his small improvements, inventions, projects, even a small airship. With a pounding heart he told her what he would become, what future he was moving towards. And united with her! But then he suddenly remembered that once on the Hetzinsel she had abruptly changed the subject when he started to speak about his innermost thoughts. She had been very distant towards him. Probably she hadn't thought about him at all since the last time she had seen him. His vivid imagination now seemed shameful to him, degrading, like an all too easy victory, a kind of fraud. Yes, that was easy, that was no kind of art, to imagine love. But to experience it! ...

Slowly he walked away from the window and began to undress. He did not re-light the candle. He really had no pleasure in life at all. The love of his mother, Olga's friendship, were such ordinary, obvious things that they were not able to touch him in his current irritable mood. Then a small hope rose up in him – Irene. Strangely, he had completely forgotten her since he came into the house. Now he remembered once again the whole afternoon, her puzzlingly quick changes between mockery, nervousness and warmth; her quick-wittedness. He looked forward to the next morning at the Manor House; that would be interesting. And then the company which she had spoken of. Suddenly, as he was falling asleep, an idea came to him – it would be good to send Gretl a postcard every now and then. She will see that I am enjoying myself and every time it will bear the signature of Irene. That will impress her! When he had been in Prague and out on excursions, and Gretl was not there, he had sent her a really impressive picture postcard – in fact that had been the purpose of his excursions. And so, thinking about his time in Prague and his beloved, he drifted off into dreamland.

The Manor House

Early the next morning Hugo peered from the final stretch of the path through the spa park into the open area that lay between the two wings of the Manor House. He cautiously moved forwards, looking into the beach chairs on the loge sections of the open veranda. Nobody. He retraced his steps, dawdled around the colonnade and the theatre, studied the barometer, and then went back again. Finally, at around ten o'clock, he saw Irene coming down the open stairs alongside the ramp. He rushed up to her, as though he had just arrived.

'Have you already been bathing?' he asked.

'I'm not unwell,' she replied emphatically, 'only my mother is here for the cure.' But she was not looking good; her skin had a greenish tinge and there were deep circles under her eyes as though she had had a sleepless night. He studied her as she sat down in a beach chair and pushed a folding chair towards him. Her hair did not seem as light as it had the day before and she had piled it up in a strikingly severe style, a narrow column; it was centre parted and fell down in big waves close to her eyebrows and down as far as her neck. She had thin arms, a small breast, a long neck rising up from her narrow back and wore a pale yellow blouse adorned with lace and embroidered flowers. All her limbs moved gracefully but sometimes gave one the worrying impression that they were not quite connected to the rest of her and that she could easily fall apart. She must be handled carefully, thought Hugo, instinctively translating the physical into the spiritual. He longed to try out his delicate touch on her like a soothing remedy. In the meantime she had moved into a corner of the wicker chair and spread out some open letters in a row beside her. 'My post for today,' she said smiling proudly and at the same time self-mockingly, as if to cancel out any negative impression he might have of her.

Hugo was not feeling in the least negative and said, 'That's wonderful.'

Visibly touched, she stopped being so defensive and volunteered: 'They're just from girlfriends, mostly in England. I actually spent a year there.'

Hugo was wide-eyed with surprise: 'In London?'

'We lived in the country, near London. English country living is the best in the world. You can't imagine. Everything is 'comfortable'. She pronounced the word in the English way. 'I pity anyone who has not known it.' She told him about her experiences and Hugo listened eagerly. Her observations were sharp, surprisingly almost masculine, and Hugo wholeheartedly applauded them. He had never heard a girl make such witty and independent observations. Then she went through her other letters. One friend had written to her from Ulm inviting her to visit them that winter. Another invited her to go to her place in Hungary for several months. 'She is so fond of me it is almost unbelievable. She does everything for me. And when I am with her she neglects her husband and children ...'

'She is married?'

'All my friends are married. You will soon hear the same of me. It will soon be all over Teplitz ...' She frowned and broke off. 'And this too is an exciting letter.' She picked up the last one, folded it and put it in her bag, while she simply bundled the others together in the largest envelope. 'I've got enough there to last me for a few days. You have no idea what I would give to have it all over with or be away from all the gossip. But these letters make me feel good again. My friends are so attached to me and I don't know why. Well, perhaps I do. I have always been very generous to them.'

In Hugo's eyes she appeared to be generally loved and desired. He hardly dared to say anything. 'Did you have someone you liked most – a best friend, as they say?'

'Yes, and no.' She said nothing more for a long time. He understood that. Could there be simple answers to such complicated matters? 'I did have one, but at the moment I am very annoyed with her ... it's always the same story. It all hangs together. In my life everything has to turn out strangely. Frieda Schwarz, don't you know her from Prague? You must have known her as a child, the beautiful Frieda Wantoch?'

Hugo kept shaking his head.

Irene was charmed by his ignorance and began to tell him about Prague society. Oh, she had mixed in the best circles in Prague ... or so far as it was possible for Jewish women to do so. She divided German society in Prague into classes; the top one consisted of the aristocracy and the best Aryan circles. Then came the big businessmen, the rich lawyers, the top financiers, and the richest Jews together with the good

Christian middle class. She calculated that from then on the categories were divided according to the dowry of the daughters. The boundaries were determined by steps of thirty thousand Gulden and the participants kept strictly to the rules. Hugo was on the point of saying that she had made an exact science out of it when she herself said, 'It's an exact science.' This accord pleased him so much that he made an effort to contribute something from his own experience to the theory. 'For example, on our tennis court ...' That didn't interest her, though, and she carried on speaking. Naturally there were exceptions for particularly beautiful, lively or otherwise esteemed people. Sometimes there were some really surprising cases of people who moved in much better circles than they were really qualified for. 'Like me, for example,' she told him in a matter-of-fact tone. 'I was brought in by my friends. The writer Hahnenkamm was one of them – do you know him? But of course you don't know anyone ...'

Hugo apologised and said that he had read some of his poems.

'What! I haven't read anything of his. That has nothing to do with it. I have never been interested in literature. But how we laughed together at the balls. Then there was his friend, Baron Havatschek, the mystic, the most elegant man in Prague – tall and broad-shouldered. He fell madly in love with me. That was the strangest thing. Once I even visited him in his apartment in Prague, obviously not alone but together with Frieda. He has a skeleton in his drawing room and pictures of Indian gods. When I had to go to the sanatorium in Lahmann, last year, he followed me there ... I must show you a photograph of myself from that time, dressed for a ball.'

'Were you in love with him?'

The Manor House

'No, not at all. It was only friendship on my side. Basically I have only had friendships with men in my whole life. It doesn't work out with girls!'

He heartily agreed with that: 'They are too stupid, too ordinary, too emotionless, don't you agree?'

'And above all too jealous. They offer friendship, but when the first man comes into view, the first love, it's all over.'

Deeply immersed in her affairs and interests, he asked, 'But did you have only friendships with men or have you also been in love?'

She looked at him askance, almost insulted, but then she smiled pityingly as if he could not possibly appreciate the depth of the love which she had experienced. After a pause she carried on without answering his question: 'Now the only friendship I have is with my brother. I have educated him, made him what he is. It's a pity that you won't meet him. He is in the Alps …'

He found it painful that she did not seem to number him among her friends. Had she perhaps forgotten what she had said on the previous day? It seemed to him as unlikely as it had then that he would ever be close to her. Such a significant person, such a circle of acquaintances … He looked at her sadly. She was more beautiful when she spoke like that – so lively and clever. Her cheeks dimpled and her grey eyes opened wider. He was sure that her beauty was not the same as Olga's or Gretl's; it reminded him of the refined marmoreal charm of certain busts of Schiller. All the same, that particular type of girl appealed to him today, as much as it had on the previous day. As she pulled another beach chair closer saying, 'Now we are really hidden,' he ran his fingers through his hair with excitement.

After Irene had spoken of Prague society, she went on to talk about the mixed society in Teplitz – the simple local people who lived content in their own company, the wealthy who intentionally lived in a closed community, and the many who looked for excitement among the spa guests ... and found it. 'There are my cousins for example who are happy to listen to the boring speeches of Herr Nussbaum.'

'Who is he? You already mentioned him yesterday.'

'He speaks even more about me. He is in love with me ... and has his own reasons for associating with my cousins.'

'What are those then?'

'I suppose you'll think I'm making it up if I don't explain it a bit more. Normally I make a secret out of everything. But this isn't really very interesting ... Herr Nussbaum is actually a Teplitz man, but after a romantic youth he married a Christian woman somewhere, I think it was in Chemnitz, and is himself no longer religious. In brief, his relations who live here – his father and brothers – are known as a very Orthodox family, and they cut him off. As far as they are concerned he no longer exists. Initially that didn't seem to bother him. Now that he is older, he seems to have enough money to live as a man of independent means. His wife has died and he is trying to renew his ties with his blood relations. Something awful must have happened between them in the past, but I don't know what it was exactly. Perhaps they threw him out or beat him! You know what these old Jews are like; they tear their clothes as they do at a funeral if their son has had himself baptized. Recently a very old rabbi threw himself out of a window when he received such news. So Herr Nussbaum is in a state of enmity with his family; he is cursed by them and consequently he hates them. I believe he is entirely ruled by a thirst for revenge combined with a certain free way of thinking, adopted partly from natural inclination and partly to antagonise his own people. He now burdens me with it too, endlessly ...'

'*Antieft*,' added Hugo dutifully.

'Because I seem to be the only intelligent audience here. They tell me he only comes here to Teplitz every year to annoy his brother. He is the most regular visitor to Teplitz although he does not need the cure. He comes every year with his son, who is a real cretin, and does his best to get himself noticed here. Last year he went to great trouble to have one of his comedies put on at the town theatre. It was called *Outdated Laws*. It was very transparent, of course, and caused a real scandal. And that is Herr Nussbaum's life's work. He is planning a public meeting for this year; he will talk about enlightenment or something like that. He only wants to annoy his relatives. I have to know all about it, and I even have to read the comedy ...'

'So it's literature again.'

'Yes, literature runs after me, as always, although I remain indifferent to it. How are my cousins involved? That's simple. He needs supporters among the local community. And naturally they are suitable. My uncle is even a member of the local council. His every other phrase is "our venerable and revered spa town". And what do they get from him? They are searching desperately for husbands for their eldest daughters Lotti and Alice. Teplitz has already been scoured and they have had enough of travelling around. But Nussbaum mixes with the spa guests and is himself a potential match.'

'But you said yourself that he is old—'

'So what?' Irene suddenly became serious. 'Do you have

any idea what a good marriage prospect is for a girl from a good family? He is rich, a widower, an imposing figure—' She spoke in a shrill, scornful and insistent tone; and it seemed to Hugo as if she were speaking about her own situation. Her travels, her foreign friends, the nervous collapse, Lahmann, even yesterday's scene with the waiter – it all became clear to him. But he didn't have the time to clarify things in his own mind because she insisted: 'You must have seen him yesterday—'

'The gentleman with the forked beard?'

'That's the one! Isn't he tall, and doesn't he have broad shoulders?'

It occurred to him that she had already mentioned those two manly attributes twice in the conversation. His thoughts took another direction then. Wasn't it astounding that he personally had been almost completely left out of it? True, he had a tendency to be dominated but no other conversational partner had ever controlled him to the extent that Irene did; she knew how to ensure that they both focussed only on her relationships. At the same moment as those two things became clear to him, he said, without thinking it through, 'Obviously I am not very tall ...'

She looked at him in surprise and then laughed at him with such abandon that he shuddered. 'No, you're definitely not. You're a dwarf, not a man!'

He was astonished and hesitated. He had not exactly been insulted because she had just told the truth; he was abnormally small, taking after his mother. But something else seemed to have suddenly become clear to him: Irene was in love with Herr Nussbaum. She was jealous of the cousins. That was her secret. And suddenly he realised that he had nursed hopes of somehow winning Irene's love, almost unconsciously, and against his better judgment. A part of him was passionately attached to her but he had only just realised it as the hope disappeared. He told himself that he shouldn't show anything or give himself away, not hesitate in any way. He stuttered: 'I am still young.'

'Yes, you might still grow,' she said, with brutal honesty. 'How old are you then?'

'Over seventeen, almost eighteen ...'

The number seemed to disturb her. 'So young ... I am almost twenty-seven.' And as she gave herself over to sentimental thoughts, she remembered the emptiness of her life and a proud look came over her face which seemed to say: 'I am not like other women. I admit to my age. I am something special.' And even if her expression had not said it, Hugo would have felt it. She seemed someone to be esteemed, this being with a dazzling spirit, a model of her sex. In a clumsy attempt to smooth things over he declared: 'I would never have thought it—'

She scowled at him: 'Thank you. Thank you very much.'

He had been serious, but out of affection for her he attempted to extricate himself: 'Naturally only outwardly. Intellectually you are so mature ...'

'No, no. Don't try to comfort me. I am not the emancipated sort, I hate all that business. A woman has other things to worry about than being intellectual. One has to shine like the sun.' She said that in one of her own particular ways of speaking. It seemed to him that she had invented that way of speaking years before, to help her through other failing relationships, and that she was honest and uncompromising enough to use it against herself now that the right time had come. More than ever her attack on him pained him; she would not accept even flattery from him. Hugo tried one more tack: 'The waiter of yesterday seemed to be of another opinion. He thought you were like the sun.'

Her face lit up, and he congratulated himself on saying the right thing. 'And Herr Nussbaum...' he continued.

'Look, he's searching for me over there.' She pointed through the gap between two beach chairs at a bearded gentleman who was busily inspecting the loges. Without actually saying that Hugo's remark was correct, she carried on in a friendly tone: 'Let him! We will stay here. We will keep together, against everything, against the whole of society if need be. Would you like that?' Just like yesterday he thought – so whimsical. It seemed high-handed of her to assume that he might wish to exclude himself from society on her account. However, a new feeling of pleasure overcame him as she drew the beach chairs closer together and began to mock his rival: 'He has an orchid in his buttonhole – *à la Wilde, à la Grossstadt.*'

'How dandyish his stick is,' Hugo observed. 'Only actors carry sticks with a silver handle like that.'

'In short – a comedy writer.' She made no secret of the fact that she found her own observations particularly apposite.

'And that is his son? With the railway timetable in his hand?'

'Yes, the red-faced idiot. He knows all the railway stations and trains of the world by heart. It's the only thing that interests him.'

'Perhaps he wants to travel, to run away—'

'Perhaps. His father did.'

'And who is the man next to him?'

'He belongs to Herr Nussbaum's group. Herr Demut. He

always wears that short brown overcoat, which has never been fashionable but could perhaps become fashionable.'

Hugo snorted with laughter: 'That's good!'

She carried on relentlessly: 'Officers who have been pensioned off and impoverished aristocrats dress like that, don't they?'

'Yes, you are right. And who is speaking to them now?'

'He is an eye doctor. He arrived here yesterday. His name is Dr Taubeles or Taubelis, or something of that sort. I just call him "the moustache trainer". Do you know why? His moustache grows over his upper lip, dark and bushy. You can't see his lower lip at all. And that gives him a rather malicious, grim look; although in actual fact he seems to be good natured. We had a very amusing conversation with him yesterday. And you know, I think that malicious and yet good natured look also appears in all those who have their moustache trainers on. I know it from my brother – those tight lips, which seem barely able to suppress a reckless word, almost tortured; and then the eyes, childlike and contented ...'

'Moustache trainer. I will remember that for our secret language.'

The group of four men seemed to be about to leave. Flora Weil, the middle of the three Weil sisters, came up to them.

'And do you know what I call her? "The baby" – so small and fat in her white linen dress, like an infant which someone has swaddled too tightly. One imagines that at night all the bound mounds of fat reshape themselves. Isn't it grotesque how women put on weight when they have passed the first flush of youth ...'

She threw herself with increasing abandon into jokes about fat women, which was obviously one of her favourite topics. Hugo listened enthralled. He had never thought about such things, since so far all women had been something of an unknown quantity to him and seemed to be much of a muchness. Perhaps because he knew nothing, everything seemed newly clear to him when he allowed himself to be led by Irene. She had clichés, set phrases and metaphors at the ready. 'I was always top in mathematics at school,' she cried to his astonishment. He had always thought that kind of material was the opposite of mathematical. He glanced away from her for a moment. Herr Nussbaum and his companions were just leaving the courtyard. Then the happy realisation dawned upon Hugo that Irene preferred him to Herr Nussbaum. Strangely, his increased confidence led him to become more argumentative and, with a glow of pride, he became convinced of the efficacy of Irene's methods. He gained renewed pleasure from speaking charmingly and light-heartedly about everything, and yet with a certain scepticism, hinting at a deep underlying seriousness. He enjoyed flitting from one topic to the next, and listening to her replies. He became heated and was completely engaged.

'We mustn't chatter all day,' she said at length, putting on her gracious salon smile. She stood up to leave and Hugo accompanied her as far as the drive. 'Till tomorrow morning then,' she said. 'I must spend the afternoon with my mother.'

'Are you going on an outing?' he asked anxiously. He would have liked to see her in the afternoon too, although it would have been impossible for him.

'No. I hate outings,' she continued in the same vehement style of speaking. 'Only native Treplitzers or highbrows do that. I'm going to stay around here. When could it possibly be enjoyable to go to the Mückenturm or to the Schweisserjäger?'

She pronounced those names so emphatically, stressing their literal meanings, that they sounded like threats. Hugo found her manner illogical and almost unscrupulous, and yet so compelling.

Then Olga appeared on the road which was some distance away. She was passing by just at that moment and when she saw that Hugo was about to take his leave, stood and waited patiently. 'Someone is waiting for you,' Irene said snidely – she had a sharp eye for that kind of thing.

'I haven't asked anyone to come here.' For a moment Hugo was undecided. Then it seemed to him that it was incumbent upon him to give to Irene, who had on his account neglected Herr Nussbaum, a sign that he valued her. He therefore deliberately prolonged the leave-taking. And Irene, who immediately grasped the situation, also remained standing there, stretching out her sentences and suddenly in no hurry. But she seemed to be less interested in securing Hugo's good will than in triumphing over the unknown girl. 'Who is that girl?' she asked with such contempt as if she knew her very well and had, God knows how, heard a lot of bad things about her.

'She is a close acquaintance of our family. She is living with us now.'

'A real healthy Jewish country girl,' said Irene. 'Hips like a big calf, eats for three, heavy food, two fingers thickness of butter on the bread if possible, does the work of four people, makes homemade wine, prays morning and evening, shouts around the house ...'

'You see all that in her?' Hugo said defensively. 'As it happens she speaks very quietly ...'

'But definitely in dialect.'

Jewish Women

Hugo moved the conversation on to the gentleman who was by now speaking to Olga. It was Herr Klein, a local book seller, who had the previous year asked for Olga's hand, but who had accepted that she was still too young. He seemed very pleased to have come upon her by chance. She indicated to him that she was waiting for Hugo. He was very willing to wait with her, if she would allow him to ... For a while the two young people walked up and down on the pavement, while Hugo and Irene talked to one another and pretended that they had not noticed anything not only to those who were waiting but also to each other. Hugo in particular was carrying on a lively and energetic debate. Eventually it went on too long for the good Olga and she went off with Herr Klein. A minute later Hugo called out his last 'auf Wiedersehen' to Irene as she fluttered away.

The Ascent

From then on Hugo called at the Manor House at ten o'clock every morning.

Sometimes he spent time with Irene on the forecourt. Other times she invited him for a brief walk, but only when her mother was there. She did not join them, but walked behind them apparently without getting bored. That particular way of being protected, 'chaperoned', was almost all that Hugo now remembered of the other young ladies he had associated with. One was never oneself entertained by girls; they all made it clear that one had to entertain *them*. Hugo realised that in the company of ladies he should not reveal too much about himself, not be too 'serious' if one could use that word in connection with young ladies. It is true that some men in his tennis group behaved freely and said whatever came into their heads. They felt in their element with an audience of teenage girls – like the fat *Couleur* student for example. He amused everyone so much when he casually told jokes or imitated his former religion teacher. Hugo admired those people without understanding them. He imitated them and whenever he visited Gretl he armed himself with a store of gossip, anecdotes and funny turns of phrase which he used even though his attempts lacked conviction. Occasionally they were successful but mostly not. He pushed himself forward, but the impression he gave was not of someone vivacious and endlessly entertaining. He could never say what he really thought, but had to work out how the *Couleur* student would have interpreted something and responded. In order to profit from all his efforts, which were clearly intended to impress, he had to dress them up to look as though they were not only amusing but effortless and that he was enjoying himself. His head would start ringing and there were moments when he simply stepped aside and stared into the trees. With Irene, by contrast, he was able to relax. His favourite topics were the same as hers and he had no need to prepare the conversation in advance. Freed from concerns about what he was going to say, he was able to focus his attention on the conversation itself. But in spite of that relief, of which he was barely aware, Irene's femininity still had a hidden charm, something to dream about.

They went to the gardens of the Clary Castle. They saw the swans gliding over their own reflections in the ponds, while the trees rustled overhead and reached out to them. Irene admired the aristocratic air of the place. In the dairy they had discovered the beauty of whitewashed ivy-covered walls. She stood in front of the sweep of the 'threefold' columns[14] and sensed their similarity to the style of building in Prague even before she had heard the name of the architect: Mathias Braun. She was equally charmed by the *Biedermeier*[15] style of the old town Baths, with their simple columns. Hugo was surprised by the way Irene, a visitor, could show and explain Teplitz to him, a well-established resident.

The Ascent

At the same time he found a certain illogicality in the fact that she continued to look down on the Teplitz inhabitants even while openly admiring the place which they had fashioned and built. She did not understand this objection. And even if Hugo conceded that it might be a superficial judgment, every day there were new things which confirmed him in his perception of her. One moment she praised the poet Hahnenkamm and the bohemian life he led; the next she said: 'One should be solid, get married' and defended that against everything Romantic, which she considered was only a bluff. She found Herr Demut charming because of his elegance, but sometimes called all elegance laughable – arguing instead that vitality was the most attractive thing in the world. But Herr Nussbaum's vitality got on her nerves. Doctor Taubelis, the 'moustache trainer', was too jokey, too caustic. But she was delighted when she herself struck home with a caustic remark. Hugo decided that her opinions were immovable and not shaken in the least by the fact that they were sometimes contradictory. From then on that remnant of feminine obstinacy which he observed in her formed one of her most attractive features. He told her so. She was entirely in agreement. 'Yes. Where would we be if women were not first and foremost women?'

What was strangest was her preference for things requiring precision. Of the arts, she only understood and loved architecture, and of the sciences, mathematics. 'And what about physics?' he asked. 'There is too much guesswork in that subject. That is not science.' He thought her response justified, to some extent. Once, early in the morning, he found her reading a book entitled '*What does a Woman need to know about the Civil Code?*' She told him that for a year she had attended a course on national economics in Berlin taught by

Dr Alice Salomon. She had also had some practical experience of social work. However she had no sympathy for the Women's Movement. 'You can't be a sun in a *Reform* costume.' She laughed at the Suffragettes, but went into raptures about beautiful dancers such as Liane de Vries and Ruth Denis. He understood that. She was not what one would call a clever girl; not one who played a musical instrument, devoured literature and accumulated all kinds of knowledge. She understood that being clever was not the most important thing. She detested the smoking of cigarettes, riding bicycles, playing the lute and free love – not to mention Russian women studying in Zurich or Schwabing[16] morals. Her handwriting was small and delicate, contrary to the modern trend. Sometimes it seemed that she represented the views of an older generation. On best interpretation she seemed consistently to defend the principle of femininity. What she recognised as of value were: race, life and fire, tact, gracefulness, the culture of the instincts and the utmost delicacy and thoroughness in intellectual matters. Enthralled, he suggested that they study together, starting from the beginning, with Kant, for example, as the basic foundation.

'Is he good?' she asked.

He thought the question both outrageous and justified. 'I don't know. I don't understand everything of his. In fact almost nothing ...'

'Probably he didn't understand himself either.'

'No, no,' he said. She laughed and allowed her high spirits, which she also thought inappropriate, to be suppressed by him as he solemnly continued: 'He is difficult to understand if one reads him on one's own. I have always thought that it would be easier for two people together.' She was entirely of the same opinion. She also agreed with him that one should once and for all seriously engage with philosophy. 'Once in a lifetime, however difficult it is.' However, she concluded by postponing the undertaking until her return to Prague, since the summer holidays were not really the right place for it ... And in the meantime she would continue with her sharp observations, which were also a sort of 'philosophy'. Hugo was pleased that she considered it obvious that they would continue to meet in Prague.

He took all of her emotional outbursts seriously, and the attention which he gave her aroused in her a feeling of friendly gratitude. She waited impatiently for him every day. She needed him as much as he needed her and she made no secret of the fact. She showed him that he was her priority. When he came to the Manor House she immediately left any group she was with. Only once, when Alice Weil brought her a letter, did she leave him in a flurry. That was the single occasion. 'Who is the young lad?' asked Nussbaum with open irritation. 'He is a very intelligent man,' she retorted. They all looked at him when he appeared. Irene acknowledged that he was important to her by immediately running across the courtyard to meet him, carrying a book which she had previously hidden from the others. Conversely she felt that her reputation was enhanced by those regular visits, which were only on her account. And Hugo kept his distance from all the others; partly out of lack of interest, partly from shyness and partly because he thought it would be a compliment to Irene. He even greeted the cousins only from a distance. She praised him for that, saying: 'One must avoid too much contact with relatives.' She gave him the idea of wearing ties that matched the colour of her clothing. And she laughed merrily when after a few days people noticed it and were taken aback. She also told him that her mother did not find her association with him particularly edifying. 'Why?' he retorted and thought that from then on he would always feel terrified in the presence of the dark lady. 'You are naïve. Are you going to marry me?' He was stunned and lowered his eyes as though caught out. 'My mother thinks I am mad on this matter,' she continued, 'which amuses me a great deal. Everyone must be a little mad if they are to be worth anything.' 'Everyone?' he said thoughtfully, as a few contradictory remarks which she had made on the subject occurred to him.

He particularly enjoyed talking to her about ladies' clothing. She had given her outfits names like 'falling leaves', 'the snake', and 'happiness'. She knew the best views on the latest fashion, and was interested in the traditional costumes of the past. He didn't really understand why he found her chatter about ladies' stockings and ankle-boots, stitching and buckles, so pleasurable. To himself he called it silly curiosity and snooping. He told himself that there must be something sensual in it but while he clearly acknowledged the charm of her feminine illogicality, on this occasion his ability to rationalise failed him. I'm still too young he would decide in conclusion and 'young' meant that he had a surprising insight into many things and none at all into many others. It is often just a matter of pure chance.

She showed him a photograph of herself in a ball gown and even gave it to him. Her figure was shown in profile – supple, and apparently standing on tiptoe although the picture was cropped at the waist. Her hands were behind her back and her face with its sweet eyes turned towards the onlooker. From then on he thought that he could see the real person in those eyes which were yearning and yet calm, but only in the expectation of all her hopes being realised. The smooth young features in the photo seemed to be transferred to her. Almost every day he found new beauty in her. Had he become accustomed to what he initially considered a rather disconcerting nose and her pinched lips? He particularly liked to see her in a grey dress which hung loosely and was fastened with a belt at the back. He discovered that it was a 'Russian jacket'. And on one occasion he was really stunned to see that her hair which usually looked brown flashed with gold highlights. 'It was washed today,' she explained to him. The thought went through his mind: 'What these women know and how much is going on in their heads!' Subconsciously he ascribed the things that he noticed about Irene to all women and then back to her but multiplied a thousand times and to greater effect. When he gave her blue-veined hand a farewell kiss, the clover-scented perfume on her hands went to his head like wine.

'Was it love?' he sometimes asked himself. It certainly wasn't like the passion he had felt for Gretl, but still much closer to that than to indifference. He regretted that even on this matter his lack of experience told. And was she in love with him? Did it mean nothing that she had given him a photograph, spoken of friendship, arranged further meetings? He felt that with the first sign of her love his world would become 'brightly lit up'. It seemed to him that it was his duty to love such an outstanding, refined and intellectual (although not in the usual sense of the word) young lady – the former lover of a poet, Baron Havatschek. He was now astonished by his coolness towards her and reproached himself for it.

She was receptive to him – showing a warmth tempered

only by good manners. He felt emboldened enough to be open about his talents which he had previously carefully hidden. He had an inclination to noble-mindedness, to heroic deeds and passion. When he spoke of heroes, great men and of the happiness of all mankind, his dark eyes blazed. Then his small body seemed sturdy, and full of compact strength, his face boldly chiselled, ready for self-sacrifice, his splendid brown hair with its springy curls and his small but thick moustache, defiant. One could see there was nothing mean about this young man; his fire and his imminent maturity promised great things – Irene also felt that. It sometimes amused her but she held back with her jokes, almost with a certain anxiety for him. So their walks passed peacefully and happily, and often with a light poetic lustre. How perfumed were the meadows with their long lines of mown grass! And then those swans which sometimes plunged their heads down into the water so that only a small heap of white feathers remained swimming on the surface! But usually they moved forward in unselfconscious happiness; the black markings on their faces made their eyes invisible and gave an impression of untroubled calm, their swimming more like sleeping. Behind them the water flowed at a wide angle, in shining folds. Irene gazed at them. Hugo found it wonderful that they could be quiet together.

 They needed only a few words to convey their mood to each other. She didn't allow her secret to be revealed although she frequently alluded to it. But Hugo suspected that a headache, which grew worse in the course of a few days, was somehow connected to it. Then came rainy days. Irene experienced the weather differently here from at home. The rented rooms were really only set up for staying in during the evening. She sat near her bed on a chair which was only intended for putting one's clothes on. There was no table. If she wanted to read, she had to rest the book on the narrow windowsill, or push the bedside table to the window. Only a little light came through the window which looked out onto roofs and chimneys. The doors opened directly onto the hotel corridor so that one was unable to leave them open. If one opened the window a cold wet flood blew in; one was closer to the inclement sky but the light in the room was not improved. Irene sat and waited with an impatience verging on anger. She had put her book aside, and kept looking at the blackness of a skylight through which she could see the rain blowing past in diagonal lines. But, apart from the grey sky, the weather did not look too bad. How quickly was the rain falling? It was not possible to estimate, one could only see some indistinct movement. With nothing else to occupy her mind she took pleasure in seeing the rain falling fast and then slowing down. But when she occasionally ventured out into the park, she saw that the sand was of a darker colour than normal and smelt damp. Drops fell on her umbrella and quite enormous transparent ones came down if her brolly touched the bushes or low branches. For a few days she and Hugo did not see one another. Then she sent him a note – an invitation to tea, sealed with violet wax. He was delighted and came in excitement, determined to be a model of good behaviour on the visit. The ugly room seemed significant to him, a new experience. She apologised for its narrowness, saying she would show him her room in Prague which was quite different. It was her sanctuary and he would be one of the few who had been allowed to enter it. She described it in detail: her pictures, the furniture, the antique silk-covered divan, the caskets filled to the brim with

Jewish Women

mementoes. He would certainly see a great deal there, a great deal. He felt honoured and listened to her intently and even when her mother intervened in an unfriendly manner, and asked if he knew where Lindengasse was, he did not allow his anticipation to be diminished. The tea gleamed like honey in his little cup. Irene refused to add rum to hers. 'If only I didn't have such a headache!' she groaned and pressed her lips together. He suspected some emotional pain behind the physical discomfort. Under the table he secretly pressed a sharp thumbnail into the flesh of his other thumb, and prayed to God, or some other unknown powerful being, that his pain might be a substitute for Irene's. He must suffer and thereby free Irene from her pain. He had done that as a child when his dearly loved governess had been ill.

Frau Lucie

He went home that evening glowing with happiness. The evening meal had barely been served when his mother asked, 'And for how long have you been going around with women?' It was a question Hugo had long been expecting, but so long as his mother did not broach the matter, he had naturally said nothing about Irene. He didn't know that his mother had only just that day heard about his relationship with the family Popper in a note she'd received. The good Olga had said not a word about his encounters at the Manor House.

'For about fourteen days,' he replied calmly, and only feared that his tone might reveal that he had certainly associated with her for fourteen days but had only really got to know her that day.

'I have nothing against your associating with women,' said his mother in a trembling voice. 'It seems that it has to be like that with you young people. I'm only worried that you may have begun a little too soon ...'

'But you yourself allowed me to go to the dancing classes in Prague.'

'Yes. And perhaps that was a mistake ...'

'I asked you in a letter and you were even enthusiastic about the idea.'

'I only thought that you would polish up your manners. Also I thought that your being a recluse was not a good idea, didn't I Olga?'

Olga was startled: 'But Aunt, I don't think it's so bad.' Then she went completely red, right down to her fingertips and looked into her plate.

'Well, Olga, you are a grown woman now. Why are you staying so aloof? It is the opposite of what you are doing, Hugo. Herr Klein was here today and wanted to invite her to join his tennis group. But she went and hid in the kitchen, and when I fetched her, I couldn't get her to say a word!'

'But she didn't say no?' cried Hugo eagerly. He had suddenly had an idea.

'No, she didn't.'

'But one can't run after men in that way!' replied Olga in a strangely deep voice. She had grown up in the confines of a small country town in which extreme aloofness was considered to be the first duty of a Jewish girl. All men were to be seen as the enemy, and there was not much socialising to be had. She had a strong character but was modest through and through. What expression would Irene have used for her? thought Hugo. He himself would compare her, stimulated as he had been that evening, with the daughters of Jerusalem whose chastity was praised in the Bible. She reminded him of the cedars of Lebanon, of the lives of the patriarchs in tents in the desert. Today her jet black hair stood up stiffly in a peak and was well brushed and shiny. It looked as though no wind could have disturbed that firmly fixed hair style under which her narrow white brow shone like a half moon.

'Who is talking about running after anyone?' the little lady said with a wise smile. 'We have an old saying, '*Zu viel und zu wing is ein Ding*'[17] But her worried mother's heart turned again to Hugo, although much of her afternoon sermonising had been directed at Olga. 'But why did you seek out that one in particular to run after, Hugo?'

'Do you know her?' cried Hugo.

'Not her – but I knew her father earlier on, when I was single. And then my cousin Flora has told me about her ...'

'Aha, the fat one ... and what did she say?'

His mother shook her head in consternation. 'Nothing pleasant. All in all I have the impression she is some kind of blue stocking.'

Hugo embraced her in delight: 'Mama, you are such a charmer, such a charming little Mama.' He stroked her cheek while she kept murmuring, 'But what is this all about?'

'Don't you know – blue-stocking is such a delightful word, so *Biedermeier,* from when you were single – perhaps in those times when Georges Sand went around in men's clothing. And the best of all is that Fräulein Popper is exactly the opposite of what you are talking about. Or, put another way, she knows all the worst aspects of a blue-stocking. "Blue-stocking" – what a wonderful word! One can see a lady inventing it disapprovingly over knitted stockings. Perhaps she has the temperament of an emancipated woman, as we would describe it in the style of our own decade ... but she carefully fights everything within herself which could remind one of the behaviour of an emancipated woman. And what does she get in return? The next man comes along and hits the target in the middle, in the black. Such a blue-stocking! Mama, mama, I love you so much—'

She stroked his hair. But Olga had listened to him carefully, so much so that the strong bones under her eyebrows grew more pronounced as concern furrowed her brow. Then she said: 'Hugo ... listen to me ... I think she is an egoist.'

'Aren't we all egoists, each in our own way,' he replied to the new attacker, determined to defend his ideal against all comers. But he felt the weakness of his counter-move and at the same time, nostalgia for that serious study of Kant passing through him and he asked: 'Anyway, what do you mean by 'egoist'? It should be more closely defined.'

'Well, I think she is using you,' said Olga, who had obviously thought hard about the matter. 'She goes around with you because she hasn't got anyone else.'

'Aha ... no-one else ... as it happens all kinds of people are running after her?' He thought of the waiter, of Herr Nussbaum. At the same time he found it pleasant and appropriate to his sense of justice that he was now defending Irene against Olga as he had recently defended Olga against Irene.

'Yes. Flora already told me,' said his mother, slowly and seriously, 'that Fräulein Popper is a bit ... hysterical ... and always thinks that every man is courting her.'

'Look ...'

Caught in the cross-fire, Hugo went quiet.

'Anyway, she has had good reason to be hysterical,' continued his mother. 'The poor girl has already had enough misfortune in her life. I feel really sorry for her. Flora told me that she was engaged last year and everything was ready for the wedding. And then the other side suddenly went back on it. All at once the dowry was too small. Apparently the bridegroom, a lawyer called Winternitz, was a rogue who had left another girl high and dry under the same circumstances, in Pilsen. For months he went arm in arm with Irene through the streets, the announcement of the engagement had been put in all the newspapers and the wedding invitations had already been printed. I heard that the Poppers had even rented an apartment for the young couple in readiness. Flora told me everything. And what trouble they had persuading the furniture dealer to take it all back! I can imagine that something like that would make anyone feel low.'

'These men,' said Olga, 'I don't know what I would do to someone like that …' Her dislike of the whole sex was given new fuel, further confirmation.

Hugo was silent. Only now did he understand Irene. So that was her secret. How could he have taken the flirting with Nussbaum seriously! He now saw her clearly as an innocent victim. Oh, to be able to help her, rescue her from the bad memories, and lead her into a new and carefree life. And how silently she had suffered. So she was a heroine and had lived up to his image of her. Her occasional caustic remarks and her ironic outlook were now, suddenly, entirely understandable. How could a heart which had been squeezed and broken bear to encompass new ideas! It was even a wonder that she was still alive. And her headaches … her evil mother who didn't understand her … Frau Lucie went quiet and was upset when she saw his serious face: 'Didn't you know until now …'

'Well,' he responded, coming out of his train of thought, 'you feel sorry for her yourself.'

She shrugged her shoulders: 'The world is bad … things like that happen every day.' And her small face, with all its delicate wrinkles and corners, suddenly looked hard as stone or a clenched fist, it was so rigid.

'Do you know what,' he continued, picking up again an idea which he had already had. 'Dear Mama, you must get to know her. That would be the best thing. I will introduce you. Her mother asked me only today to introduce you to them at some time ...' Irene's mother had in fact, in spite of her habitual icy reserve, said something of the kind that day. 'The whole thing is very simple. Tomorrow afternoon we are going with Olga to the Königshohe where Herr Klein plays tennis with his friends. Olga will surely let herself be persuaded to attend, won't she? Assuming, of course, that the weather improves. And on the next court the group from the Manor House will be playing. I will arrange for you to meet Frau and Fräulein Popper.' He was completely taken with his plan, which in addition to having the goal of drawing the families close together, offered another possibility: that from then on he could also spend the afternoons with Irene, assuming the mothers got on with one another and Olga allowed herself to be detained on the neighbouring court.

'You're a good boy,' said his mother with feeling. 'Just be careful that it doesn't happen with you as it did with Hans.' Hans had been Hugo's elder brother who had died six years ago. 'He was also one for the ladies, and particularly the weaker ones, the ones who needed help. That's why I was so alarmed when that letter came today. Women drove Hans to his death. I'm constantly thinking about it today – I don't know why that is, but I can't get it out of my head!' As if to give herself some relief, she carried on. 'For months he pursued that actress and protected her from her director. What didn't we say to him, but all in vain! I know that he just wanted the noblest things in life, poor Hans. He loved art, beauty and the ideal. She must have been a very beautiful girl – Henriette Collina

– according to what I was told.' 'But leave that now, Aunt. We know it all ...' Olga anxiously put her hands on her shoulders to comfort her, but Frau Lucie couldn't be stopped. 'In the end Hans was shot in a duel. And not by the director – that's the worst part of it – but by some foreign officer. It was never really clear exactly what happened!' She put her handkerchief to her eyes. She had put her other hand on the table and Hugo stroked it. Suddenly she cried out, 'If I lose you as well, Hugo ... you are the only one I have left in the world ...'

He tried to make a joke of it: 'You're just jealous, dearest Mama ... *na, na.*' But his eyes were wet. Once the conversation had turned to unhappy themes, it had aroused sad family memories, dreadful events that were scarcely believable and yet often happened in the world.

After they broke up Olga caught him on the stairs and asked, 'Do you want some new candles?'

'No, I have enough.'

She looked deep into his eyes: 'I know. I saw. Don't be angry – I count them every day when I clear up. You haven't used up many, not even one. And you mustn't misunderstand me; there was no other reason when I said today that she is using you and that she is an egoist. I thought that she was preventing you from working so that you can entertain her. Are you angry with me for that?'

'But Olga ...'

'Perhaps I am doing her an injustice. One should never think badly of anyone.' She became strict again out of sweet concern for him: 'But you really haven't studied much. How will the examination go after the holidays?'

He had long been prepared for that criticism. 'It doesn't make any sense to be cramming in July, you know. I would forget it all again. I have thought hard about it. I will begin in August, and you will be astounded.'

'All right,' she said hesitantly and left him, only half reassured. 'So ... good night then.'

'It is very good of you to check up on me so much,' he called after her, forcing warmth into his voice, because a certain irritation had risen in him which he immediately decided was unjustified. 'Thank you very much Olga. Good night!'

The Tennis Court

In the morning, lying in bed, Hugo could see the sky was blue. At first he was sorry about that, because he realised what he owed to the rainy days with their cosy mantle of gloom from morn till night – his intimacy with Irene. Then he remembered the new appointment, on the tennis courts, and he jumped up happily, in tune with the cheerful weather.

He discussed the whole plan with Irene at their morning meeting. She was fully in agreement with his suggestions and in the afternoon he drove his mother and Olga to the Konigshöhe. His mother's words of the evening before about the unfortunate fate of her eldest son had made different impressions on the three people present. His mother, who was not melancholy by nature, had been to some extent relieved of her fears by having spoken about them. And now having raised the matter in her own words, and having examined in detail the circumstances of the misfortune, she became aware of the significance of the differences between the situation of Hans at that time and Hugo's now – particularly their disparate ages and the difference between the girls. But Olga was of a less volatile disposition and was still suffering from the shock which her kindly nature had endured from the violent shattering of the family peace. Lastly, Hugo, newly enlightened about his own passionate nature and his present difficulties, took a calm and considered view of the day. On the journey he did his best to prepare his mother. He acknowledged in advance that Irene's way of speaking might initially seem rather pert and her mother's natural reserve more like arrogance, but asked his own to make allowances until she got to know them better.

Irene never played tennis. She hated the sport as a new and graceless exercise and couldn't tolerate the efforts one had to make. She much preferred to walk around the courts in the afternoons with one or more of the gentlemen. However, as previously agreed by them, she was on this occasion standing alone by the entrance gate and when she saw Hugo arriving she ran towards him.

'I can see that you ...' Then acting as though she had just noticed the ladies accompanying him, she politely ceased to address Hugo. He quickly made the introductions and, with a show of respect, Irene kissed Frau Rosenthal's hand and greeted the silent Olga in a friendly manner.

At Irene's pressing invitation all four of them walked up to the tennis courts together.

On a bench to one side sat Frau Popper and Frau Weil. They were sisters, both dark-complexioned and dressed in dark clothing. Irene dealt with the situation skilfully. It wasn't clear whether she had given them a signal or whether the two of them had stood up politely of their own accord. In any event, the next moment they were all standing together in a group.

'Do you like it here in Teplitz?' asked Frau Lucie.

'I am quite satisfied,' answered Frau Popper drily, 'what

more can one expect ...'

'The weather hasn't been very pleasant up until now,' interposed Frau Weil, as if she had to mediate between her sister the visitor and this local lady. 'One can hardly be blamed for not being too enthusiastic.'

Irene took up the topic of the weather. She spoke with markedly more animation than the pleasantries required, clearly intending to liven up the conversation. 'But what more could you ask for? Today is the best weather in the world, glorious sunny weather ...'

Hugo noticed with surprise that the conversation had not moved any further forward. He wondered when they would begin to speak about something else. They had all thrown themselves into the topic in order to soothe Frau Popper's feelings since her remark had been harmless enough. But she herself did not seem to need any consolation, and joined in the talking as though there were a fourth person to console. It seemed to Hugo that there were suppressed yawns accompanying every word, and the atmosphere of his Prague tennis days seemed to have returned. And then he looked in surprise at his kindly mother whom he was used to seeing only in friendly company. Here she was tense and cold. And Frau Popper, whose stifled sobbing over her prone daughter he seemed still to hear, faced her with indifference like a stone wall. Those two caring mothers behaved as though their hearts were fixed only on their own families. They opposed each other, as if with heartless bodies. With their weapons and armour they seemed to be openly hostile to one another, not, as it were, because they knew each other but on the basis of previous bad experiences. Solemn-faced, they jousted verbally as though they had kingdoms to defend from one other.

On the courts no-one was playing as yet. Herr Demut and his brother were marked out as the only serious sportsmen there by their clothes. They wanted to play a singles game together. 'The women just make mistakes,' they declared, 'and you can't really have a proper game with them because all they want is to cause a disturbance.' 'Just so,' retorted Dr Taubelis, 'Their primary aim is to disturb and they can only do that if they join in the game.' Alice and Flora Weil protested against the verbal attacks launched by the three men and focussed their attention on one or the other in turn. They seemed to want to prolong the break indefinitely if it gave them the chance to talk to the men. They had already put away their equipment while the men continued to gesticulate with their racquets, tennis balls at the ready and words like 'play' on their lips. Only the older Fräulein Kapper seemed to take the matter seriously. She had a shrill, already old-maidish, voice and sad, small black eyes and seemed to take the matter seriously. She was really angry and tried to achieve some order. Her younger sister Kamilla was sitting stiffly on the second bench along, in front of the tent. Nussbaum and his friend Pitroff, a young Russian, were standing next to her and every now and then they bent down to say something to her. She smiled, but at each approach seemed upset, offended almost, that anyone should dare to disturb her. She persisted in her lofty silence while at the same time there was a trace of satisfaction in her smile. She turned her whole body to look up at the person speaking to her, and as it were, straightened up with difficulty. From the combination of offended and flattered an impression arose of indescribable, almost unbearable, affectation. The tastefully calculated simple elegance of her clothing contrasted with her naïve behaviour. Her face was the prettiest on the court, or at least the most easily appreciated at first glance. It had a smooth and well-modelled symmetry, a fleshy uniformity, so it was easy to see why the two men were making such strenuous efforts with her.

Hugo had half turned his back on the mothers in order to study the silent, indolent girl who stirred in him faint memories of Gretl. Irene was talking loudly behind him. He had been so affected by the revelation of her secret the day before that she now seemed to him like a saint or a martyr. But today's cheerfulness, albeit as thin as candlelight, her gift for conversation, the friendly superciliousness she exhibited towards the mothers with its echoes of great balls, of political conversations in which she had participated, had all driven away his devotion only too quickly. That pained him, although for her sake he felt he should be pleased. While he was immersed in these contradictory feelings, staring at the grey floor and almost hypnotised by the white chalk lines, he suddenly felt something cold on his neck.

He put his hand to his collar. It was water. He spun around. Then he saw Elsa Weil looking at him, the youngest of the three sisters, an eleven-year-old brat. Her whole face was screwed up in hilarity but she was not making a sound; her slender body was bent double and shaking with the effort of suppressing such mirth. The child's shining eyes were open so wide that the whites showed in a ring around the brown irises. She had sidled up to him undetected and fired her fully-loaded water-pistol. He looked at her in embarrassment and whispered: 'But Fräulein ...' with the same awkwardness he felt before many local girls, because he wasn't sure whether he should introduce himself formally or treat their mutual acquaintance as a given. And what a forward child! He was distinctly irritated, particularly when he saw that, emboldened by his politeness, she was aiming her pistol at him for a second time. Should he box her ears, run away or shout at her?

Fortunately Irene noticed his predicament. 'Stop it, will you, you little monkey! What an urchin!' She darted forward and chased the enemy away. The girl whirled around on the tips of her toes so that her skirt billowed up. She was still wearing socks. One could see her slender bare calves, looking like delicately carved wood, and her lovely rounded kneecaps – all brown from the sun and showing new and old grazes. At a safe distance she turned round again and made a face at them before she ran away. Her brown hair was loose and only restrained by a light green bow. It flapped like a short cape around her shoulders.

'She will be prettier than her sisters,' said Irene, 'one can see that at first glance. She's such a wild little thing but one can't help liking her. I was like that when I was small ... Did you hear that Elsa recently let off some gunpowder caps in the theatre during a quiet scene? And once she bought the best fruit at a delicatessen, whole baskets full, and had the bill sent to her house. She plays such pranks! Yet she's top of her class at school.'

'Then the teachers must have a lot of patience with her,' growled Hugo, still rather irritated as he tried to dry his neck with his handkerchief.

'A bright child,' said Irene, closing a subject that didn't particularly interest her. With a sideways glance in the direction of the mothers, she turned to her own matters: 'So that's all in hand. Let's leave them to it!' she said and steered Hugo over to join the young people.

Herr Nussbaum was the first to be introduced. Hugo

found him not nearly as laughable as Irene had depicted him. Did she perhaps see everything ironically? He had a full beard which had been firmly brushed into two points, large dark eyes and a strong if crooked nose; all in all he made a thoroughly respectable impression on Hugo. Nussbaum complained that once more he had had to postpone his public meeting by a week because the authorities had put such difficulties in his way. He spoke in a deep and ponderous voice, and seemed to be perpetually addressing himself to a large audience. Convinced as he was of the effect he had, he didn't seem to attach much importance to the words he chose but reserved his main efforts for making a kind of emotional appeal, constantly bemoaning his own ill fate and suffering. His eyes swam hither and thither; his hands trembled. He allowed a small element of self-deprecation, or a joke, to creep in from time to time, as though duty bound. But in the next sentence the inner turmoil of his freedom-loving soul showed through, even more painfully than before; his struggle against the whole of society. At a superficial glance one could take him for a poseur. But it quickly became apparent how serious and innate this tragic role was for him. It was hard to imagine what he would be without that underlying element of tragedy. That fighting attitude was, as Hugo realised, the connection between him and Irene. It became clearer to him as he got to know other people on the court, what the nature of her association was with each of them.

With the older Demut brother she spoke about Coalport's *Elegance* porcelain and a new Operetta figure in the range. The younger Demut didn't seem to pay her any marked attention. Neither did she seem to have any connection with Dr Taubelis apart from sharing the occasional joke as could now and then

Jewish Women

be heard. He constantly spoke against tennis and advocated a good game of bowls, which he was already looking forward to. He hadn't forgotten there was one that very evening. He invited Hugo to come along, giving him a hearty slap on the back. If people hadn't constantly addressed him as 'Doctor', it would have been more likely that with his loud behaviour, and his strong red face, he would have been mistaken for a commercial traveller.

'Tell me,' said Hugo, drawing close to Nussbaum who was standing nearby, 'what are you actually going to speak about at the meeting?'

'Against Zionism,' came the ready reply.

'And why are you against Zionism?' asked Hugo in all seriousness, hoping to learn something from him.

While Nussbaum made sweeping hand gestures in preparation for his reply, Irene interrupted with her own ready opinion. 'But one must be against Zionism. One just must, as one must be against the Women's Movement.' Her decisiveness cut off Hugo in mid-sentence. With a contemptuous shrug of her shoulders she seemed to be saying that she considered that bringing any evidence or logical reasoning to the matter was superfluous, uncivilised and even uncouth. Inwardly Hugo did not agree with her, but he had become accustomed to her way of seeing certain things at certain times as axioms, and to her attitude towards those axioms; he felt a vague anxiety and dared not speak further. Anyway, the matter was of no particular importance to him, just something to talk about.

But Nussbaum carried on speaking undeterred. 'Zionism is a reactionary movement which is all the more dangerous for creeping in under the guise of progress …'

Hugo wanted to say that a general comment like that

could be made about any type of movement. But he held back because, at Irene's behest, he considered the subject as closed. To his astonishment Irene turned to him and said: 'Look, I told you already – it's just the same with female emancipation. Reaction masquerading as progress. Yes, that's very well put ...' So she doesn't follow her own rules, Hugo thought to himself. I am more 'Irene-like' than she is. And felt a little ashamed at the realisation.

Nussbaum set his face in a serious expression, obviously wanting to respond, then suddenly slapped one hand to his neck. Little Elsa Weil had crept up close again and, standing on tiptoe, sprayed him from behind with her water-pistol. As she pulled the trigger, her red lips pouted further and further from her pale face until they resembled a little snout. Nussbaum took hold of her hand firmly, like a man who knows how to deal with any situation. He smiled good-naturedly and tried to pat her head. She shook it angrily and screamed while struggling to free herself. Her thin wrist reddened under his thick, knotted, brown fingers.

Josef, Nussbaum's son, had arrived at the same time as Elsa. Like his father, he was casually but elegantly dressed as befitted a bachelor. The impression given by his worn clothing was enhanced when he said: 'Papa, could you please give me a Krone?'

Nussbaum, visibly annoyed, turned on him, saying: 'Not again, surely. You received your pocket money only yesterday.'

'And he bought me a ball with that,' babbled Elsa cheekily as she sprang to Josef's side, having finally managed to extricate herself, 'there's not much one can do with a Gulden.'

'Littl'un,' warned Nussbaum, in faux-friendly fashion. And then, in a distinctly unfriendly manner, said to his son while he handed over the money, 'Here are twenty Kreuzer, you won't get any more until the fifteenth.' Although possessed of a large fortune Nussbaum was distinctly miserly, as is often the way with people who live off their wealth without doing anything to add to it. To be forever eating into capital puts them in a permanent bad mood. This strictness towards his son compared unfavourably with the warmth he liked to exhibit in general. Getting it wrong, like the mothers, Hugo realised.

'He'll buy me more caps with that,' said Elsa. 'Isn't that right, Josef?' She hung on his arm, craning back her neck to peer into his face, enquiringly and seductively. 'And later on he will marry me ... Isn't that right, Josef, you will be my husband?'

The overgrown lad looked back at her fondly and replied: 'Certainly, Elsa.' Leading her to a bench, he put down the large bundle he had been carrying under one arm. He had brought her his entire collection of books about Red Indians and volumes by Karl May. She was thrilled. Throwing herself on them, she began to rifle through her haul and shout out the titles: '*In the Land of the Skipetars* ... *Winnetou* ... oh, you're so nice to me, Josef ...' He calmly showed this or that to her and kept putting the other volumes, which she'd scattered over the seat, back in the right order. The youth appeared somewhat awkward to Hugo but there was no sign of his being the idiot Irene had portrayed him as. He began to distrust her judgment.

Irene approached the bench. As so often happens when children are present while general conversation fades, Irene took advantage of the opportunity to adopt a child's outlook herself and began to praise other examples of Elsa's conspicuously bad behaviour. 'Did you hear about Elsa and the big nose?' she asked them all. 'She recently met a man in the spa park whose nose was greatly enlarged by cancerous ulcers.

She looked at him for a long time and jumped around until he asked in a friendly way what she wanted. She answered that she just wanted to see whether each of the growths on his nose had its own pair of nostrils ... such perfect callousness!' Irene laughed aloud, and louder still when Hugo reluctantly joined in. Elsa listened as if it had nothing to do with her. She stood motionless and stared calmly up at the sky. There was a yellowish light in her eyes, as if whipped up by the wind currently blowing across the court and tugging at her skirt. She held it down firmly, palms against her thighs as she sat down. Then she wedged a fold between her knees and sat back with her hands folded behind her head. Her flashing eyes became placid, as if merging with the sunlight which lay on her smooth cheeks. Irene turned to Josef next, speaking in the simple way which adults adopt who think they are good with young people: 'What kind of books are they?'

The lad's damp, red and shining face, with its dull blue-grey eyes like clouded water-drops, turned to Irene with an awkward rolling movement inside his collar. He followed up the motion of his head by taking a clumsy step in her direction. Josef had an oddly determined-looking gait; he kept his fists clenched, his upper body leaning forward as he took big steps. He often looked around him in a frightened manner with a jerk of his head. He stood up straight, and seemed to pull himself together although there was no obvious occasion for it. 'Here, Fräulein,' he said to Irene with slow emphasis, almost effusive but in a quiet voice, 'are the strangest adventures in the world, the greatest deeds, the harshest deprivations.'

'Well,' laughed Irene, 'that wouldn't interest me at all.'

'Not interest you ... America, the Savannas, the Sahara Desert?'

Irene prodded Hugo with her elbow as she asked the lad: 'So, do you believe that everything in those books is true?'

'Why not?' said Hugo, in order to give Josef more time since he was clearly struggling to follow.

'It's not only all true, Fräulein,' said Josef, his face glowing with conviction, 'it has been personally experienced. I have visited Karl May in his villa in Dresden, I have his autograph, and I have seen his silver gun and the Henrystutzen[18] ...'

'Not only true, but personally experienced,' joked Irene. 'What do you mean by that?'

'What have you got against him,' said Hugo to her quietly. 'It's nice to see such youthful enthusiasm ...'

'But he is driving the girl mad,' hissed Irene and Hugo was at a loss to understand on what basis she was making such a judgment. One moment she was defending Elsa's unusual character, even, it seemed, her amorality; the next she wanted to keep her safely in a bourgeois environment. How could those two approaches be reconciled? With a friendly nod, Irene roused Elsa from her day-dreaming. 'Will you read these books? Which one will you read first? ...' She looked down at the girl benignly.

But Elsa replied pertly, 'That's none of your business. Whichever one I like best I will read first. I read what I want to. Isn't that right, Josef ...'

Josef didn't understand the situation and said seriously, 'I would recommend reading them in order, beginning with the first volume.' Although significantly older, he seemed less mature than Elsa who was bent on driving away her cousin with dark looks.

At last Hugo was able to walk alone with Irene up and down along the court. He told her that he didn't feel comfortable among those people; in fact, he was really disappointed, having imagined that the afternoon would be very different. 'But in what way?' 'I don't know. Just different.' She said he was suffering from mild depression, and told him that life was more complicated than he imagined. Those words hit their target. He was pleased that Irene felt it necessary to instruct him and to clarify things for him. And with regard to the complications of human interaction, of social gatherings – that one must bear them with fortitude rather than getting into weak-willed moods was also his proud, firmly held opinion in spite of himself. No shying away from uncomfortable facts, no dizzy-making happiness. And so he listened while Irene expanded upon her favourite theme, which was the structure of society. Here in Teplitz she had already found castes. 'Look at your friend Olga,' she continued rather spitefully, 'she immediately found her way around at the second court, but not with us ... the country bumpkin!'

In fact, immediately upon arrival, Olga had been noticed by Frau Fried, Klein's sister and warmly invited to join another group, but she did not go without having first asked Frau Lucie's permission. Herr Klein, whose business prevented him from being free until the evening, was for the time being not present. 'Oh, how pleased he will be when he comes,' declared his sister. And Olga, quickly finding her way around, borrowed some tennis shoes and a racquet from the wardens, and was soon playing enthusiastically. The general consensus was that she had a definite natural gift for a clever stroke and all the men were happy to instruct her. She proved to be both grateful and determined. She sprang about freely, and gave it her all. Her cheeks were already glowing as red as strawberries. She constantly asked: 'Am I holding the racquet correctly? Like that? If I hold it lower down, I can't manage ...'

'See how she walks!' said Irene critically. 'So proudly ... She goes around as if she's in a dancing class ... and so tightly laced. Don't you have the feeling that you can hear her corset screaking with every step. It pains me just to hear it ...'

'You don't seem to like her very much.'

'What do you mean?' said Irene with a toss of her head. But, she couldn't stop herself from occasionally peering through the net which divided the two courts. Olga's unaffected good nature, to which everyone responded, had raised her acquaintances' spirits. All the men were looking after her and when Herr Klein eventually arrived he had an uphill task in commanding Olga's attention. They laughed at him and said: 'First come, first served', while Olga vivaciously tried to make peace, gave orders and shouted above everyone else. And all this unaccustomed exuberance seemed to bubble up unbidden and with the same naturalness as her usual air of calm competence.

Hugo turned back to his own court. The two Demuts, whose white tennis shirts hung half open on their chests, were either stretching up, or running with huge strides, and sometimes almost lying on the ground. To smash an unreturnable ball close to the net on the opponent's side of the court they stretched upwards, and to reach a difficult side shot they stretched out incredibly long arms. No point was too far away for them, no serve too quick. Their sleeves were rolled up; on their bare brown arms the muscles visibly bunched then released. With their wild movements and their ruthless running hither and thither, they seemed like wild animals in a cage. The women who were more quietly involved in the game seemed more like the indifferent spectators who were standing around. The light began to fade. The persons standing still and dressed in black looked like towers while the two players dressed in white were like seagulls in flight, racing between them, and circling round them.

'What madness,' sighed Irene, 'what is it all for?'

Hugo felt that she was getting closer to his mood although coming from the opposite direction. For him, looking at those physical exertions gave him a desire to charge about in the same way. 'What is the matter with you?' he asked sympathetically.

'I feel so weak,' she said, almost fervently, as she looked at the show of strength on the one court and the enjoyment on the other. 'Doesn't it smell of sweat here and other human odours? When I look around me, everything seems so fragile. Everything ... my own mood included.'

'It makes me think of death,' whispered Hugo. 'In a hundred years' time, what will remain of all that we are looking at?'

She shivered: 'Something has upset me, I don't know what ...'

'Nerves?'

'You can call it that if you like, I seem incapable of uttering a proper sentence ...' She turned to him and asked warmly, 'Are you coming to the bowling alley this evening? We won't be disturbed there. Here there are draughts and everything is in a muddle.' She pulled her shawl more closely around her shoulders which as she leaned forward seemed even narrower than before. 'Are we leaving soon?'

'It's true Fräulein Irene, now you can see it as well ... we two don't belong here. We are another type of person entirely ...'

'In every way?' she asked him confidentially.

He nodded calmly and silently.

The next moment, startled by a loud peal of laughter from nearby, she let fly at him: 'Oh, you men, in one way you are all the same!' and looked over at Olga who was doing waltz steps with one man while three others stood around them. She peered at them for a moment and then turned away, as if to avoid the cause of her bad mood. 'It's outrageous – this preference for plumpness!' She considered for a moment whether she should press her hand to her own meagre breast. Then she did it and almost hissing said, 'In sexual matters, you men are infuriatingly alike, all of you!'

Hugo protested.

She pretended that she had never counted him among the generality of men. He was alarmed by her dismissive look. Then as if in acknowledgement of this, she lowered her hand from her eyes and presented a more friendly face to him. She was breathing heavily and, as if seeking salvation from him as a trusted friend, said: 'This evening, don't forget ...' He happily returned her gaze and at that moment he felt that his worth in the world was significantly higher than it had been, that he was acknowledged and had almost achieved what he most wished for. Inclining their heads towards each other the pair stood to one side of the court, silhouetted against the evening sky like two swaying pillars. They fell silent, having recognised their mutual loneliness.

In the meantime Olga had returned to Frau Lucie who exclaimed: 'How hot you are!' Nussbaum praised Olga and asked her to play with them next time. Dr Taubelis invited her to the bowling that evening. Irene, who had joined them, directed a long disdainful glance at the steaming, shining and happy creature. Hugo drew her away. Naturally he didn't reproach her for the fact that her theory of the separation of Teplitz society had collapsed so quickly; on the contrary, he tried to get her to see the funny side of Herr Klein who was constantly bowing to Olga. He felt that she needed comforting.

They started to leave and Elsa used the general disorder to put her water pistol into action again. This time the younger Kapper sister was the victim. She had just wandered slowly to the tent and seemed to be annoyed that Pitroff was bent over his racquet press, while at the same time thanking him most graciously with a bored smile. Then came the jet of water. Indignant and now really offended, she turned on Elsa. But then she immediately turned away in contempt and one word came from her mouth whose full lips had remained closed for almost the entire afternoon – *Chutzpe!*

But this time the matter didn't end there. Frau Lucie had perhaps been irritated by the boring afternoon which had weighed heavy on her lively, happy heart and she said in a tone which was both friendly and reproving at the same time: 'Little girl, you should have your knuckles rapped for that. Who is allowing you to behave like that? Such a joke is ...' She had meant to say 'all right once' but strengthened her warning by saying '... not right. And when it happens several times ...'

Frau Weil was dismayed and, as though Frau Lucie's reprimand had been directed at her, took her youngest aside and began to rail at her about a thousand old offences, going from one to another and not even restraining herself from cursing. The whole group was embarrassed and impatient and seemed to fear hearing more family revelations. Josef stood next to Elsa with his bundle of books under his arm as if guarding her and ready at a sign from her to take them all

Jewish Women

on. But Elsa stood there calmly and with downcast eyes. She looked modest and innocent, staring at her shoes which she slowly raised and lowered until her heels bored into the sand. A strand of hair had strayed over her shoulder and onto her breast; her long eyelashes fluttered and cast delicate shadows onto her smooth cheeks.

Frau Lucie was astonished by the havoc she had caused and turned to leave. She pressed the others to do the same so as to disperse the crowd around Elsa. She called to Frau Popper who turned aside, muttering something about 'people who would do better to look after their own children and not involve themselves with other people's affairs—' Finally Dr Taubelis brought the matter to an end by lifting Elsa onto his shoulders and carrying her homewards. She began to cry up there. Josef wanted to rescue her and rushed after them. Elsa squirted the remaining contents of her water pistol in his face and laughed so loud with the pleasure of it and kicked so hard with her feet that the Doctor was glad to put her down again.

'It seems to me that we didn't have much luck with our mothers,' said Irene to Hugo.

She seemed to feel even more agitated and weak in the press of people.

In the meantime Frau Popper had quickly found an opportunity to take revenge for her wounded family pride. As the groups mixed together on the way home, someone expressed surprise that Pitroff already knew Frau Lucie. Unsuspecting, she responded: 'One of his acquaintances lived with me in my house – a Baroness.'

'So, you rent out rooms,' cried Frau Popper. 'I didn't know that. I could have rented from you. How much do you charge *pro Saison?*'

The Tennis Court

And while she suddenly played the customer, and moved Frau Lucie from an equal to an inferior place, someone whom she might possibly help to earn money, she found fresh opportunities to make malicious remarks. It was embarrassing for everyone and they wanted to change the subject but Frau Popper pretended to be in earnest and didn't stop putting questions about costs and conditions. Out of politeness Frau Lucie had to answer, although several times she mentioned that at the moment there were no vacancies. The charged atmosphere would definitely have ended with an outburst had not an unexpected incident taken matters in another direction. Suddenly Irene looked at a man who had just passed by, screamed, leaned on Hugo and swayed. Naturally he had to help both her and her mother who seemed frightened to death and completely transformed. He bundled them into a droshky and they drove off.

The Bowling Game

Frau Lucie and Olga refused to go to the bowling game with Hugo. Their excuse was that they were too exhausted. So Hugo set out alone. In his anxiety he took the long way round and the first thing he saw was the Manor House. Her window was dark. Had Irene recovered and gone to the bowling? Or had she already gone to sleep? He was alarmed. Clearly she didn't take their arrangement as seriously as he did. If she was unwell she obviously had the right to stay at home; although he would have gone wherever she told him to, even if he were seriously ill. He wondered what he would do with himself there if he did not meet her. He had probably annoyed his mother and Olga for no good reason. He tried to recall the way they had looked at him when he left. They clearly believed that he was bewitched by Irene, and in love, which in fact he was. Did it look as if he were running behind her all day like a little dog? He thought hard about it but couldn't remember what their faces looked like because he had been in such a hurry. And, thinking back, he wondered if perhaps he was more in love with Irene than he was prepared to admit.

Because only then did he realise that he had not given any thought to his mother's worries and loneliness. He had only been concerned to get away and to be with Irene again as soon as possible after the brief interruption of the evening meal. A cold shudder ran through him at that thought. He was in Irene's power and she treated him like an exigent goddess. But at the same time he felt affection for the frail creature that she was, for her weakness that afternoon on the court and her fainting fit on the road, which now seemed to him like the ultimate consequence of her weakness in such a rough environment. How much he would have liked, there and then, to be able to talk to her about it.

The beach chair in which she usually sat was empty, but now the moon was tinting its sides with a heavenly clean blue-white light and throwing its shadows into relief so that it looked like a boat – the little cabin of a gondola. How nice it would be to lie back in it and, to the accompaniment of the oar strokes and singing, be wafted through the cool air to those fantastic places of which Josef had spoken. He had found the boy pleasant, Hugo thought to himself, more so than all the other people at the tennis court with whom he had recently become acquainted. Josef was a pure soul with open enthusiasm for life in his still unlined face. Without really knowing why, he somehow connected Josef's character with Irene and adorned his beloved with the same virtues, though without any inference that she had previously lacked them. The two persons became one and inseparable, merging into a glowing image and with that image he passed ecstatic hours somewhere in India, by moonlight. He had waited his whole life long for that moment, always in the knowledge that it would come, that it was destined to be. An innocent and honest happiness that did no harm to anyone and yet was filled with the joy of the struggle, and achieved by effort, after conquering all evil – under flowers and a roof of dried reeds. Perhaps I am sleep-walking, he thought, as he jerked himself out of his fantasies, the full moon has always had that effect on me. Suddenly he was filled with impatience. Why wasn't he already at the bowling alley next to her? Why was he losing valuable time? He began to run but whatever speed he gained was too little for him. He galloped through the dark and deserted park, over narrow bridges, and around the winding flower beds. He didn't even slow down on the street until he stood in front of the tavern *Zum Hufschmied*.

He walked through a dark corridor, musty with the smell of the taproom. The floor seemed to move as though laid over a swamp and the walls were damp with beer, undermined and decaying. He could already hear the slow rolling of the balls, the crack when they hit one another, the light crashing sound of the falling skittles. Hugo went in, but nobody noticed. Dr Taubelis had just thrown a 'nine' and so they shouted out and raised their glasses. He had to put ten Kreuzer into the cash box 'to celebrate'. With his jacket and waistcoat unbuttoned, cigar in mouth, and his legs set apart, he stood at the end of the alley and put on a serious expression as he bowled, though inwardly quite pleased with his success. Irene had also applauded him. Then she noticed Hugo who was taking off his overcoat and was looking around, undecided as to where to hang it. She came towards him.

'You have recovered already?'

'It was a small nervous crisis, nothing more,' she said. She seemed to be strangely exalted, as if lit from inside. 'Let's stay here,' she said in a lively tone, 'so that we are alone. Over there one can't get a moment's peace.'

He sat down at the table. He laid his overcoat on a chair, unconcerned. He gave a nod in the direction of the other people and then looked his beloved in the face. Soft music began to play inside him while she looked back with a friendly smile.

In the large hall there were only two or three gas lights near the alley, so that the lower half of the long table, which had no cloth on it, remained quite dark. Hugo and Irene sat there. On the other side of the table, in a small lit-up space, the others were moving about between the run-up to the alley, the podium where the scores were chalked up, and the upper end of the table where the beer glasses stood on a red cloth. Many of the ladies sat around, while others looked at the next person to bowl. The men were playing *Honneur* and seemed very serious about it.

'You're not leaving, Pitroff?' shouted Nussbaum. But Pitroff couldn't be persuaded to stay. The younger Kapper girl hadn't appeared. She had let it be known that she was too tired. Elsa was also absent. 'Where is little Elsa?' called Nussbaum, who apparently felt embarrassed on account of his son. 'My youngest has to stay at home as a punishment,' declared Councillor Weil. Josef immediately gathered up his things and left; he had been sitting patiently at the table without daring to ask. Without paying any attention to the others, he disappeared with Pitroff. Hugo followed him with his eyes, and was surprised how little he empathised with him now, in contrast to the deep sympathy which he had felt earlier in the park. A good lad, but there were many like him in the world.

'The two lovers. Isn't that funny?' said Irene and spoke as calmly, as if she and Hugo had been talking the whole time.

In fact they had both fallen silent, as if moved by the same powerful feelings and quietly watched the players from their dark retreat. Hugo had hoped that a significant word would have broken the silence. But he knew how to control himself and quietly asked, in the same tone as Irene: 'Why?'

'It's precisely the two girls least in need of them who have admirers – Elsa and Kamilla, the youngest ones,' she said pensively.

'You're speaking like a mother,' he responded and grasped the glass which the waiter had put on the brown table. *'Prost!'*

Irene looked at him in astonishment, a little vacantly. Then she smiled, 'Wait a moment, I'm fetching my glass …' She got up and then, enchanted, he saw her coming back with light bobbing steps, as if blown by a breeze, holding the glass in front of her in her hand and leaning over it in a small sweet anxious moment. He had only seen her by day before, never in artificial light. And now he had to admit the yellow tone flattered her unexpectedly. For the first time her grey eyes showed up in their true colour a glorious blue. Her skin and her hair were also shining, and her lips were red and moist. 'Now I'm drinking with you,' she said. 'To your health!' And gaily touched his glass with hers as she sat down. She rattled her glass on the small table and pursed her lips to whistle briefly.

'You're in a very good mood today,' he observed, and it really seemed to him that in the lamp light her inner mood was also of a livelier colour than usual. 'It seems to me that the old song fits you well, the one my mother always sings: "By day I am hectic, by night I'm electric".'

'Our mothers!' she cried. 'Yes, that was unfortunate what happened today … but yours is really so friendly, so sensible … I am ashamed of mine. It is a problem I often have to contend with. My mother has a certain aristocratic pride, I have to admit. But in fact she has nothing to be proud about. It's just baseless arrogance, the kind I have often noticed among Jewish women. They imagine themselves to be unapproachable, just think they are better than everyone else, and carry on believing that, forever, although there is nothing to reinforce or strengthen it …'

'Perhaps that is the only kind of well-founded pride,' laughed Hugo, 'when one doesn't need any evidence for it.'

'Very possibly. But it's not very nice, not very pleasant for those involved … What will we do now? Well at least we still have our mornings together.'

He found the way in which she spoke about them, as natural allies, to be very gratifying. He would have liked to kiss her hand for it. 'I would be happy to make my afternoons free as well,' he said to her laughing. He had the impression that he need only say the right words to draw her from her elated and lively mood into a permanent close relationship with him. The words were on the tip of his tongue but he found he couldn't say them. In the meantime she turned back to more neutral but none the less friendly matters. 'But you should realise that my mother didn't mean anything really bad. I will apologise for her to your mother if you like …'

'That's really not necessary.'

Irene carried on with her high-spirited chatter and said, 'It's not as if there's anything to it; there's nothing special about our situation. Between you and me, we are solid middle-class but nothing more. The fact that I have moved in upper class circles, and to some extent been able to introduce my brother to them, is down to me alone.' She told him about her triumphs: how she had danced with Baron Havatschek, and recited poems by von Hahnenkamm in a fashionable club; and how Willi Karhoff had wanted to have a duel over her ... 'We'll also dance today, won't we. You'll dance with me Hugo,' she cried, leaning close to him. He could feel her breath on his face and her loosened hair gently wafted against him.

'What's going on with you two down there?' called Nussbaum. 'Always alone together. Won't you come and play with us for a bit?'

'Certainly,' said Irene and got up with alacrity, almost dancing. Hugo followed her.

'Match!'

Councillor Weil and Dr Taubelis were the captains. They called 'heads or tails' and the Councillor had first choice for his team. He chose the older Demut brother for his side, while the Doctor immediately chose the younger one. The two tennis players represented a different type of manly strength, a modern one that was necessary for this occasion. Their muscles were particularly suited to bowling. Also, because they were not known for giving much attention to the women but were focussing all their efforts on the sport, they were considered to be good material for the match. Nussbaum was chosen as the next most desired participant because bowling was his particular sport. He bowed to the Councillor as though a great honour had been conferred upon him, and eager to get down to the fight, had already started weighing a ball in his hand. Everything went so quickly that Hugo, who had been torn away from his pleasant conversation, barely found time in the general confusion to explain that he had never rolled a ball before and certainly not hit anything. 'All the better,' cried the Doctor, 'that way you will balance out Fräulein Irene. She just fumbles with the ball, and that kind of thing.' He chose the elder Kapper sister who was continually shouting that they shouldn't forget her and boasting about her skill. The two Weil girls were allocated to different sides on the basis that they were of equal strength and finally only Irene and Hugo remained. Each team claimed that they should be allocated to the opposite party. Irene's mother, Frau Weil and the Kapper husband and wife, who were not playing, remained seated at the table. 'Should we send him in first?' pondered Herr Weil and Demut, and then turned to Hugo. 'Come on, lad, you're going to be the first to bowl.'

Hugo stepped up to the alley. He started, as he had seen the others do, by moistening his hands in the blue enamel wash-basin which stood on a chair near the run-up. Then he inspected the balls in the wooden channel and chose the smallest. 'Take a bigger one, it knocks them down better,' advised someone behind him. He did what he was told, and then suddenly regretted that he had dared to come here and get involved in things he knew nothing about, and also that he had never before taken the opportunity to get some practice at bowling. His heart was beating fast and he was afraid of disgracing himself in front of Irene. If only he knew where she was standing and from what vantage point she could see him. He focussed his attention on his back, how to position it and which part of it she would see. He saw the alley in front of him and it looked endless. Its grey concrete surface shone eerily in those areas which were lit up by the three glaring lamps above. Those three shiny parts broke up the stretch and increased the appearance of its length. The last and strongest lamp threw its light over the skittles and a pale girl was arranging them. Then in the shadowy distance she scurried off to one side. Hugo realised that he must now begin since nothing was

The Bowling Game

hindering him. The blood rushed to his head and he wished for the strength of a woodcutter, a giant. 'Don't do a *Brandeis* or you'll be slaughtered,' called the Councillor pleasantly. But Hugo had already thrown the ball and without knowing what it was, had in fact done a *Brandeis*. This meant that the middle three skittles had fallen and the group was now split into two halves. It was divided by a broad furrow which caused great difficulties for those following him because even those balls which were well aimed were inclined to run through the middle of the skittles without bringing any more down. 'So we've got the hole already,' grumbled the captain with ironic satisfaction. 'Still, not a bad throw for a beginner.' He put his hand on Hugo's shoulder but Hugo was satisfied and would have been happy to retreat. 'Another go now.' Encouraged by the praise he doubled his efforts and knocked down two more skittles which earned him the lively admiration of everyone.

'Now what do you have to say to me,' he said, turning to Irene and beaming.

'Good luck!' She lifted her glass with a deprecating smile.

Because he had shown some aptitude, he became interested in the game. There was a feeling of rural German comfort to it, which pleased Hugo. Here he felt he was among brothers, without any distrust or anxiety. He went from one person to another, clapped them on the shoulder and spoke freely with them. At the same time he was constantly thinking about Irene who was speaking to the mothers, without taking any notice of the game. How pleasant it would have been to have exchanged a hearty handshake with her! And he was beside himself with amusement when he saw Nussbaum dramatically doing some magnificent bowling. His speciality was the rubber ball. He let it glide smoothly from his hand. It came

Jewish Women

on so slowly that the bowling girl stayed in the lane. Everyone laughed at the comical sight although they were well used to it. Although it rolled slowly the ball crashed into the skittles and brought down one, two, six with astonishing power. Nussbaum always waited until the rubber ball was thrown back to him. He scorned the others. Mysterious, heavy and fat, warty with grey bumps, it lay in his hand. He smiled at it modestly and it seemed to smile back at him.

Now the other team were on and everyone did their best. Only Irene's delicate body was almost thrown to the ground by the ball. She was obviously struggling with the game. Her pitch hit the wall a short distance in front of her. 'Missed!' cried Hugo. 'Everything is allowed in a game,' said the Councillor. Then Irene missed every time. He thought it was cunning, small-minded and to some extent cowardly to conserve her own strength in that way.

But he was not able to repeat his previous performance, his luck had deserted him. However hard he tried he was unable to bring down another single skittle.

Nussbaum lectured him: 'It often happens that beginners succeed with their first throw and then there's nothing more. It is a psychologically understandable fact, inasmuch as ...'

Hugo found it dreadful to hear him orate with the same expert knowledge about bowling as he had in the afternoon about Zionism. Provocatively he said, so that Irene could also hear, 'It seems to me that you are promoting the sacred doctrine of liberalism even in bowling...'

Nussbaum was astonished, and said, 'How is that?'

'Well, it's obvious.' Hugo was pleased with his own observation. He had the feeling that with a bit of thought one could make some sense of it if one wanted to, although as

The Bowling Game

yet he hadn't found any. Sensing a lively exchange developing Irene drew closer. 'You have theories for everything,' Hugo continued brusquely. 'You want to help everyone – to save the world and all its treasures.'

'Please!' said Nussbaum, turning to him, both offended and unctuous.

'A rubber ball … a comedy writer,' said Hugo, getting ever more heated, until nobody could understand what he was saying.

Because it was now his turn to bowl again, Counsellor Weil took Hugo by the hand. Ponderously he drew a chalk line in the middle of the alley. 'You must look at that, at the board, not at the ball. That is your biggest mistake, youngster.' 'Look, this is how a practical man speaks,' said Hugo turning angrily to Nussbaum again. He threw and missed once more. Sullenly he stepped into the background.

His enthusiasm had quickly faded. He looked at Irene, who was sitting at the table supporting herself on a small pink hand and leaning closely towards her mother. It was as clear to him as it had been at the tennis court that he and she did not belong among these people and their common amusements, but in another dimly lit place, fanned by romantic breezes; perhaps in Nice, he thought. He approached Irene from behind as she bent over like one of those narrow bridges in the park, and he whispered in an almost inaudible voice: 'Fräulein Irene …'

She quickly turned round to him with a movement which suggested she wished to embrace him. He felt that this was perhaps the word, the intonation which they had both been waiting for. He ran, rather than walked with her back to the dark end of the table, though admittedly not so far down as they had been sitting at the beginning; that would have been too obvious. But there was at least one empty chair between them and the others. Her eyes glittered and her small face suddenly seemed to widen, stretching right out to the walls to either side of them, so close did she come to him while she asked: 'Did you see my fiancé today?'

He looked at her in complete astonishment: 'Who? ... No.'

She didn't explain anything further. She assumed that he knew everything that was going on. 'What did you think then? That the nervous shock I suffered today was for no good reason? No, Dr Winternitz went past me as we left the tennis courts. It was obvious he was waiting for me ...'

'But I thought ...'

'Yes, yes, the engagement was broken off. A long time ago. But that's just it ...'

'I will protect you, if you wish. I will challenge him to a duel. Whatever you want, I will do it for you. I know how to guard you against such a rogue!'

'Don't be childish, Hugo. What have they been saying to you? My former fiancé was not a bad man, although everyone says that of him.'

'But didn't he deceive you, betray you?'

'He loved me as no man has ever loved a woman. Oh, if only you knew, Hugo ...' She pressed her hand on her breast. 'But that's the worst of it: our story is not yet finished. He is still in love, he follows me everywhere! He pesters me!'

'And you?'

'I have never stopped loving him. Now you know everything.' She let her hand fall from her breast to her lap and sighed. 'What happened between us no-one could ever describe. So many things. Even my former friend Frieda Wantoch played a role and not the most sympathetic one. But the main problem was that his partner – he is a lawyer, you see – holds most of the capital in the business, while Heinrich just works and works. His partner didn't want him to marry a woman with only a little money. He would rather have dissolved the partnership. And then there were his relations and the relations of Heinrich. There were endless torments and intrigues. You can't imagine. I myself said, "It won't have a good ending, Heinrich. How could I face you afterwards?" Yes, Heinrich was weak, but not a bad man, not that. They would have defeated the strongest person. Those reproaches, day after day; those tiresome events, one catastrophe after another and no end in sight.'

'But what about the girl in Pilsen?'

'Did you know about that as well? It was something quite different from the gossip which went around. She was mad. And not metaphorically, like we all are more or less, but really afflicted. Should he have married her regardless? It was an unhappy series of events, nothing more. But as I have already told you, it's always been like that in my life. Nothing straightforward, only complications. Isn't it odd too, how one still has a certain relationship with one's disengaged fiancé? Not directly, obviously. But Alice Weil corresponds with Frieda, and Frieda still maintains her friendship with Heinrich. She got to know him through me. Now she is married anyway and he helped with that, strangely enough, but I am not in the least jealous of that. And so it goes on: a confusing web of relationships. I know, for example, that since we broke off our engagement, a lot of rich young women have been introduced to him and he has refused to consider any of them. I know that he is always informed about everything that I do, who I am associating with and so on. And he doesn't leave me alone …

although it must be permanently over between us. Look, we once broke off our engagement because of his relatives but then were reconciled. It makes me so furious that he is just as unhappy as I am, that neither of us can find any peace—'

Hugo thought about it for a moment, remembering Flora's words to his mother, and wondering whether she didn't perhaps imagine this admirer. But Irene had already discreetly passed him a letter under the table in which some words were underlined in blue: *'the person in question also recently spoke about going to Teplitz for the summer holidays to see Irene again and to speak to her.'*

'Now what do you say about that? Do you understand that?' whispered Irene, then immediately sat down and flashed a glance at Alice. 'If she knew I was circulating her precious secrets—' Hugo was surprised and found those asides somewhat unimportant compared with the earlier revelations.

Completely stunned by learning so many new things at once, Hugo looked around. Over there in the light a new game had begun but they had not invited the two of them again. People jumped back and forth, swung their white-sleeved arms, and shouted all at once. While he was repelled by their strange behaviour, having found himself in the midst of them and having joined in with their lives, he felt tied to those people of whom he had known nothing three weeks before. It could be that on summer holidays, getting to know people happened more easily than it did in Prague. Or perhaps Irene had been a major contribution. For a few moments he felt that these human figures, in addition to their earthly meaning must also have a divine existence connected to his while their mere transitory existence remained always immaterial to him. Somehow, in higher and purer regions their souls, together with his, moved through space like transparent spheres and that endless sweet meaning and movement over the clouds was real life, true life, while what he saw in the tavern was nothing more than gross disappointment. Also Irene and her torment, her heartache that seemed so strange to him, were nothing more than an illusion, while the real Irene, that wonderful shining ball, that was close to him and that loved him as he loved her, glowed and glided next to his sphere somewhere in the distance and wonderful music came from both of them whenever they touched.

He turned to her but she was in a state of excitement, swept away by her revelations and in a kind of rapture. She carried on speaking: 'But that just can't be. I would rather die than go through such days and nights again. I love him very much. But in the end ... if it can't be ... one must pull oneself together, fight on and get up on one's feet again. Everyone must look after themselves. I will be strong. Anyway it was already dark. Perhaps it was him – the figure was very similar, the broad shoulders and upright bearing – or perhaps I was mistaken. Maybe I imagined it because I have been thinking about him the whole afternoon. Well, that's over, and I won't think about him again. I will begin a new life. Kant, mathematics, whatever you like ... Hugo you will stand by me, won't you? You will stay with me?'

He did not hear her clearly. Her words had caused a wave of contradictory feelings to flow through him. Sometimes he felt moved; sometimes let down again. But the last sentence had filled him with pure joy. He nodded silently as if requesting her to carry on speaking.

But Alice had sat down at the piano. The game was over, people wanted to dance, the fathers wanted to play cards for a bit. A new waltz from *The Count of Luxembourg* rang out.

'Shall we dance to this, Hugo,' she cried, and then got up and reached out to him.

He held her in his arms. She was light and moved in such a way as to feel weightless. Although she was taller than him, he held her firmly and guided her so that he could turn her to the left. He used all his skill so as to show his desire to serve, his dedication. He was a very skilled dancer and she was a gracious one, but there was something a little insecure about her steps, perhaps too flexible. They were in full swing. He drew her with him in ever faster and bigger circles so that their feet only briefly touched the ground. He held her at a distance and used all his strength to twirl her around him. He had the impression that she was flying away from him and he flew after her. He led her right into the corners, with narrow turnings to use all the space and a feeling of masterfulness rose up in him. He closely and elegantly avoided the other pairs, he paused where necessary or wheeled around. He knew how to find the right places where there was most space and there he made some wide turns as if in a shout of victory.

They came to a standstill, hot and exhausted. 'You dance wonderfully,' she cried, 'just like the Baron.' The compliment – the first she had paid him – had him blushing deeply. 'Let's carry on,' he shouted. They danced again until everything began to swim around them.

Then they stopped. They laughed and looked towards the other people. They talked and laughed some more.

Irene clapped her hands together and skipped and jumped behaving as though she were unhinged. Suddenly she stopped and looked at him with real affection: 'The little Baron.'

He trembled as he accompanied her home. When they

The Bowling Game

parted he kissed her hand. And then – then in the darkness, as she left, he felt her stretch out her hand behind her, grip his and then gently stroke it. It was the first unambiguous sign of love that she had given him.

He stood on the same spot where three hours ago he had so longed for her, in front of the same beach chair. Then he ran back into the park, much too excited to go to sleep. So happy love does exist, he said to himself; that close affinity between unhappiness and love, which had seemed inescapable to him until now, was not after all inevitable. There could also be love and happiness, love and joy together. And he reminded himself how young he was, how quickly he had arrived at the greatest happiness. Love and happiness both, at sixteen years old. He kept repeating those words out loud to himself ... and he had told Nussbaum what he thought of him. He called to the moon, the same one that had recently witnessed his ruminations on what life really meant, his doubts and his complete breakdown. Now everything was flowering anew for him, everything was full of hope, everything only beginning when it had seemed to be at an end. Today he had spent the whole day with her, morning, afternoon and evening until midnight. That whole time together with a woman, the same one, always knowing what she was doing and always seeing her! He pondered it and then he unwittingly slipped into a loving thought – that it would be wonderful to have that forever. In short, to be married to Irene. In Prague he had had to struggle just to be able to speak to his beloved, or to be alone with her, against her will and after a thousand tricks which she never condoned. But Irene was not hostile towards him, not putting up resistance; she facilitated their meetings, she wanted them. Now everything was flowing forward unhindered and

Jewish Women

his youthful soul flowed with it in a flood of gratitude. It had only been a delusion, those ideas that happiness would never be his, that perhaps nothing like that existed in the world. Now he no longer felt shut out from normal life. He called the trees by their names and counted the stars. He hung over the waters of the stream like low hanging foliage and kissed it. He saw his curls merging with the little white clouds in the sky and he put in his hands so that he felt his fingertips drawn by the precious metals and warm medicinal springs deep down in our Earth.

Gretl

The next morning the matter seemed clearer to him but no less satisfying.

When he thought about it, he realised that half of yesterday's plan – to bring the mothers closer – had failed. By contrast, the other half, for which he had not had high hopes, had succeeded. Olga had 'thawed' as Frau Lucie joyfully expressed it, and even asked to join Herr Klein's tennis group. Hugo accompanied them and while his mother remained at Olga's tennis court, he slipped over to meet Irene. Every morning he stationed himself punctually outside the Manor House.

They spoke a lot about love to each other, but never of their mutual feelings. Irene talked very freely of her one-time fiancé – the last barrier to her secret had definitely fallen. Hugo copied her and talked about Gretl. They dissected and extolled those feelings, but there was an unspoken agreement that they didn't apply to each other. But the agreement did not have the effect of a partition which kept them apart but was more of an affectionate bond. Although both pursued a different ideal on another track, nevertheless they went forward hand

Jewish Women

in hand, and exuded an atmosphere of loving warmth. At least that was how Hugo saw it. Their conversation was intimate, full of delicacy and mutual consideration, and with the deepest heartfelt emotions which moved him, whoever they related to. He felt very good in that passionate atmosphere. He also hoped that Irene would be aware of his reserve and understand his true feelings. But how could he make them clear when she was always sighing after her Heinrich! So he stayed with Gretl, inwardly uncertain whether his affections were still fresh or whether he had overcome them.

'Do you know what the most beautiful thing is,' she said during one of their walks in the Castle gardens. 'How one speaks when one is in love! One speaks to the loved one as in a melodrama.'

He had never experienced that. But, shivering with delight, he ventured, 'You mean you draw out the words and wait for the music to begin?'

'Oh, no. You actually hear the music! It is like a harp in the soul, playing quietly while you speak to its accompaniment.'

'Speak quietly or loudly?' Hugo asked, going along with her fantasy which he was enjoying.

'Very quietly, extremely quietly, because one wants to hear the music all the time and it isn't very loud …' She trembled and smiled. 'Those were wonderful times.' She plucked a leaf off the next tree they passed and pressed it to her nose, slowly inhaling its green perfume. He saw the fluttering of her closed eyelids, with their many tiny lines, smoothed out by the sun and the light reflected from the leaves.

Every day she looked eagerly through the list of the spa guests. The name 'Winternitz' did not appear. But he could have registered under a false name, which seemed more likely.

Gretl

Several days went by. There was no sign of Dr Winternitz. Gradually she conceded that she must have made a mistake on the evening of the tennis match. Anyway, what was it to her? Gone and forgotten! Hugo who was plucking up courage again, encouraged her in that approach. If she started speaking about him again, he reminded her with: 'But you didn't want to think about him again.' Sometimes that resulted in her giving him a scornful warning look.

She was obviously bored if their conversation veered away for any length of time from her own affairs of the heart. He felt to blame for such mistakes and made strenuous efforts to compensate by trying to identify with her earlier relationships with such questions as: 'And how was it in fact? Was Herr Dr Winternitz completely different from the Baron or Herr Hahnenkamm?'

'Obviously.' She wasn't particularly surprised at his having guessed correctly. 'There was perpetual war. Naturally, my fiancé didn't want me to go around with those irresponsible people any more. He talked to me at length about family life and so forth ...'

'And whose side were you on?'

'What a question! Obviously I entirely agreed with my fiancé. Just to annoy him I occasionally allowed myself to be accompanied home by the old group. Then he became so jealous, so furious ... but those elegant "gypsies" seemed laughable to me compared with him.' Her memories came flooding back so vividly that she stopped speaking.

Sometimes, as a kind of quid pro quo, she encouraged him to speak about his memories. He began with perfect composure: 'I often went early on Sunday mornings to the Hetzinsel. The fast flowing water shone in the morning sun; it pushed its way past the watermills and then cascaded over the wooden dams. I often stopped and stood looking down from the bridge and noticed how dark green and brown it looked in the shadow of the trees and so still at the edges of the island that it looked like firm ground. It gave me the impression of being somehow divine. I imagined being able to walk over the water just in shoes, bend down and scoop up the water in my hand to quench my thirst. Then we youths would lie down in the grass near the tennis courts and wait for the ladies. One of us, a *Couleur* student, told jokes and amused us all. We also talked about a lot of indelicate things which is normal among men. I felt the cool dew on the palms of my hands, on my forehead and something health-giving from the warmth of the sun in my whole body which ran smoothly like a machine. We lay on our backs and looked up into the old chestnut trees and did not look at each other as we spoke. We just talked into the air. Sometimes we got up and walked along the paths or went to the comfortable old restaurant where we drank small glasses of light beer or ate buttered bread. They were wonderful times. I felt that boundless power was growing within me, something unconquerable, as though I was preparing in the best possible way to win Gretl for myself once and for all. But when she appeared it all came to nothing. It even changed the strength which I had mustered into weakness. It depressed me because it had an effect but in a different way from the effect it had on Gretl. She did not appear to notice any of nature's strength as I approached her. With that failure came things which were outwardly amusing but very painful for me. For example, on one occasion Gretl and I were going alone together for a walk, outside the tennis courts and along a narrow path on the edge of the island. We could see in the distance the

Belvedere, the Hradschin and the Elizabeth Bridge, and in front of us were the waters of the Moldau in all its shining breadth. There was also a small rope-making business under the trees; a worker was standing there and pulling a rope over a wheel which was turning with a whirring sound. He was walking backwards and seemed to be pulling more and more rope out of the wheel. That workman made a big impression on me. I couldn't say exactly why I had that impression or of what it consisted. Perhaps it was because I was walking with Gretl and that shabbily dressed man near me was working so hard and because, in spite of all the idleness and wealth and the beautiful girl by my side, I was so dissatisfied and unhappy. Perhaps what I have been saying is not clear, but you can imagine, Fräulein, how it was – Gretl looked so pretty, with such rosy cheeks; she gave me so much pleasure. And the sun was shining through the leaves which were fully grown and a cool breeze was coming off the river and from the grass …'

Irene had sufficient good taste not to interrupt his excited account. But when she realised that he couldn't see a way out of the business with the rope maker, she interrupted with: 'I can very well imagine. Such things cannot be described … Now tell me about something else!'

He threw her a grateful glance and carried on more calmly: 'I can't say that she was unfriendly or cold towards me. Sometimes she seemed to be actually encouraging me. She was also moody and arrogant. Everybody paid her compliments on her beauty and she deserved them all. But for me there was constant change between being favoured and rejected. Sometimes I was deeply unhappy and sometimes she said something kind, for example: "Herr Rosenthal, I will see you again tomorrow," or "Would you like a piece of croissant?"

breaking off a piece of hers. For weeks I eked out a miserable existence on such remarks, recalling them again and again. It was far removed from the ideal of happy love as I'd imagined it – nothing genuine. And most of the time she was merely indifferent to me. For example, I had chosen a bench to be our favourite during our brief excursions in the pauses between games. There we sat, she and I. It wasn't isolated, everyone could see us, and we only spoke about mundane things. There was really nothing special about it. It was just the fact that she went there with me, as a favour which she bestowed on me. And the bench was not in fact my favourite place but I called it that and deliberately represented it as such so that we had something to share. And I asked her to have an affection for the bench as well. I said that I would visit it when I was older because of the memories and so on. On one occasion we approached and found the bench already occupied. I was distraught and pointed it out to her while we were still some distance away. Then she said, 'Can you see how upset I am!' She was so cold and sarcastic. I could not have felt worse if someone had just knocked me to the ground. For days I couldn't get those words out of my head. And something like that happened every now and then ... But the worst of all was the *Couleur* student, whom I actually liked because he was a witty and pleasant person. I don't think that he was in love with Gretl – at least not in the same way that I was. But she ran after him all the time; by which I mean that she loved to hear him telling jokes. She laughed so merrily and all she ever wanted to do was laugh. I don't think that she was in love with him but she certainly preferred him ... I often said to myself: "I'm going to finish with this, I would rather not go on; the pain is worse than the pleasure." I told myself that

Gretl

she was not as beautiful and attractive as I had imagined. It was purely my fantasies that had turned her into something so beautiful and so rare. But I had to admit to myself that giving up my fantasies would be harder even than giving up reality. I would have had to have destroyed what I had built around her so enthusiastically, the thing that was dearest to me, my own feelings. And at the end of the day, what is reality and what is fantasy? Why had she captured my imagination in that particular way – why her and not someone else? *Gott im Himmel!* To be going around Prague without having anyone with whom one could talk to about those thoughts ... and more importantly, not to be able to tell her how I felt about her, because she laughed at me so much if I tried to begin any such conversation. She just started to laugh ...'

'That must have been a really dreadful relationship,' said Irene. He flinched to hear such an accurate description, but he didn't quite understand the significance of it. Had Irene really grasped the meaning of his account so well that she at once understood how demeaning the relationship had been, how pernicious? Did she sense how laughable and contemptible he had appeared to the group with his sentimental love? Had she immediately understood all the humiliation of his misfortune, the details of which he had kept from her? Did she mean to indicate that she herself had experienced much more love than him? Or did she take it rather more superficially and was she, when all was said and done, even a little jealous? Or all of those things at the same time? He pulled a picture postcard out of his pocket, wrote a greeting and asked Irene to sign it with him.

She turned it over. The other side was blank. 'I don't sign cards without an address on – one must know with whom one is corresponding.'

He calmly took back the card and smiled as he wrote Gretl's address on it.

Irene signed it without saying a word. And then after a moment she said, 'Would you marry her, this Gretl?'

He hesitated, then said 'I'm not sure now whether I still love her so much …'

'But what I mean is *then*. Did you want to marry her *at that time*.'

'Obviously. If I had been in a position to do so.'

'Does she have money? What would she bring?'

'I don't know … but does that make any difference? I think not very much.'

Then she looked at him with real joy, almost moved, and said: 'Hugo, do you know what a fine person you are …?'

He understood her immediately. She was thinking of her fiancé and the breaking off of the engagement. He felt the need to help her and the best ideas came to him very quickly. 'I don't understand … "fine"? What does that mean? What does fineness signify in this context and why exactly are you praising it? Let's assume that I am giving up ten thousand Gulden for Gretl's sake while another person might prefer to give up the girl rather than the ten thousand Gulden. One quickly reaches the conclusion that I value love more than he does – I feel it more deeply, at least ten thousand Gulden more deeply – and that is what you meant to express by the word "fine" – finely organised. But, *du lieber Gott*, one is assuming without any evidence, that for me and the other person money has the same value. But perhaps that very presumption is basically wrong. Perhaps then thousand Gulden mean the same to him as many millions do to me. So it is possible that he has the stronger feelings for money, and also for love, for everything.

Gretl

The importance of money is a very personal thing; that is what I have often thought. People are so illogical. Personally, I don't find anything dishonourable about avarice, although it is quite foreign to me. Take our Jewish businessmen for example, who think only about business day in and day out, about earning and money. No-one in the whole world has been so badly treated as they have, no-one treated with more injustice, so looked down upon. But money represents all the pleasures which one can obtain with it – travelling, clothes, often health, a happy family, a fine house. So, in short, fine things. And anyone who loves money, actually only loves those fine things. Therefore it is foolish to overwork in a business, because these businessmen – and I include lawyers among them – would give up more pleasures than they would acquire and would not be in a position to enjoy the fruits of their labour through overwork. So it is impractical behaviour but is it dishonest? Why dishonest? Why contemptible? Unless one loves money for its own sake rather than for the fine things it can buy. Because money is an ideal, something unreachable, never to be satisfied. And so I would like to know, by what right can one have an objection to that ideal any more than to all the others which are just as futile but which drive men to make enormous efforts. In this scenario money is an ideal just like any other and to me there is something heroic about it. Perhaps I'm not expressing myself properly. But tell me, wasn't it like that for you? Haven't I got it right?' He looked at her meaningfully. 'Either beautiful things or money as the ideal – did one of those two passions also have an effect then?'

She stood there looking serious. 'No. Nothing had any effect. You can't begin to imagine. You are simply too young. God knows! You probably believe that you are thinking in an experienced and pessimistic way, and that you have no more illusions and everything looks clear to you. But in fact you have no idea what goes on in the world. It is always like this with young people. They think they have left illusions behind them, but in fact they have them all ahead. Absolutely no idea. You have no conception, Hugo, of how bad the world is.'

'Mama recently said the same thing to me,' he said in a quiet joking tone, striving to suppress his emotions.

She shook her head and looked down on his light brown curls in a melancholy way. 'No, Hugo, just remember one thing. You are too good. It will go very badly for you out in the world.'

The Snake Dance

But not every walk passed so harmoniously.
When Hugo told her once more about his limited experiences, she interrupted him in irritation. She called them 'mere trifles' in comparison with the scale of her worries. She asked him about his social circles. She was able to reel off whole lists of distinguished acquaintances and with each name she asked him, 'Do you know him? You really don't know anyone.' With painful eagerness, she returned to her days of triumph. At a masked ball the Governor devoted himself entirely to her. It was even reported in the newspapers: 'The dashing Greek woman who was enthusiastically courted by a high-ranking dignitary etc ...' Her stories always seemed to be challenging him, seemed to be asking imperiously: 'So, where are your adventures, your successes?'

'If one doesn't enjoy life to the full ...' she cried. An actor, a friend of Hahnenkamm had even fought a duel over her.

'With the Baron,' he added.

'How did you know that?'

'I heard about it.'

He never felt the need to hurt her, to take revenge. On the contrary he wanted to please her in all gratitude. 'I have had my romantic moments,' he said. 'We young men all have a longing for the exotic. Particularly at night, while walking through the streets. You feel: Here is just the place for all kinds of nonsense. Everything looks so orderly; citizens sleeping safely in their beds, behind the stone walls of the houses. Everywhere is empty. And the strangest things come into your head – about doing something big, against all common sense. For example, we were recently walking in the Obstgasse. We talked about great events, like the discovery of America by Cortez. The ground had been opened up as part of the relaying of the pavement; there were stones lying around in heaps. I don't know why but it seemed to me like an intimation of chaos, in those well-ordered streets, a bit of wilderness where one could do something or experience something surprising. I climbed up and looked down into the dark hole. Believe me, at that moment, madness was almost upon me. I could have jumped down into the hole …'

'And what did you do?'

'Nothing.'

She laughed maliciously: 'So you did nothing. That's the difference between you and Cortez.'

He felt hurt and cried 'What should I have done! It wouldn't have made any sense. I just wanted to give you a feeling for the mood, that bohemian mood …'

'Is that what you call bohemian!'

He conceded. Anyway, he hadn't had an opportunity as yet to make an extravagant gesture. But he knew a good device. 'When I find life boring and empty, then I pull my lower lip into my mouth and feel it with both rows of teeth. Look, like this! And then I think to myself what a wonderful example of life that lip signifies, how wonderfully it is constructed, from thousands of cells, and so supple as well ... how much about it goes unresearched and unexplained ... and at that moment it is incomprehensible to me how anyone can find life uninteresting.'

'You are very modest in your enjoyment,' she said in a critical and reproachful tone. 'That is a very cheap pleasure. Everyone has a lower lip.'

On other days she moved the focus of her criticisms away from him and onto people going by. At a symphony concert, she once said about Flora Weil who was visible in the distance: 'Look! That long brown coat makes her look a lot taller. Narrow and dark – perfectly contrived to that end. When I saw Flora today, I immediately thought: "My God, how much taller she's grown!" But close up she seemed even smaller than before. Do you know why that is? At first one is fooled and adds something – like in an equation – then one notices the mistake, and subtracts, but that time more than one had previously added. One shouldn't use the most extreme measures – that is the lesson to be drawn. An observer must always be able to say to themselves: I could take it a bit further if I wanted to. At the moment when the observer realises that everything has been done that can be done, the effect is zero. A tall feather in the hat, for example. Can that make you look taller? On the contrary, it seems to shout: I would love to be so tall – it is like an outstretched arm.'

Although he enjoyed listening to her comments on clothes and found them very apt, it pained him that she didn't take account of the fact that he himself was short. She was always making fun of short people; and it was embarrassing because he couldn't help feeling affected by it. But he didn't dream of paying her back with an obvious comment such as: 'May I ask what that has to do with any equation.' He respected her mathematical pretensions. But she carried on: 'You should watch your tailor more closely. You don't get broad shoulders that way.' She pulled a horse-hair out of his jacket, which had come through on the padded shoulder. He blushed, not having realised until then that his jacket had been made fashionable by those means.

'I have more to think about than my clothes,' he said defiantly and then used the last weapon at his disposal. He told her his 'secret' and hoped that he would thereby make an impression, completely overcome her with his pain. She listened to him. Then she said: 'You are a *Realgymnasiast*—' She obviously wanted to say something nice, to remind him of their first meeting. But in that moment it seemed dreadful to him that she was thinking more about her misfortune than his unhappiness. How different Olga had been with her hand-wringing! She wasn't unsympathetic and asked him for more details. But as he tried to compare Irene's misfortune with his, she was almost outraged and would not accept it.

He didn't want to look small, and so he began to speak about his plans, his inventions. He wanted to be an engineer, and somehow change working methods by introducing wonderful automatic machines and thereby making everybody happy. In the meantime he had made only a new model of the Neffschen Hammer, a circuit breaker, of little significance. He himself confessed that it was little more than a toy.

'Whereas literature pursues me,' she sighed, 'I always have luck with poets and such people, who really don't interest me …'

The Snake Dance

'But I ...'

'Well, that's literature, my dear, what you are speaking and thinking about. Making people happy is a fine notion, of course ...'

He pressed his lips together in a serious expression and then began to tell a lie: 'But you have completely misunderstood me, Fräulein. I don't want to make money from my inventions. If in addition I benefit mankind, that's good. But more than anything else I want to be great, famous. You recently told me that things would go badly for me. Do you realise that I found that very offensive? Why should they go badly? Do you think I am incompetent? Oh, I can put up a fight! I will succeed. At the moment I am thinking about an aeroplane. I tell you, Fräulein, quite contrary to your assertion, it will not go badly with me. Never, I swear to you. I can promise you that. I feel that I am called to great things. I will rise in the world. Ministers will wait in my entrance hall. That's how far it will go!' His voice took on a steely tone as he rushed on: 'I will work ... but every man must have hope you know. Something to inspire him. And even if it seems almost impossible, I must tell you that it is you that I have fixed on to be my hope. I strive for you when I work. It's you I want to conquer ... perhaps you will laugh ... I am deliberately not looking at you. It's good that I am at last able to tell you what my feelings are. It's better than being forever ambiguous. So, I see a bright future for myself. You and me together. Not in Prague among our lacklustre acquaintances, moving in a small circle. No, it is to be a life of high style; always travelling – spring in Egypt, summer at the North Pole, winter in Paris. Heaps of money. Perhaps, when the mood takes us, waking up in luxurious beds in sunny Nice. Would you like that? Tell me, wouldn't you enjoy that? I'm not asking you if you think it would be possible. *I* think it's possible and that's enough for me. I am only asking if you would enjoy it, Irene. Listen ...'

This was a declaration of love with any doubt. Flattered by the outburst of youthful ardour, she laughed heartily and said in a sonorous voice: 'Certainly, Hugo. Something like that would be entirely to my taste.'

He breathed deeply: 'Thank God ... it's yes then ...'

He went home in a state of high emotion. His studies now seemed childish to him compared with such great undertakings. His head was burning with unimaginable events and he had to sit there and cram for some wretched examination retake. To make it even worse, when on one occasion he had said to Irene that he intended to begin his cramming, she had said, 'What for? You would do better to work on your inventions.' She had meant it as a joke, and he understood it as such, but nonetheless it prevented him from studying. He was also like that when he came back to his room in the evenings from his dangerous conversations with Irene. He was always on his guard throughout, otherwise she humiliated him. His head felt so weary that he didn't have the capacity to absorb anything. Finally he made up his mind and set a candle aside with the intention of throwing it away in the park the next day. The next morning he said to Olga, 'Hey, today I began—'

He often saw his friendship with Irene as a meeting of souls. He could hardly wait to see her again. Sometimes she hurt his feelings so much that he found her dreadful. He alternated between happiness and fear. And then, in consequence of a not particularly significant coincidence, a third feeling was added. At Irene's suggestion they often visited the place where they had first met. She made a real cult out of everything which related

The Snake Dance

to her life-story, finding it all very significant, meaningful, even mysterious. On the way she told him, yet again, how fine and necessary it was to be scintillating in company and how much she valued liveliness, cheerfulness and spiritedness as the most important qualities. She mentioned, in passing, that her mother's family probably came from Greece – hence the darker skin – and that she herself felt a strong inclination towards the south, towards dancers like Ruth St Denis for example, and that she also had some talent for dancing. They had just arrived at the glade where Hugo had met her for the first time when Irene suddenly pulled a pin out of her hat. Then she laid the hat on the ground and put the shiny glass knob of the hatpin between her fingers, so that it looked like the ring which Ruth St Denis wore when she did her snake dance. And then she began to imitate the writhing movements of the dance. Suddenly she stumbled over a tree root and was brought to the ground in the middle of a sinuous, graceful and quite artistic pose. By coincidence it was in almost the exact spot where she had lain on the earlier occasion. Even her hat was lying next to her as it had been then. In that moment Irene acquired another quality – she seemed comical to him. He told himself immediately that it was all coincidence and that anyone could stumble in the woods or while dancing. But the coincidence of all those things – in his mind's eye he could also see the waiter in a tailcoat – had such an irresistible effect that he could hardly prevent himself from laughing aloud while he helped her up. And what made it even more difficult was that she herself didn't seem to see anything in the least comical about the situation. Whether it was to skilfully cover up her accident or from real self-assurance she carried on praising St Denis.

From then on he noticed many things which had not previously occurred to him. They went down to Prasseditz, to the workers' village. A small child was being pushed past them in a pram; it had open patches on its face as if a cheese grater had been drawn across it. 'Did you see that?' said Irene. 'So? Don't you know that it's a sign of syphilis.' And by the way she stressed the second syllable, he immediately realised that she had read the word but had never heard it spoken. And now she casually used the word to show how broad-minded she was – but she got it wrong. It was exactly like her falling over in the middle of the dance. Hugo found it funny. He immediately felt inclined to argue that the rash was due to some illness other than syphilis, having completely lost respect for Irene's judgment by now.

Whistles sounded. 'Six o'clock,' he said. 'The workers are going home.' 'If only all workers were free after six o'clock,' she sighed. He felt that this reference to her Berlin courses, spoken without any sign of emotion, but just for the sake of saying something, was more damning than anything else she had said so far.

On another occasion it annoyed him, that when they went past the Seume monument,[19] she said with a certain pride, 'I haven't read a word of his!' When they came to the Golden Ship Hotel Hugo said, 'Goethe lived here. Did you know that?'

'I'm so pleased!' she said and laughed.

'And it doesn't move you at all that *The Wandering Bell* was probably written here?'

'Such a childish poem!'

He stopped speaking for a while. But she had recited the stupid poems of Hahnenkamm, although she confessed to understanding nothing of literature and not to be interested in it. He put that to her now.

'That is something else. That was a social occasion,' was the reply.

And how she showed off her knowledge of languages! With her London 'finish', she regarded it almost as an insult if someone else dared to say anything in English. No-one could say either a French or an English word in her presence; she immediately let fly at them and corrected it. She even shouted her corrections of pronunciation across the tennis court. On some days she had a mania for translating, for no good reason, every significant word that came into the conversation into French or English. She did it both as a tiresome personal exercise and to demonstrate the correct spelling. If one talked about *furchen* she said loudly, in an aside: furrow, f-u-r-r-o-w. On such occasions she seemed to Hugo to be like a governess. On one occasion she astonished him by pronouncing the word 'pathos', not in the usual way but with a short 'a'.

'Do you also know Greek?' he asked

'Oh, no,' she said, and straight away began to recite the first verse of the Iliad. '*Menin aeide thea* – my brother taught it to me. I don't know more than that.' Hugo wanted to say something about the Greek language, since her family probably came from Greece but she stopped him. She only seemed to be interested in what she had already learned, as being essential to conversation, but not in learning for its own sake. He had already noticed that about her earlier on, but only now did he sum it up in one stark word – 'comical.'

In a mood of uncertainty, on one occasion he asked Olga: 'Do you really think that Fräulein Irene is beautiful?'

'Oh, yes. A very pretty girl ... and really elegant.'

He realised that if she had been a man he would not have

found her intelligence attractive. He couldn't picture her as a male friend, though. Did that speak for her or against her? Strangely enough he discovered that, although he had noticed her comical side, it strengthened rather than weakened his overall feelings for her. He didn't love her any the less because she had shown her human side. On the contrary, he saw in her faults and weaknesses the sad fate of girls, particularly Jewish ones, who had been brought up with no other purpose in mind than marriage. When that game was unsuccessful they had to struggle through life with an inadequate education. Irene was much more mature than others who shared her fate, and there were times when she had a clear understanding of her inner self. Her desire for independence and her strongly developed self-confidence helped her. But it was precisely this self-confidence that in other ways made her laughable. She fluttered before his eyes in every possible colour and was always worth seeing.

One occasion in particular which he shared with Irene made an unforgettable impression on him. He went to the Manor House on a Sunday. He came across her sitting with her cousins in a loge on the veranda. The latest edition of the *Prager Tagblatt* had just arrived and the girls were crowding around it. The older cousin, Lotti Kapper had found it and with astonishing speed opened it up at the right page and thrown all the others on the ground. 'So, guess who,' she said turning to the girls standing around her. 'Erna Burok with Adolf Meisel, General Manager of the firm Moller & Co., Berta Jeiteles …' 'She went to school with me,' cried Flora in anguish. And when the list of engagements was finished they all wanted to hear it again, reached out for the paper and wanted to read it for themselves, to be absolutely sure of the latest news. Irene laughed excitedly: 'We've been left behind.' 'We've been left single, we're on the shelf,' wailed the others in chorus. As if in a round dance of despair, they lifted up their hands and danced around the newspaper, giggling and crying at the same time. Even Kamilla Kapper, usually a very reserved person, gave a slight sigh of agreement.

Irene went up to Hugo, whom she had only just noticed. He was standing there in total astonishment. He had never imagined that such things as a list of engagements, which he found completely uninteresting, could affect other people so deeply.

Irene looked at him: 'You seem surprised. Didn't you know *that each of these girls you see wailing, is acknowledged to be brilliant.* And they all bewail that brilliance which is left to wither without any chance of expression. Each of them, even if you can't recognise it, could love so warmly and delicately, love with their whole being and develop the best side of their personalities. But the world rejects what they are offering. That's how it is, dear Hugo. You have no idea of the tragedy of the daughter of a family today. She grows up in the bosom of her relatives, watched and protected and surrounded by all of them – but while she is still growing up, she is exposed to the hardest possible struggle for existence. That is the fraud. The apparent security and the real struggle underneath it. Who will look after her if she doesn't get a husband? And yet the appearance of security, of the familiar family life without worry – I can't quite find the right word – must be maintained. And the worst thing of all is that the girl must remain passive throughout the struggle; she cannot involve herself actively. She must rely on the protection of her relatives, can't protect herself or engage personally in the struggle. All that protection offers only something negative ... wonderful!' she laughed bitterly. 'Before I set out from Prague, I was at the wedding of a friend. She is twenty-nine years old and was marrying a fifty-five year old man. He is still healthy, but just think of it – fifty-five years old – old enough to be her father. He already has four children, including three daughters of marriageable age. How they carried on in the synagogue! I was quite beside myself. It was a very strange wedding. The bride just stood there, barely taking any notice of him. She plucked some flowers from her bouquet and gave a pair to each of us. When her "bridegroom" eventually came up and asked her why she was doing that, she said, "It's for luck." Then he said, "Then I'll give my daughters some of that too," and took a handful. I noticed only one of the daughters kissed her hand; the others just pressed it lightly.'

'Why was that?' asked Hugo who understood very little of the whole thing.

'Now they must obey the new wife who is no older than them and call her Mother ... I don't know. I love my father very dearly – but if he did something like that, got married again – I don't know – I wouldn't speak another word at home.' And she looked at Hugo angrily as if he were in some way to blame for the fates of those strangers.

He told her that he didn't really understand her. How did she want the world to be? If older men re-married, wasn't that good for women, there would be more prospective husbands for them.

'You have no feelings,' Irene said to him abruptly.

He realised that he was in the wrong but thought she was also doing him an injustice. He tried to put it into words: 'It's strange. Until now I thought that I had more feelings than

The Snake Dance

you—' He wanted to add 'at least in such matters' but kept silent because he could see that she was working out her ideas. After a moment he added, without any particular meaning or conviction: 'Anyway, ignorance is no excuse.'

She quickly took her leave of him and returned to her cousins.

On that afternoon she seemed particularly attractive to him. Caught up in feminine affairs which she experienced as directly as any other woman, and yet at the same time standing aside from them and looking on as an observer. If that difficult stance, which was so far from his understanding, appeared rather laughable, he told himself that the fault lay with him rather than with her.

Although her not entirely praiseworthy qualities caused the pleasure he took in her to increase, they also caused his anger and concern to mount in equal measure. So long as she entirely impressed him, he allowed her to laugh at him without making any protest. But now he found it offensive that she lorded it over him and everyone else while she had an equally defective character. On one occasion he used her mocking of Nussbaum as an occasion to defend himself. 'Doesn't he look as though in the next moment he will say: "*So soll ich leben*" or "*Gotteswillen*" she sneered.' Hugo responded by saying, 'What's the matter with you? You despise everyone. You think they are all worse than you – perhaps the reason is that you have a bad character yourself …'

That remark had an unexpected outcome. Irene went white and looked at Hugo, speechless and trembling. Finally she pulled herself together and said, 'What do I have … tell me again?'

'A bad character,' he repeated without showing any sign of

remorse. He thought she would not take it too badly because she had often portrayed slovenly people, confidence tricksters and swindlers as charming. And anyway an expression like 'bad character' did not require fundamental ethical debate or deep study of Kant to give it meaning. But Irene flew at him in a rage. 'So I have a bad character ... then why are you still going around with me. No-one ordered you to. What do you want from such a degenerate person as me ...'

His ears rang. 'Go away, leave me alone!' He tried in vain to calm her down. He begged for forgiveness. She grew even angrier and went away without saying goodbye.

'Was that one of those huge rows that sometimes happen between lovers?' he asked himself, not without satisfaction.

On the next day she was as cheerful as ever.

'But why did you get so excited about that expression yesterday?' he asked at an opportune moment.

'Well – because I experienced a similar scenario with my fiancé on one occasion. He reproached me in the same way, with exactly the same words ... Was it a coincidence? Obviously he immediately retracted it. But the memory upset me so much ... Don't be angry!'

He went home that evening feeling more disappointed than ever. He meant so little to her that she wasn't even annoyed with him. He could bear the fact that she did not love him, but not that she couldn't even be angry with him on his own account but always in connection with that man! No, no. He suddenly saw everything very clearly. This wasn't real love either. He had once more tried to love, but it was not more than that. And falling into Irene's way of thinking he told himself that his love had been somehow too early, *praematurus*. That Latin word seemed to him to be entirely suitable and to explain everything which he himself had previously found unclear.

Now many things became apparent to him. He had forced himself into that love, persuaded himself on the basis that one should not miss the opportunity with such a clever and unusual girl. But now he reproached himself. Wasn't it irresponsible to want to be in love at any price. Perhaps he really was too young and immature. Why not instead peer into the distant heavens, busy himself with stamp collecting or football. In God's name, did he really have to be in love? Was it so essential? He despised himself. Could he not wait until the right one came along, or must he run after substitutes in childish impatience, just like a boy? And what in the end had come out of devoting himself to this substitute? ('It serves me right,' he thought angrily. His heart boiled over with rage at the scale of his own modest demands. Can one ever be understanding where ideals are concerned!) What had come out of it? He still couldn't even say '*Du*' to her. He hadn't kissed her once. How often she must have kissed Dr Winternitz, he thought. On one occasion she had stroked his hand when they parted; that had been the high point of her love. Perhaps it is only the circumstances which are to blame, he told himself, because she is taller than me. How could I draw her to me and kiss her. Physically it is just unthinkable ... But no, their conversation had never been so affectionate that a kiss would have been the logical outcome ... It was only ever perspicacity, mockery and dissection. Looking back he found that their whole association had been sickeningly intellectual, although there had been some pleasant episodes – at the bowling game for example. No, he didn't want to be unfair; there had been many such episodes. And the age

Jewish Women

difference had been so ridiculous. A failed Gymnasium student and an old maid unite against society – how devastating! Thankfully, Dr Taubelis, who always teased them, hadn't realised the extent of their bond. There had always been something unnatural in their relationship and that had made him irritable with her and his affection weak ... but why was it so? He didn't want to consider Irene's actual faults. Beauty, youth, spiritual perfection – the strength of his infatuation had enabled him to overlook any lack of such qualities in Irene. But now he was able to define her: She is clever but incapable of any noble deed. That seemed to him to be her most significant characteristic. There was nothing particularly good about her, no kind heart, self-sacrifice or noble deeds ... only considered and contrived stuff; caustic, calculated eroticism. Her belt buckles, her enamel purse, her unusual watch – all so self-consciously original! Hadn't he developed a headache when she showed them to him, as if they had been in a museum ... or better still a specimen cupboard? And in the same way she assessed their companions: He is an intelligent man – why hadn't she ever said: A great and noble man! No, no, enough of that. *Amor praematurus.*[20] It had all been an unpleasant dream, a nauseating error. And that evening he reached for his books for the first time and began enthusiastically to prepare for his examination.

Visiting the sick

However, this new awareness did not really change Hugo's situation.

Irene clung to him. And he understood for the first time that there was something more to the relationship than his reason could grasp. Why did he experience pleasure in her company regardless of what they were talking about? Was it like that for him because until then he had rarely spoken to girls? Did he like her or not? Where did the happiness come from which he experienced when he saw her approaching? And why did he find it so painful that she was usually unfriendly towards him now, and that the lovely days of their relationship seemed to be finally over?

Conversation between them had become ever more barbed. Irene seemed to set out to annoy him and he couldn't muster the strength to defend himself. He even found her unpleasant on occasion and experienced slight physical unease in her presence – for example, at the way her hands were always cold. He was very aware that she bound him to her more firmly with insults than she had previously with her flattery. He still felt compelled to visit her at particular hours, any other use of his time seeming empty by comparison. Then he had to listen to her, parry her blows and cleverly fend off her attacks. Nothing else was of such all-consuming interest to him so much as how far she would go in her enmity. And he reached the conclusion that he would not have put up with all that, if she had not been so much older than him. There's no shame in it; she is like a teacher to me, he reassured himself. This feeling dominated him more than he was prepared to admit. It was also the case that in comparison to her, he had always felt more hopeful and happy. What more could she expect from life? However much she insulted him she could not reduce him to her own state of misery. As the happier party he felt himself obliged to be more generous towards her. Out of sympathy he restrained himself from sharp retorts and recovered his equilibrium. And there was always the faint hope that once again they would have a sensible conversation. He looked forward to it so much. But time and again his hopes turned into angry hate when he found himself painfully enmeshed once more in a bad-tempered conversation, overshadowed by her threats.

She went into raptures about her former fiancé. She harassed Hugo with, 'He was much better than you.' 'In what way?' he responded calmly, always trying to contain her outbursts and thereby limit the damage. She took great delight in enumerating them. 'Firstly he was taller than you, far more handsome, more manly, cleverer ...' 'Also cleverer,' said Hugo, shaking his head sadly. She laughed: 'That's the worst isn't it? Much cleverer, which is the most important thing. What didn't he know and what hadn't he experienced, from travelling and in business!' 'He was much older than me,' he protested. But she wouldn't tolerate any contradiction. 'I didn't know him when he was your age. But I am convinced he never talked such nonsense. You are a complete child!' It was as if she wanted to revenge herself on Hugo for her own unsuccessful life. Hugo was surprised by his outward show of calm, while inwardly everything was falling apart. 'Well, sometimes it is good to be a child, and unspoiled.' This only provoked an outburst of scathing laughter: 'Unspoiled ... unspoiled ...'

It was often on the tip of his tongue to say: 'Why do you still speak to me when I am worth nothing.' But something held him back. Why did he associate with her even though she was unbearable and he hated her? Perhaps it was for the same reason on both sides. And it was then that he realised that it was not simply chance that had brought the two of them together. As happens everywhere, not only in Teplitz circles, two wounded hearts had met and tried timidly to hide their pain under the veil of a secret. Hadn't that been the first thing they had in common: unhappiness which one had to be ashamed of – an engagement broken off, an examination to retake! Certainly at the beginning their association had seemed to be a matter of free will. But that was only the outward appearance. It had been the workings of fate, necessity, their staying together dictated by the invisible forces of the whole of society. They belonged together and must stay together. And perhaps that feeling of obligation had smothered what remained of the genuine affection which they had once felt for each other. As was often the case with married people, thought Hugo. His idea of marriage had changed so much since that moonlit night.

And isn't that humiliating for me – he wailed to himself – so young and already a victim of so much misfortune.

He was still convinced that he was destined for greatness and worldwide renown; but he now began to resent that premonition, which had not so far proved to be true in his life, as another cause of humiliation.

While Hugo blamed them both equally for the lacklustre and dishonourable state of their relationship, Irene did not seem at all inclined to consider herself as in any way degraded or humiliated. She viewed him as a kind of toy, to be cherished sometimes and discarded at others. In her eyes she remained always the central figure, the principal one, in both good fortune and bad. She sometimes indicated that she saw this summer's episode as only one of many such in her life and certainly not as the most significant. 'So, for example, did you have just as much feeling and sympathy with your new acquaintances last year?' This was Hugo's way of putting a general question, carefully and anxiously, so that the answer would only be relevant to him. That perpetual game which brought him only new defeats, was deeply appealing to him – full of danger, and joy in his own torment. This was not the right way to win her heart, he told himself firmly – he should have talked proudly about inventions and a life of greatness; but that would have seemed to him dishonest. No, he wanted to move her, to bring her back to love in a straightforward way by his own essential character. Only that would satisfy the craving in his heart. But she remained merciless. 'Last year? Oh, I felt a lot more then.' And she told him, with clear pride, that she had been very friendly with the famous tenor Gartenfels and his lover. What characters they were! Such children of nature, so spirited! His legal wife had even come later to Ostende. In vain Hugo asked himself what kind of attraction there could be in such company. Although he didn't know those people at all, he was inclined to think that the tenor was stupidly proud, his mistress ordinary and his wife weak-minded. Hadn't Irene in any event been entirely superfluous to this trio? Hadn't she just pushed her way in? He couldn't imagine what her role had really been even though she portrayed it as important and multifarious. She achieved at least one thing by telling him this story (which was perhaps her intention), namely that Hugo saw her in a newly cold and clear light that left him with a better understanding of their recent estrangement. And a certain grudging respect for her, although not in the way she had expected (because the tenor didn't impress him at all) came back to him again in a round-about way.

Every day when letters arrived for her she found an opportunity to boast to him about her far-flung friends and acquaintances. In the winter, she said, she would probably travel to Ulm, to stay with a female friend of hers. He glumly reproached her by pointing out that in that case nothing would come of their plans to study together. He begged her with an anxious look for some reassurance such as: postponed but not cancelled. 'Well, there are other things in Prague which would be more important to me,' she replied sharply, as if his reproach had been an attack when in fact it had been made out of love. He pondered anxiously. It seemed to him that now he could, with one sentence, seize everything by the roots and in one movement remove all misunderstandings between them. She wouldn't be able to evade him now: 'Do you think, that it ...' But even as he spoke his courage failed him and the sentence turned into something infinitely more down-hearted as he started it again. 'Isn't it true that you also believe that there cannot be any real friendship between husband and wife!' He hoped that she would understand the implied compliment which lay within it, namely that he had left out so many links between his question about their projected winter studies and this one, relying on her intuitive understanding.

But, she was unperturbed and answered, 'Obviously not.' And she immediately proved that by relating episodes from her earlier close relationship with Frieda Schwarz. How well they had understood one another and how well they could guess each other's minds in every nuance. They spent whole days together. Every word cut him to the quick. He didn't want to believe that she was now denying him friendship, as she had earlier denied him love. She didn't even seem to be aware that she was trampling on his feelings but carried on talking about her memories of Frieda as if it were a neutral theme and without relevance to him. Her attitude suggested that she was expecting psychological interest and gratitude for her detailed information. He was already burning with dejection. Once it seemed to him that she was speaking about personal things in the way that refined people would – he would gladly have given all their high-flown discussion for a single scream, or some other sign of intimacy. 'So it was a better understanding than you had with me,' he finally said, quietly, his boldness accelerating into rashness. He could already predict her response: 'Better in every way.' And she smiled innocently as if she wasn't causing him any pain, not even wanting to give him the right to speak, to feel pain, to be disappointed. She seemed to imply: 'Yes, what else did you imagine ...'

In addition she had adopted a habit in recent days that affected him most painfully. For no reason she would suddenly fall silent and interrupt his ever-anxious chat with terse critical comments and assessments: 'Very good ... that was average ... ouch! ... banal!' Was she really a governess? Or rather an evil princess to whom a court jester played simply because it was his duty or because he was paid and had no right to be respected or even spoken to on equal terms. The outward form of their association contrasted strangely with those discussions in which he so ardently and unsuccessfully pursued some praise or kindness. Hugo was the reserved one. Sometimes he even avoided her. She immediately sent him a note inviting him to call again. She spoke to him on the street and asked him to visit. Loyal Olga, even while she basked in the admiration of her gentlemen acquaintances, had not given up on convention and was very surprised by it all. 'She's not the least bit embarrassed. How can she run after a man like that?' Hugo had difficulty in justifying Irene's behaviour. She was the stronger party, although it pleased her to behave as though she was more dependent on him than he on her. He finally understood that. 'She controls me so much that she doesn't lose face when she gives up the outward appearance of it and briefly plays the weaker role. Even that small weakness is a measure of her strength. Just as a lion tamer puts the lion's paws on her neck ... Yes, yes, I've been trained.'

On one occasion while they were carrying on a painful conversation they passed the train station and met Josef and Elsa going hand in hand through the station grounds. 'What are they doing here?' said Hugo. 'That dunderhead wants to be a railway conductor,' claimed Irene. 'Can you believe he's the same age as you, Herr Hugo?' Hugo was enraged. Now he detected malice in every one of her comments. But she was not as consistent as he supposed – she didn't even take that as seriously as he did. She carried on: 'How differently human minds can develop over the same period of time.

One shouldn't measure age according to the number of years which have passed, but by other indications.' From there she proceeded to talk about one of her own favourite theories which she often used to refer to, but Hugo who had drifted off into his own moody train of thought, couldn't take his eyes off the strange pair. The clumsy youth striding out in wide baggy trousers looked at the girl with moist besotted eyes. She was wearing a red linen dress with white spots. It hung down stiffly without any pleats almost without touching her slim and as yet undefined body. It was very long and only tied loosely at the hips with a belt of the same material so that her waist seemed unnaturally wide. But for that reason all her movements were free and forceful; she swung as she walked along like a dangling rope. Her skirt was quite short, pleated and sloping down at the sides, and when she ran became almost horizontal like a twirling ballerina's. Her kneecaps could be seen protruding from her thin legs. They were strong and round, with that particular attractive movement which they have in young people. She tugged at Josef, pulled his watch out of his pocket, ran ahead and then hung on him again when he quietly and calmly caught up with her. She laughed – perhaps at him. Then, surprisingly, she walked quietly by his side again. Her hands were pressing down on her belt, as against the railings of a balustrade, which made it sink down further. She gave her companion a wild look and pushed up her elasticated sleeves, which were already short, to reveal deep blood-red rings on her bare arms. She is obviously controlling him as Irene controls me, thought Hugo, and it is just as embarrassing. As had happened before, he was gripped by a deep sympathy for the tall defenceless youth. But at the same moment something flashed into his mind. 'No, not defenceless, no.' And before he had taken the next step, and while looking at the young couple tussling and laughing as they disappeared into the trees, he made a decision. On the first of September I will make some excuse and travel to Prague where I can prepare for my examinations in peace.

He was already studying every day, not much but at least regularly. It seemed like a sweet betrayal of Irene when in the evening he opened up his physics textbook and began to carefully read the simple sentences, working out the formulae and memorising them. Force, mass, velocity, effect. He was captivated by those very limited things which had their own independent value, without Irene's love, and oblivious of what Irene thought and whether Irene even existed. It was a landscape which was completely independent of her, a cool landscape into which he could escape. But while he was energetically and joyfully building up a picture of finally escaping, he suddenly realised that he would not actually succeed in doing any studying. The thought, the desire, was like a thin skin which gradually turned into a hard shell around his studying and wouldn't let him get through. It was Irene who was stopping him again, she had just changed shape. In despair he struck the table with his fist so that the lamp shook. He reached for his book again but it had all been interrupted. With difficulty he found the place but gave up after a few words in boredom which he interpreted as tiredness. He would start again tomorrow.

Oh, the agony of learning. Always stuffing oneself with new knowledge, always having to take something new into one's head! It seemed to him like the worst of all kinds of work. For while all other workers have free time after their day's work and can forget all the efforts they had to make, the

Jewish Women

success of the student depends on constantly remembering the effort, never forgetting. Even when he wasn't at his books, yes, precisely then, he felt obliged to test himself from time to time to see whether he still knew this or that formula. He asked himself unexpected questions. When he was walking alone or on the way to Irene or back from seeing her, he repeated whole sections of what he had been studying. If he could not remember a particular theory he immediately lost all confidence in his memory. There were moments when he was truly convinced that he knew nothing at all, not the slightest thing. And even as he recited part of the material to himself it seemed to him that in the meantime, precisely at that moment, he had forgotten another more important thing. His work was truly an uninterrupted effort from which he had no break in which to recover. While all other work ultimately decreases the more one does of it, in his case the opposite was true. With every day and the longer he worked, there seemed to be more of it. It just piled up and gradually stretched itself like a grey veil in front of the world. Nothing could be allowed to divert him from it, to take his mind off it. In fact, the very point of the exercise was to grow to love that veil and keep it constantly stretched out! Every minute in which he thought about something else, something pleasant or natural, seemed to him, when he considered it seriously, to be a minute lost. It was about doing oneself harm and then holding on to it as if it were a pleasure, becoming fond of it with the same passion, blindly.

Certainly in Irene's presence those conflicts disappeared behind more immediately pressing pains. And when he wasn't with her, then he was often tortured by the poisonous idea that during that time, Irene existed, was doing something, was

Visiting the sick

walking around somewhere nearby and gesticulating with her hands. He imagined her reality and it seemed unthinkable to him then that he could not see her, that she remained at a distance, that such an important sight could be taken away. And buried in his books he began to feel not only pain from Irene's absence, but also from all the proceedings in the world which he could not see and about which he could not think because of his studies. For example, the fact that an express train was just drawing into Munich's main station lay like a stone on his chest and made him feel breathless. It was as if he felt responsible for everything which was happening on earth, as if he must think about everything to keep it running in the right way; he must look after the provisioning of the big cities, pull boats through locks, bring the corn in at the right time, as if nothing could function without his involvement – as if he had at least to have everything in mind if he couldn't actually be there. That anxiety grew in him to the same extent as the other anxiety grew, namely that in every moment he must think of nothing else apart from his studies. Those two delusions, each the opposite of the other, were pulling him in two completely different directions.

How hard it was for his knowledge to advance in the midst of that struggle. He remembered that during his school days he had learned much more easily ... and he knew why. Then he had heard about physics for the first time and read about the subject with interest but superficially. But now he had to penetrate that tangle of things which sounded familiar but which were deeply unknown, and to understand completely hitherto pleasantly vague and formless ideas. And to work through all this and discover that he still only understood half of it – which meant in effect less than nothing – was unbearable.

Jewish Women

In this mood, in which he found himself to be pitifully in need of help, it hit him twice as hard that Irene did not support him. Yet she mustn't know about his suffering. He was convinced she would only laugh at him. Yes, he said to himself, it's the same as with Gretl. One must not go to a woman when one has a heavy heart. They don't offer consolation, or give one strength; on the contrary, one must have a surplus of strength when one goes to them. They don't give, they only take. And then he saw, in the midst of his darkness, that out in the light and without a care, or in any case far away from his worries, Irene was chatting with other people. First Dr Taubelis, then the older Demut and then Nussbaum, all drew near to her; and how gaily she entered into all the pleasant diversions of a summer holiday. She was there at the Venetian nights, the little *Redoute*, at the bowling evenings, at the *Drahrerabend*. If she had only behaved in friendly fashion towards him, Hugo would not have begrudged others a share in her favours. But now that he had been hurt by her, every kind word which she bestowed elsewhere was painful to him. He hated everyone who crowded around her in a group. It was true that she sometimes seemed to be left out, ignored by everybody, pushed firmly into the background. But on most days – whether it was by pure chance or a delusion of his – he saw her surrounded by admirers, giving her moods free rein like a spoilt child with everyone obeying her. On those occasions he would have liked to have taken each of them aside and asked: 'Do you love her? What do you see in her? Do you feel close to her? What has she said to you?' And then angry curiosity filled his heart which caused him to feel all the pains of a thwarted lover although he had actually not been in love for a long time.

Visiting the sick

On such days he came home with a dark expression. 'Something has made him liverish,' joked his mother good-naturedly. 'Why are you so down, Hugo?' Olga asked him in a quiet and friendly way, her hand on his shoulder. It hadn't helped that before he came into the house he had been determined not to allow anything to show. Then anger at his own failure and his weaknesses broke out at those words. Until then he had successfully restrained his anger at the afternoon's events, but now it made no difference to the outcome. He slammed doors and refused to answer any questions. He could see no way out, even if he told himself a hundred times that Olga and his mother were good to him and were in no way to blame. He was so burdened with the feeling of suffering an injustice that he found it necessary, even against his own will, to be unjust.

Oh, to escape, to run away – such ideas were howling inside him when he was sickeningly isolated, shut up in his little room. An overwhelming nostalgia for forests filled his heart, for running over green and healthy glades and down hills, and for the timeless pleasure of quietly stretching himself out in the sun with a light breeze blowing. Oh, nature – the stormy landscapes which Irene did not like, those excursions which she despised – that would have been his happiness. Riding, swimming, fencing, wading through murky swollen streams, drying wet clothes by running for miles in the hot sun, eating hard bread and gnawing the bark of trees, sleeping on a bed of moss under the twinkling stars! Where were those great joys, those escapes, worthy of a man and a full life? He lifted up his hands in ecstasy. It was impossible, unthinkable that he should pine away there in unhappiness, in this narrow bed, when he felt inside himself the temperament ideal for a great love and deeds which would kindle his innermost core with the flame of satisfaction. Because that was his desire – once and for all to shine bright in the greatest magnificence, come completely out of himself, and spin around in a raging vortex whether it led to his ruin or to his death. Not be for ever protecting himself and pining away in creeping nostalgia.

He came to his senses painfully. What he wanted was perhaps not the way things went those days. Until now he had always been full of the confidence of youth; had the notion that he ruled the world and that everything in it was happening as he wished it to; that evil and petty things were only taking place because he closed his eyes to them from time to time, out of leniency or inattention. Now suddenly the whole world seemed to have fallen through his hands. He became aware that he was powerless and that evil and harm, to which he had paid little attention previously, were ubiquitous. He began to scent them out everywhere and even with a kind of painful lasciviousness to wish his struggle against them to be over. So he was barely surprised when on Irene's birthday, and as he was looking for her in the courtyard with a bunch of flowers, the porter came towards him with a note. He quickly unfolded it: Irene was ill and she asked him to come up to her room.

He went in. She was stretched out on a divan in a pink and yellow dressing gown. She turned towards him, her white face looking smaller than usual and, in her indisposition, so overshadowed by her dark blonde plaits that her eyes looked like two holes to the right and left of her narrow nose. She stretched out her hand to him and it felt cool and moist. Tears immediately came to his eyes, and he bowed to her silently so that his emotion wouldn't be noticed and laid the bouquet sideways on the table.

Visiting the sick

She followed his movements with her eyes and nodded in thanks with a weak smile on her pale lips.

It affected him deeply. 'Has it come to this,' he said quietly.

She looked at him and it seemed to him that until then her eyes had been closed. 'I have had a morphine injection.' There was a kind of pride in her words. Then she said, 'Sit down!' in exactly the same painfully satisfied tone. He felt pleasantly touched that a chair was standing ready next to the divan.

'Is your health often as bad as this?'

'Not without good reason.'

She blinked at him, inviting him to enquire further. Just as she did in the beginning, he thought to himself – but he did not give way. He looked around at the room and it aroused in him memories of his first visit on the rainy days. He had not been here since then. In order not to give way to sentimentality he carried on: 'Did you have a disturbed night? Did you not sleep well?'

'The doctor had to be called in the middle of the night!' She lifted her head a little by supporting it on her raised hands. One wide sleeve fell back to her elbow so that her white arm was exposed. A faint perfume seemed to come from it. She stayed motionless in that position and looked into Hugo's face as if she were seeing him for the first time, as if she were solving a puzzle. He realised that the two of them were alone together, undisturbed for the first time. He was confused: 'I imagine that it must have been very unpleasant …'

She coughed weakly and then laid her head down on the pillow again with her arm underneath it. 'Particularly on a birthday,' he continued. The next moment he regretted the comment because he feared it was her birthday which had so upset her. She had often told him how sad getting older made her feel. To cover up his slip he kicked the table with pretend clumsiness, and grabbed the bottles which were standing on it. 'I almost caused an accident,' he laughed.

'It wouldn't have been so bad!'

'Are they actually medicine bottles or perfume bottles,' he said eagerly. 'In a lady's room all bottles look like perfume bottles to me.'

'It's medicine,' she responded softly. 'If you really want perfume, then please open the cupboard over there.'

'But what for?'

'Just do it,' she said faintly.

'But why? I don't want to put you to trouble.'

'No. You are not putting me to trouble ... the key is in the lock.'

He walked up to the cupboard and opened it. Pink and white dresses ballooned towards him, released from their close confinement. A hat fell off a nail and had to be caught. 'There's a casket down there,' Irene said directing him from the sofa. There were some blouses that rustled as he pushed them aside and also some belts. Then he brought the casket out: 'Have you got it?'

'Here it is.'

'Give me your handkerchief.'

She sprinkled a few drops on it.

'Thank you very much. How delightful.' He immediately put the handkerchief to his face to show his joy.

'You really like it?' she said pensively.

He stared at the floor in front of him without answering. He was completely overcome by a feeling of unutterable melancholy. After a while she took a sheet of paper from the table and held it out to him. He looked at it. It was the list of spa guests. 'Read it!'

A few lines in he came upon the name: Dr Heinrich Winternitz from Prague, Lawyer.

'Is it him?' he asked quietly.

She nodded.

'So that's it.' He heaved a sigh, not of relief, but to convince her, with the slightly unusual sound, that she had his sympathy. It irritated him that once again that other person was arousing feelings in her which should have belonged to him. But he immediately told himself that if her behaviour was forgivable, then certainly it was today, when it was the result of some change or unusual event. The episode in the night had obviously been caused by it.

'What will happen now?' he asked with concern.

'How do I know?' she said looking anxiously at the ceiling. When a fly came through the window she flinched and waved her hands in front of her face. Hugo stood up to chase the insect away. 'Anything is possible ... in the kind of life which I lead!'

He didn't know what to say in reply. He sat down again. For a while both remained silent.

'Can I help you?' he eventually asked.

She shook her head.

In that moment he felt that time was passing and that nothing was happening to bring his goal nearer. The idea came to him that a superficial observer, an outsider, would perhaps have found the situation awkward. But while he tried to understand what exactly the thoughts of the observer would have been, he realised how unimaginably far, laughably far, from awkward the situation was. It was serious, human, moving – everything but easy. He felt sorry for Irene. At the same time he thought how horribly she had sometimes behaved towards him and felt the need to bear that in mind. And yet he felt that it was his duty to console her. But – wasn't it unwise to think only about her wellbeing (as was his natural inclination) and to neglect his own interests, to destroy himself? Perhaps it was a more important duty to make a bold move and change everything for ever. And at that same moment he felt a bodily weakness sweep through him as if he had already been infected by her.

'Have you already seen him?'

'No.'

Without wanting to, he had to keep mentioning the man, his fortunate rival, although it was obviously not in his own interest. He even felt that it wouldn't have served any purpose if he had not mentioned him. And he felt consoled by the fact that he was speaking, if not in his own interests, then in Irene's. Loving his neighbour in the absence of anything better to do, he reproached himself and carried on: 'Perhaps he has already left ...'

To his astonishment Irene kept her gaze fixed on his face and changed the subject. After a pause she said, 'You don't look well, Hugo.'

He was so moved that he could have thrown himself at her feet. Unless it was just a good move on her part.

'What's wrong with you,' she said softly.

'With me? Nothing.' He had been so often disappointed that he automatically held back. I've had my fingers burnt too often, he thought.

'I had already noticed it. Recently I saw it all the time. Several times I meant to mention it to you. One just forgets. We live in such a mad rush ...'

He interrupted her with, 'Fraulein Irene, it is very kind of you to think about me. I mean, that you have given thought to me and my situation. Perhaps you shouldn't speak so much, it's tiring ... please, just stay lying down ... may I straighten up your pillow. Seriously, don't talk so much. Stay quiet and you will soon be better.'

'You are very attentive, I have always known that.' She obeyed him because she was tired and laid her head down again. 'But there's something not right. With all your excellent qualities, I don't know how it happened ... there is only one thing I can say in all good conscience: It is not my fault!'

'Certainly not,' he hastened to say. 'I never said that it was. No, it is not your fault. Not mine either. Basically, no-one is at fault for what he does ...'

'No. It's not my fault,' she repeated and shut her eyes.

'Look Fräulein ...' He rested his hands on top of one another in his lap and bent over. 'I am burned out ... burned out. It's a terrible feeling ... youth lost, like an extinguished crater ...'

She smiled: 'Please! You are still so young. What can I say?' He felt that she was veering away from what was actually troubling him. It was so difficult, in vague words and half meanings, to remain close to one another in a matter which had not been expressly referred to. And while gloomy but not especially unpleasant thoughts went through his head, he forced himself to make strenuous efforts to maintain the mood so as to reach some final conclusion. 'I don't mean it like that. Not the years but the feelings. One lives and hopes; hopes for great things and to see it always turning out differently. That is painful ... a miserable life. It would be good, just once, to spend a really happy day. Pure nonsense when it's expressed in that way. But yet, what a difference between a fresh, green heart, a thing of lush foliage and flowering stems, and one that is so burned out—'

She looked at him and nodded assent: 'Yes, yes!'

He wanted to say more. But everything that came to mind seemed unsatisfactory. 'I must prepare myself to be able to explain it better ... because it contains my whole view of life ... what lies deep within me.'

'Well?'

'You don't believe it ...'

'Yes, I do. Carry on speaking. I won't say anything. You are right, it is tiring. Right at the beginning you said something like that when you came in: "Has it come to this!" What did you mean by that ... I mean ... I understand it perfectly ... but I would be pleased if you would explain it to me ... what can I do?' There was emptiness in her wide eyes as she spoke those last words; deep dark rings were visible under them.

He waved his hands in the air: 'There is a gradual sinking down of everything, all is ruined ...' He had difficulty in keeping to generalised expressions. It lay on the tip of his tongue to say: When I got to know you, for example – but he was ashamed to say it out loud, to, as it were, take advantage of Irene's weakness. 'Everything is worse than we expected, and worse than we deserved. Much is promised but there is nothing there.'

'You are right. Life is just a pain.'

It was not clear whether they were both thinking of the same thing while they were talking. But the illusion of accord between them didn't do any harm. And there was at least something mutual in the resigned and sorrowful looks which they exchanged.

'When I think – good God! – with how much unhappiness one must pay for a few days of pleasure ...'

'It's like that for everyone.'

'It would almost be comforting to think that I am the only one who is feeling so bad. As I said, I am burned out.' Without thinking Hugo kept going back to the same words.

Irene lifted a finger as if she were listening to something. He stopped. She sighed: 'Look, now we are speaking as if we were in a play ... that's how it is.' In fact, until then they had both spoken quietly, not on even one occasion raising their voices.

He shuddered, but pulled himself together quickly, and defended himself almost fiercely: 'But not because we are in love. Only because we are ill. That's the big difference.'

She shrugged her shoulders.

'Did you want to say something?' he asked after a long pause.

She looked at him calmly and said, 'What would I want to say?'

'I only meant ...' He hesitated and stared into the distance. He took a tassel of the sofa cushion, divided it into strands, then put his fingers through them, carefully as if it were something important, and then pulled them out so that the strands came together again.

There was a knock at the door.

A spa attendant came in: 'Excuse me, Fräulein, are you bathing today? Shall I get everything ready?'

'No. Not until tomorrow. Thank you very much.'

The door was closed again. Hugo was afraid that Irene would be embarrassed, because earlier on she had claimed she was not ill and that it was only her mother who needed the

Teplitz 'Cure'. 'Where is your dear mother?' he quickly asked to create a diversion.

'She is bathing. This is now the time when she does. I usually bathe at eight o'clock.' So she had forgotten everything, thank heavens. He was really relieved.

'What I was just saying ...' Irene struggled to take up the thread again: 'Are you very angry with me? Seriously, have you been very annoyed with me, Hugo?'

'Annoyed?' He pretended to think hard about it. It was strange how this small diversion had derailed his own thoughts so much that he was not able to get back to them. Suddenly everything appeared plain and clear to him – the whole relationship unveiled. At the same time, he realised that in his anger he would exaggerate if he began to speak as his heart dictated. So he strove to tone down his response and said: 'I don't remember ever being annoyed with you.'

She didn't seem to believe him and protested again: 'I can't really do anything about that.' She took a rose from the bouquet he had brought her: 'Long-stemmed ... I like that. Did you know? They're entirely to my taste. I will put them into water straight away, until Mama comes.' She held the rose to her breast and put her head down to it.

'By the way, I shall be leaving soon. In eight days' time – on the first of September.' He spoke quickly as if he would otherwise lose the opportunity for ever. It seemed to him that it was exactly the right moment to tell her, when she was looking at something else.

'Why?' she retorted and looked at him enquiringly.

'I have things to do in Prague.'

'You are deserting us ... I'm sorry to hear that ... and so soon.'

Visiting the sick

He was astounded to see how hardened his heart had become. His sufferings, the bad experiences had made him apathetic. He shook his head and whispered: 'Too late ...'

She tried to make a joke of it. 'I say too soon and you say too late.' The charming smile she gave him was full of warmth.

But he was filled with stubbornness and mistrust. He repeated, with an even more meaningful tone: 'Too late!'

She looked in astonishment at the young man who was sitting on his chair and fiercely returning her gaze, while inwardly trembling. Then he took out his handkerchief and pressed it to his brow. With an anxious expression he breathed in the perfumed air and held the handkerchief to his nose as he had before. A long time passed in which he seemed to be undergoing a change of heart.

'Would you also like a rose – as a reminder,' she said reaching to the bouquet again.

'Yes, of course.' He quickly helped her to untie the strings.

'How about this one ... now you can't say that you have spent a boring time with me today without any reward.' She seemed completely changed, full of goodness and cheerfulness. However he didn't want to give way to his feelings. Tears, which had been held back for so long, gave him a pain in his head and his arteries trembled. He stood up, to take his leave: 'Thank you ...'

She looked at him questioningly.

He gave it some thought, then continued. 'And not only for the rose and the perfume. For everything which you have said today ... for allowing me to visit you. I value that.'

'Oh, come on ... I know from my own experience that visiting sick people can be very burdensome ...'

'You are quite wrong. I completely refute that.' He made such an effort that he shouted. His high voice sounded weak and strained. Irene put her hands on her ears, to make a joke of it. Although he did it in a cheerful tone, Hugo had protested with the deepest conviction. He understood all too well, that the mood of that day was perhaps the last thing which they had to offer each other.

The Public Meeting

From then on Hugo could find no peace.

The next morning, as he approached the Manor House he saw two unfamiliar men with Irene. He was alarmed and immediately assumed that one of them was Dr Winternitz. Irene had obviously recovered. The connection was clear to him. But who was the other man? In his confusion he was inclined to think that the second one was also Dr Winternitz. He had to tell himself firmly that the same man could not be there twice before he was willing to give up the idea.

Irene introduced him. They were her father and her brother Alfred who had come to visit her. They want to protect her he thought and immediately decided to add all his strength to that phalanx protecting the persecuted girl.

However for the time being it seemed that the family circle was firmly closed and not in need of any outside reinforcement. The three Poppers were intent on speaking to each other without paying any attention to Hugo. The brother in particular was showing off and shouted again and again: 'That's Jewish behaviour that is, I can't find any other way to describe it ... it's purely Jewish.'

'S'il te plait, n'excite-toi pas,' cried Irene.

'Ne t'excite pas,' Alfred corrected her rudely.

Hugo was amused. So that was the brother she had brought up! It didn't actually look that way.

The father was a tall man, with a wide white moustache and a smoothly shaved chin. He pulled himself up to his full height and said: 'Stop squabbling, you two. There's always this quarrelling. You have barely seen one another before it starts up again. I'm going to turn round and go straight back home. I'm certainly not staying longer than this evening.' He turned to Hugo: 'The two of them are like cat and dog ...'

Hugo thought it best not to make any reply. At that moment it seemed to him to be extremely important to get to know Irene's family and in that way to gather more information about her character. It also occurred to him that nothing threw so much light on a person as their relatives. Their father tried hard to keep order. Alfred resisted. And though Hugo didn't know what the subject matter of the dispute was, he was inclined to side with Alfred. Irene's brother spoke so energetically and pulled such angry faces that his broad teeth shone out. His face was brown, darker than Irene's and their mother's. A light moustache was barely visible on his upper lip. His hair was cut short and stood up thick and fuzzy so that it seemed to provide an impenetrable and almost hard cover over his head. 'You have deceived me, tricked me.' He let fly at Irene who flinched. 'You're a nervous wreck,' he said scornfully.

Frau Popper came out of the house. She knew exactly what it was all about and intervened: 'But it is in your own interest, Alfred. You will finally be free of the pain. You will be grateful to us ...'

Alfred's whole body shook with anger: 'And it has to be done here, does it? As if there were eye doctors only in Teplitz. Obviously nowadays one always has to travel seven hundred and seventy kilometres just to see an eye doctor.'

'But if an operation had been necessary, you would have needed to be near us, Alfred.'

'If only you weren't such hypocrites,' he said and stamped his foot and looked at those around him. His father had turned away and let the matter run its course. Irene didn't contradict him either. Instead she pressed her lips together in an arrogant expression as if she wanted to say to her brother that he could fight as much as he liked, it wouldn't do him any good. That made him really wild. 'I know exactly what this is all about. I'm not so stupid any longer. It's …'

'Alfred!' screamed his mother, so loudly that her son fell silent, more from fear than obedience. And then she carried on speaking, softly, but with an angry and ominous glare fixed on her son. 'You forget there is a visitor present. How are you Herr Rosenthal?' She held out her hand to Hugo who was astonished by such unaccustomed friendliness. He shifted from one foot to the other.

Alfred had pulled himself together and he began speaking again although in a more subdued manner and in a much milder and more cautious tone than before: 'We would definitely have reached the Ortler today. We were feeling so strong, not at all tired. The whole of the Dolomites had not weakened us in the least. And then suddenly a letter arrives. You spoiled all my fun!'

'You could have finished the excursion,' said Irene, with hidden irony but apparent seriousness.

"Yes – if you had sent me more money. That's always your

last resort. I will definitely not rely on you ever again!'

'Don't you see?' said his mother trying to calm things down but, it seemed, not out of beneficence but because she was aware of Hugo's presence and feared further arguments in the family circle. 'Next time is only a year away. The Ortler won't disappear.'

'God only knows where I'll be next year. Or whether I'll even be still alive ...'

'I wish you wouldn't talk such nonsense,' intervened the young man's father and immediately turned away again and drew patterns in the sand with his stick while breathing heavily.

Alfred was somewhat intimidated and said: 'All right ... but I want to be reimbursed for the journey here.'

'We can speak about that another time,' said his mother smiling, but with the same threatening look still on her face.

'And Kamilla Kapper means nothing to you? Have you already forgotten your young love?' Irene stood back a little before she shot her delicate arrows at him.

Her brother seemed to be particularly annoyed by her. His parents tried to calm him down. 'Just leave me alone ... you,' he hissed at Irene. 'As far as I'm concerned women can all be abducted – Jewish women in particular!' And he turned on his heel and left.

'Children, children, behave yourselves!' warned Frau Popper, anxious and commanding at the same time. She seemed to be the only one who found the fighting in front of Hugo to be embarrassing. Alfred was too excited and their father indifferent. And Irene? Hugo asked himself why she allowed him to witness it. But then he decided that once more it was down to her low opinion of him, as was so often the case. Today she was well again and thoughtless. He had correctly assessed her gentleness of yesterday to be a symptom of her illness, bodily weakness. *Ach Gott!* Whether it was him listening, or some child from the street, it was all the same to her. She was not embarrassed in front of him. That realisation filled his head and became so overwhelming that he was sunk in thought and no longer listening to the conversation. He didn't understand the things they were talking about and they didn't concern him either. The four of them had gradually quietened down. They asked Hugo about excursions and he answered absentmindedly.

'We must go to Eichwald sometime,' said their mother. 'It's scandalous that we have been here so long and haven't yet visited Eichwald.'

'Even Fräulein Irene can come with us,' said Hugo. 'One can go there by tram.'

Alfred immediately roared, 'I'm going on foot.'

'Ever the alpinist,' Irene said mockingly. Then she turned to Hugo and said, 'Have you noticed that nowhere are there so many stupid people as among alpinists? Of course, I don't mean Alfred, and present company is naturally excluded.' As always she claimed for her wounding insights the respect owed to objective science. 'Only one group surpasses them – enthusiastic amateur photographers. If one becomes acquainted with really insignificant people, one can be certain that within the first half hour they will turn out to be amateur photographers or alpinists. And in the worst cases, both.'

Hugo found the way her family reacted to Irene's aphorisms quite strange. Her mother listened but evidently did not understand. Her father didn't listen at all and took a certain pride in making it obvious – he clearly had better things to do. Alfred considered that everything that Irene said was basically wrong and contradicted her angrily but at the same time casually, as if it were barely worth the effort to contradict such nonsensical stuff. 'And even if you say so, what does it mean. Fräulein Irene Popper! Wonderful! Everyone is listening!' Because he exaggerated so much, Irene sometimes found it easy to put him in the wrong, although on the whole his opinions were more reasonable. He took particular pride in correcting her French.

She defended herself by saying to Hugo, 'He studies modern philology.' It seemed strange to him that she tried to justify herself and to show her superiority in that particular area, while she did not try to explain, even afterwards, the many matters of which Hugo had caught a glimpse that afternoon.

Her family did not provide a good foil to Irene's intellectuality. They didn't seem at all suited to making her particular traits believable. On the contrary, to an objective observer it must have seemed that Irene, who was the offspring of such dreary people, was only pretending to be delicate and frail, perhaps on rational grounds or perhaps obliged by outside circumstances. She did not seem to fit into that environment. And although Hugo suppressed those ideas as soon as they arose on the grounds that there was no evidence for them, some of them lodged in his mind bringing him a degree of quiet pleasure. If Irene had had sensitive parents and a brilliant brother – that would have impressed him fatally and thrown him at her feet for ever.

At the tennis courts he listened contentedly to an older gentleman whom Frau Lucie had recognised and who was taking a real pleasure in rekindling youthful memories. His

The Public Meeting

red face was fresh and clean like his white hair; his clothes were simple and durable, almost country clothes which were especially suitable for the corn merchant he was. Particularly noticeable were his thick heavy watch chain, which he liked to rattle, and his stiff round hat made out of grey felt. 'Weren't they wonderful times when we went to the theatre together! Obviously in the highest gallery, as arranged by our caretaker and costing four Kreuzer more, but it meant that we were the first to go up and get the best seats, the so-called 'standing' seats, do you remember, *gnädige Frau?*' Hugo's mother laughed happily and he pinched her cheek affectionately. 'Ha, ha! We were already there at five o'clock and had the honour of waiting from five till half past six in a tiny room, all squashed together. Or on the narrow staircase with people standing on it from top to bottom like horses at the starting gates! And then the door was finally opened and we ran, stumbling over one another, up the stairs and into the theatre where it was still dark. *That* was a struggle for human rights.' 'You always let me go ahead, Herr Popper,' the elderly lady said, lowering her head in obvious flirtation and looking to the side. 'Anything for you! Because then I often had to sit on those boxes which were really only intended for leaning on. We sat on top. I don't know if young people of today could do it. Just listen to this Alfred, and you Mr Gymnasium scholar! We kept ourselves in position with our hands pressed flat against the ceiling, no holding on as one does on a hook, but only with our hands pressed against the bare wall.' He demonstrated the position. 'And so, with our arms lifted up, we held out through the whole act. And when the curtain fell we collapsed.' He bent his legs and rubbed them as if they were hurting him, momentarily pulling a face. 'You see, Alfred, that was real appreciation of art ... but

Jewish Women

then we had the strength for it ... Slansky, Moser-Steinitz.' Frau Lucie immediately responded with other names which were unfamiliar to the rest but, when pronounced by these two elderly people with boundless feeling and ever changing expressions, sounded awe-inspiring. 'There's simply nothing better than the theatre,' sighed their father. 'It was different from today ...'

Hugo had further conversations with Alfred during the following days. He got to know him better and even went walking with him alone. Alfred was one of those young Jewish men who have a strong leaning towards the Aryan and find everything Jewish to be contemptible. However, it was not just negativity but an attitude that seemed to be strengthened by other inclinations. He was a gymnast, and president of a liberal society in which he was the best fencer. He got drunk at every important event and loved brawling with Czechs, crude jokes and stand-offs with the police. His authority in the matter of student politics was acknowledged. He didn't make a show, either to himself or to others of his particular view of the world but only occasionally mentioned it and then only in part as though it were obvious. In fact, all this was due entirely to a single theoretical work which he had read with enthusiasm some years before though only superficially and without understanding it properly, namely Weininger. He had discovered more from conversation with friends than he had from reading and cited what he had heard being cited, not what he himself had read. However, there was no disorder in his head; rather his view of life swam in a stream of practical knowledge, experiences and instincts with a splendid steadiness. He seemed terrified of women and girls and wanted only to have nothing to do with them. 'Look,' he said to Hugo, 'I sort that out for one Gulden twenty a month. Then I'm all right again!' His plan was to become a middle-school teacher and then to become involved in national politics but in a completely different way from what had been the usual path until then. His ideal was the unification of all Germans which would achieve amazing things. Perhaps he wouldn't become a Member of Parliament as that might be too difficult for a Jew, but at least a national political agent doing the legwork. That would be the most he could achieve. He had already joined an athletics club in Teplitz which was of a similar political colour. He had recommendations from leading Councillors, corresponded with organisers and never forgot to put the stamp of the German People's Council on the envelopes. His head was full of newspaper announcements, election results, bestowing of honorary citizenships, property purchases, appointments of civil servants. To all that he brought an energy and fire, which only highlighted his racial origins when he felt most distanced from them. At the tavern he asked for *Schulverein* matches. Afterwards he turned to Hugo with a smile and said, 'It's a small thing, isn't it. You are probably laughing at me but in national matters nothing is unimportant. One mustn't be embarrassed...' Sometimes he went so far as to ridicule those things and to say, '*Heil*' and '*treudeutsch*' ironically. But such occasional satirical outbursts did not hinder his efforts to move in the right nationalist circles and feel comfortable about it. He was really happy to be in Teplitz, in a German town instead of in '*tschechutzisch*' Prague, but at the same time annoyed that there were now so many Zionists there. He called the middle class 'contaminated' and preferred to speak about workers and small businessmen. He said, 'At last one can finally speak German with the people without any worries,' and was delighted by the dialect. 'How rough Czech sounds by comparison, so mean, so banal.' He harboured a deep and real hatred against everything Slavic ... He didn't pay attention to his clothing, aiming to be only comfortable and clean, anything more viewed as unimportant. He never wore a collar or a waistcoat and a loose tie fell over his sports shirt. Above it all his brown and energetic 'bandit' face was continually laughing. In addition and without paying much attention to music, he was a Wagnerian and knew the text and many motifs of the Wagner works with surprising accuracy. From afar he whistled the *Donar Ruf* or the *Siegfriedshorn* as a recognition signal. Hugo was happy to walk with him and for a while believed that he had found a person of the same mind as himself, with an enthusiasm for healthy and energetic ways of living. He learned a lot from the young man; for example, how to breathe when running long distances. The way in which Alfred explained things, in a curt and rather lordly manner, as if it were a disgrace not to know what he did, Hugo recognised as the only similarity he had to Irene, his otherwise very dissimilar sister.

'Will you have yourself baptised,' asked Hugo with interest, 'since it is, as you say, very difficult for a Jew ...'

Alfred was ready with a reply: 'It would be cowardly and for that reason I wouldn't do it. Anyway, it wouldn't mean anything to me. I am not prejudiced. And particularly because of the parents ...'

Hugo found such talk frightening. Even if he thought that what Alfred was saying was rash and controversial, he did not have the knowledge or the experience with which to contradict him. By comparison, for much of the time, although not always, he felt himself to be strongly Jewish

The Public Meeting

but yet not excluded from the nobler feelings of mankind in general. Alfred attended the university and was a grown man and Hugo could not complain about his good fortune which had brought him into association with older people whom he had to respect simply because of their age. He decided, with some pride, that it was a sign of upward striving that from his early youth he had always associated with older people. He was always making an effort, looking upwards, but it was not so easy to educate oneself that way. However his brave and difficult path was worth the effort and the many struggles.

But much in those days was beyond him. He had not been able to penetrate the family argument he had recently witnessed. That conflict was carrying on and seemed to be getting worse under the surface. It was also completely unclear to him why Alfred was pursuing Kamilla, the younger Kapper sister, so enthusiastically but secretly. How had that man who so despised women been caught by that quiet girl who immediately became unattractive when she opened her mouth and her shockingly rough voice could be heard. 'Modern women are rubbish!' said Alfred and cursed all manner of contact with them, their corsets and their huge modern hats. But Kamilla went around polished and corseted, dainty from top to toe like a picture out of *Wiener Mode*. Hugo gave up trying to understand it. Perhaps it was a relapse into youthful infatuation as Irene had suggested? It was rumoured that Alfred had challenged Pitroff to a duel but had received a clip round the ear as a response. Hugo did not dare to ask him about that. And anyway he didn't really believe the gossip. It didn't seem to him that Alfred was disposed to infatuation. *Ach Gott*, all the infatuation in the world was locked up in Hugo's breast.

Jewish Women

The arrival of family members had, in addition to many other changes, meant that Hugo could not be alone with Irene. Within a few days her father had become visibly irritated, and was constantly saying: 'My head is full of business matters and I have to stay here with you.' He left without saying goodbye to Hugo. But Alfred was almost always around. Also Dr Taubelis, who came to the house to treat Alfred's eye pain, became closer to the family than before. He participated in the morning walks with Irene and was always jovial and inclined to make jokes. But what was most noticeable was the change in the behaviour of Irene's mother. Until then she had clearly not looked favourably on Hugo, but now she was suddenly more friendly as if softened by an inner happiness. She called him 'dear young man' and often engaged him in conversation while Irene went on ahead with Dr Taubelis. Sheepishly, he followed her with his gaze. She no longer paid him any special attention, but he became even more concerned about her. How had it worked out with Dr Winternitz? Had he approached her and had they had a conversation? Hugo had no chance to speak to her. In vain he made signs to her; she misunderstood him, deliberately it seemed to him. Because there was no other way to do it, he tried to work out what was happening by studying her face. He was certain that significant things were happening in her life every day – that much was clear. He was convinced of it, not only because of its likelihood but also because of Irene's strange appearance which seemed to change from hour to hour. One moment she broke out in a burst of high spirits, and the next found her in deep depression. He tried to guess what was happening – today she had seen *him*, today a fatal letter had arrived. She was extremely nervous, clinging to trees as she went past them. She shivered in her clothes as though she were in a cold bath even when the sun was at its hottest. But he couldn't get near her, she wouldn't allow it. She had broken the tie of sympathy between them without any hesitation and without giving any thought to what might come of it. Now he felt, more clearly than ever before, that apart from everything else she had a quiet power over him – habit. Out of habit he went to the Manor House every day; he had to see her, if only from a distance. He couldn't give up trotting behind her like a poodle, exchanging a cool greeting with her, a bored hand shake, a few phrases. He was distressed but continued to fight against it. Suddenly it seemed as if every curtain had fallen away, as if he loved her again as he had at the beginning on that bowling evening. She asked him: 'Are you coming with us to Eichwald the day after tomorrow?' His heart lurched towards her. She noticed nothing, neither smiles nor hand gestures. It drove him half mad. And now that it was the last few days before he was due to leave, wasn't it almost unbelievable thoughtlessness on her part?

What affected him most was that she was associating so much with Nussbaum. Every day he publicised his public meeting, which had finally been licensed, with posters, advertisements and invitations. Hugo wondered, with astonishment, how it could have such an effect on Irene. She was clearly taken in by it all. She was always dancing around Nussbaum. When he made his appearances as a public figure she always had something to ask him, something to show him. Just as in the first days of the holiday she had put on a display of running across the whole courtyard to meet Hugo, now she visibly preferred the Councillor. The memory was very painful for Hugo, the comparison. Was Irene really so banal, he wondered, so interested in outward fame, in being noticed? Did she want to play a role at any price by the side of Nussbaum about whom she had made so many apposite jokes? He didn't really know why, but whereas on the one hand he valued her praise and her preference less, and his previous position at her side hadn't amounted to much, he was curiously greedy for nothing so much as to have that praise for himself again, and to replace Nussbaum. He couldn't stick to his books. Not another word was being learned. Oh, to be great, famous, finally significant in the world. He built a small motor, feverishly drew machines which he envisaged being finished and working, although some calculations – actually all of them – were still to be worked out.

The public meeting took place in Schönau, two days before he was due to leave. After many discussions with Irene, Nussbaum had changed the theme and spoke about 'National and religious tolerance.' His friend Pitroff would follow him with a speech on 'The persecution of Jews in Russia.' The convenors were a *Volksbildungsverein* (National Educational Association) and *freisinniger Arbeiterverein* (a liberal Workers Association). Long before the appointed hour the room was packed full. Cigar smoke wreathed up the green walls. People were eating at the tables and waitresses hurried between them wearing white aprons and with leather purses at their sides. Each carried a bunch of beer mugs in their hands. Soon more people arrived, blocked the doors and gangways between the tables, and had to be constantly asked to move to the side. They all streamed up and down like on a Corso. Only one table in the first row was left free for the Committee. It caused quite a sensation when Irene came in on Nussbaum's arm, and Kamilla Kapper behind them with Pitroff. They rustled in, dressed in striking clothes and were gallantly led to the reserved table by

The Public Meeting

the two speakers. There was an almost peaceful moment when there was only a buzz instead of loud shouting. Hugo thought his heart would stop beating.

He and Alfred had found standing room in a side gallery where they could hear everything but see very little. There was a constantly changing and limited view of the podium, glimpsed between heads and backs. Several men had sat down at a table on the podium and studied the audience below. If you wanted to look at anyone in particular, you had to move backwards and forwards constantly depending on how people were moving in the rows in front. Hugo had the impression that the arduous work involved was causing the sultry heat which had settled in the hall. He saw all the heads moving backwards and forwards, each blocking the view of the other. Every neck was sweating from the constant movement and handkerchiefs were being applied to necks and bald heads. The civil servant representing the government had taken off his black hat and placed it on the podium table. It lay there as stiff and severe as he was himself, the only person in the hall who was not in internal tumult. The members of the Committee sitting next to him took no notice of him. Finally Nussbaum stepped up. From somewhere in the front came the signal for applause. Was it Irene who had given it? Nussbaum thanked everyone. More people began to applaud. He gripped a chair and leaned on it. He then pulled the chair towards himself so that only the two back legs were on the floor. Then behind that barricade which at one moment he raised and the next lowered, according to whether he wished to draw near to the listeners or move away from them, he began to speak in a powerful but quiet voice. Hugo had to admit that it was skilfully done, but he couldn't bring himself to listen closely.

He looked around the hall in order to forget Irene's presence. The green wall opposite was divided by white pillars upon which two busts were mounted, recognisable only because of their characteristic outline: the Emperor and the Empress. Three gas lanterns were hanging together in a cluster but only one was lit. From its general appearance the room was clearly a dance hall and used more often as such than for significant events like that of the public meeting. In the corner of the podium an orchestra would usually be playing. A cry startled Hugo. Next to him in the empty gallery a small plump baby girl was innocently toddling along, the innkeeper's daughter. Dismayed waiters fell upon her and told her to leave. Some women looked fondly at the healthy child, and forgot about everything else. Most people were annoyed by the disturbance. Calls of 'Psst!' and 'Quiet!' could be heard. Inwardly Hugo had a wicked thought: if it had caused a small disturbance, then he was pleased about it, because Nussbaum was surely coming up to the punch line. But the speaker didn't allow himself to be disturbed, a least not by such a laughably small incident. He was fired up. He constructed parallel sentences which were minutes long and followed one after the other. They each began with 'You have— You have— You have!' Hugo found him boring, and he couldn't concentrate on the meaning. And what was Irene doing in the meantime? Hugo thought that every obliging smile which Nussbaum bestowed upon the public from the depths of his beard, was especially aimed at the reserved table in front of him and more particularly at Irene. And her brother was standing next to him. What should he do? Hit him? Speak to him in a friendly way? Something had to happen and Hugo thought it heaven-sent that at least her brother was there, the same blood as the

The Public Meeting

woman who was annoying him more than ever that day. In a moment when he had thought that not even the brother was next to him and he had been abandoned completely, he felt that he was about to faint. In the meantime Nussbaum had been interrupted by a burst of applause. What had he said? Hugo was so uninterested that it was impossible for him to make it out, or even to listen. It was only the applause that from time to time diverted him from his angry thoughts towards the speech. Alfred was listening. But why was he listening? The speaker said: 'And now finally—' Everyone breathed a sigh of relief and listened expectantly. Even Hugo could not stay aloof from the general excitement. Although he didn't actually listen he turned in the direction from which the voice was coming. But it had been a trick, to arouse the interest of the listeners. Nussbaum spoke on unabated and even used the trick again and once more everyone became as quiet as mice. No doubt it was a common trick among public speakers, thought Hugo. Sometimes Nussbaum raised his voice, and shouted so much that one thought he had to be nearing the end, unsparingly giving it everything he had. He received a storm of applause as a reward. He used it to rest for a moment, and after the pause, when the noise had died down, started again in a quiet voice, saving himself for the next punch line. He had carefully planned the most effective moment. He told anecdotes, and knew how to alternate seriousness with humour. The audience followed him expectantly and paid attention to all his arguments. They interrupted with shouts of agreement, in groups; this was barely noticed by him and seemed to be the normal course of things. But sometimes an individual was so excited that he answered a rhetorical question. "Do you really want—' asked Nussbaum, full of fear and indignation, and

Jewish Women

quickly went on speaking. 'No' shouted someone decisively. People laughed, but in the next moment admired the speaker even more. Then he addressed the students: 'You are only enjoying a superior position in society so that you can receive the treasures of culture and hand them on.' 'Bravo' shouted someone who was particularly deprived of education in a loud and anguished voice.

'Don't you now feel honoured to be a student?' said Hugo turning to Alfred.

'I'm not listening at all. I'm thinking about something else.'

'You as well ... what are you thinking about then?'

'When is that Pitroff speaking?' Alfred looked around the hall and only then did Hugo notice how excited he was.

'I don't know ... a public meeting like this is so dreadfully boring ... the only lovely thing around is the women.'

'Aha', said Alfred and mischievously waved a warning finger at him. 'I think you are a little woman-lover, aren't you?'

'Yes, I love women,' said Hugo and turned his back on the meeting. Here in the gallery they could speak undisturbed and he felt a great need to relieve his inner tension with some kind of emotional outburst. So he immediately confessed everything and couldn't stop himself from speaking as he hoped, by doing so, to understand himself. 'Yes, yes, I confess that I couldn't live without women. Life seems worthless and dark without them ...'

'Hey! A little eroticist as well ... hmm, I see.'

'Not at all! That's completely wrong. I'm not at all erotic. I'm surprised at it myself, but I am not in the least sensuous. You may not believe it, but I have never touched a woman.'

'How old are you then?' asked Alfred, who was getting interested in this conversation.

The Public Meeting

'Nearly eighteen,' lied Hugo. 'It's strange, everyone asks me how old I am ...'

'Eighteen years old ... Listen, it's not surprising that you're still a virgin. You don't need to worry about that.' 'But I am ...' Alfred wouldn't let him speak further, as always happened when he wanted to finish what he was saying. 'I held back until I was twenty-two. And to be honest, I'm sorry that I didn't wait longer. Women have the right to expect sexual purity from men. That is my view.'

Hugo was irritated and burst out with, 'That's got nothing to do with me.' He could see very well that what he was now doing wasn't what he had set out to do. It relieved his tension but it wasn't really right. They were, in a way, having a parallel public meeting, next to Nussbaum who was speaking to an expectant public. Theirs was in a dreary gallery in which broken chairs leaned against the pillars, which stank of wood and dust and which had old empty bottles standing in the corner. How ridiculous! But in spite of everything Hugo felt the need to speak. To speak as he had never spoken before and precisely about what was filling his heart so intensely, while nearby a torrent of words, which meant nothing to him, was being poured out into the hall. He wanted to empty out his burning young heart, to liberate it. It's true that he would have preferred to speak to Irene and to have left her brother to the demagogues. The whole thing was crazy and inappropriate, pointless from beginning to end. But it didn't matter. 'No. That has nothing to do with me,' he said, seizing Alfred's arm. 'Just understand me for once. Try to understand me. All those questions do not interest me in the least. And this is what I want to emphasize – as I said, I am not sensuous. Desires and the flesh, emancipation, sexual problems – I leave those to the philosophers. I am not a philosopher; I haven't even read Kant. What have those serious questions and discussions got to do with me. I don't understand them at all. I leave that to the libertines. Perhaps it will be different when I am older, but for the moment I can only say, in all honesty, what I feel in my honest, childish heart. Look, Herr Popper, I am *not* sensuous. But I want love, I want a heart that turns to me, a woman, who feels things with me, who thinks of me as a friend and brother – the ideal of womanhood, in a word. Look, I just love women. I respect women and, to put it briefly, I am pleased and happy that there are women in the world. That is the whole of it. Are women of any use to me? I don't know and it's not relevant. I feel no inclination to look into that question. I can only say one thing – I am grateful for the fact that they wear light-coloured clothes. No, don't laugh! Just imagine, if there were no women in the world, how deadly boring it would be. I am just happy that women exist, that they look at me and speak to me, that their opinions differ from mine and are different in a feminine way. Women are better and more perfect than men in every way; I know that, and there is nothing else that I am more convinced of. That belief is the very foundation of my life. Can you understand at all? Yes, yes. You are right. I have never known a woman like the one I imagine, I admit that. But I would claim that is irrelevant, a completely irrelevant circumstance ...'

There was a loud shout of applause nearby, into which Nussbaum shouted the word 'progress' in the loudest possible voice. Then he paused.

Hugo also paused until the hall became quieter.

Then he carried on: 'My ideal is so firmly entrenched in me – that gentle, good-natured, charitable woman – that it probably couldn't exist in real life. I keep it firmly inside me. Perhaps it is only a consequence of my limited experience of life, that I have never met such a girl. That is also a possibility. But where does that ideal come from then, I ask myself, if not from real life? I'm not so conceited to think that it is my own invention, my poetry. No, rather it works like this! I enjoy associating with women, I admire them and I always notice small things to admire about them, for example, their pleasant light clothes, their charming remarks, a quiet goodness. Their goodness, and those small characteristics seep into me almost unnoticed and are built into my ideal. To whom do I owe that ideal? To women. I owe it to them, not them to me. For that reason it is right for me to speak humbly to them, not to demand too much, on the contrary, to thank them and that's good. And I am happy to do that, and happy to be with them, very happy. Even the air around them does me good. My head dwells in dark places when I have to be just with men, if only for a short time, I get headaches ...'

'Now he's really speaking quite well,' interrupted Alfred, who had been listening only to Nussbaum after the last applause.

At that moment everyone got up and flourished their glasses. Nussbaum was led off the podium in triumph by three men. It was over. They went wild. The *Tribun* leaned on his companions with dignity and they carried rather than led him down the steps. He looked at the tumult with a calm and serious expression without even for a moment reducing the excitement and the applause with an involuntary modest smile. Irene had also stood up, stretched her arms out widely and then brought her hands together slowly, so that her applause was visible from afar, even if it could not be heard. Hugo pushed his way through the crowd. Was she handing the fellow a laurel wreath? Ah no, it was only a flower. Only? It was dreadful to be together with her in that room, between four walls, without feeling the slightest connection. He looked at the walls. Those walls encompassed her and him, and it was of no use to him. Having pushed his way along the row of pillars he finally stood opposite her, and greeted her for the first time that evening. She thanked him with a cold and absent-minded nod. He felt the ground sink beneath his feet.

Alfred had followed behind him. 'Pitroff is speaking next, isn't he?'

Hugo didn't answer. He felt a slight weakness in his heart.

'Where is the gang?' Alfred glanced restlessly round the room; he too seemed to be looking for something missing. 'There will be a barracking like you've never seen before! If it works ...'

The Russian had begun to speak, in a very different style from Nussbaum, almost shyly and with a pronounced accent. He opened his mouth wide, and because his moustache was only visible at the corners of his mouth, there appeared to be a large hole directly under his nose. It was easy to see how much effort he was making, while only producing a weak sound. All in all it was an unusual sight. After making an introduction in German Pitroff spoke Russian. At the sound of that foreign voice, which seemed to change the mood in the whole hall, Hugo began to feel ashamed. It was no longer the right moment to answer Alfred's question, so he signalled his participation with a question. 'What have you got against Pitroff? Do you know him?'

Perhaps Alfred had expected that question, because he answered very clearly and carefully: 'You tell me first, do you know him?'

The Public Meeting

'No, not at all …'

'But isn't he … apparently … Herr Nussbaum's friend?'

'What do you mean by that,' said Hugo irritably, involuntarily copying Alfred's intense studentish attitude. 'I don't know Herr Nussbaum either. Apart from the fact that we were once rude to each other at a bowling game, the man is a stranger to me and means nothing.'

'I'm pleased about that. So, I can tell you… this Nussbaum …'

'Why is he speaking at all? What is he trying to achieve with this public meeting …'

'He wants to win a seat obviously.'

'So it's nothing to do with his relatives?'

'Not at all. He belongs to the Hock Party and will be a candidate in Vienna. So he needs a letter of recommendation, such as: "Is very active in the provinces."'

Hugo thought how often he had changed his mind about that man. And probably his new view was also wrong, or one-sided at least. It really isn't easy, he thought, to make a judgment about people, particularly not for a young person. Perhaps Irene is something else entirely. His thoughts returned quickly to her.

'But I don't want to speak about that,' said Alfred. 'Come back to the gallery where we won't be disturbed … I am only interested in this Pitroff … I found out that Nussbaum has only recently got to know him. In spite of that he is introducing him everywhere as an old friend. There must be a reason for that. At first I thought that, like all rootless people, Nussbaum was looking for connections everywhere, wherever he could find them. Without a homeland, without a nation, as he is … but the matter goes deeper than that. The two of them are "free thinkers", both anti-national ... what a scandal, just think of it ... in Teplitz, in a German town, he has a Slav speaking, publicly. Just think! If a German citizen spoke in Tabor or Jicin, what would they make of it there. He would be torn in pieces, wouldn't he? But we, we are half-hearted, we allow everything to happen to us. Well, we must spoil it for them ...' He looked into the hall nervously. 'The whole thing is a Jewish story from A to Z. Will you be in Eichwald tomorrow?'

'Yes. Fräulein Irene has invited me.' Hugo was surprised at how calmly her name tripped off his tongue.

'And at the Rathauskeller in the evening?'

'No. But what has that got to do with Pitroff?'

'What! So you don't know that my cousin Kamilla will be engaged to Pitroff tomorrow evening? You didn't know? With drums and trumpets ... but it must be stopped; I will cause a song and dance today, if things work out ... '

Hugo began to understand. Love was showing through the political enmity.

But Alfred forestalled him. 'Don't think that it's about the girl. A girl, I ask you, a piece of flesh with eyes ... I just feel sorry for her. She has to accept that completely strange man, an alleged friend of the allegedly well-known Herr Nussbaum. Any bridegroom is good enough for these Jewish families. They found out all about him, of course. He has money, some yarn factory in Petersburg. And so, just like that, the girl must be sent over the border ...'

'Does she not want to go?'

'It doesn't matter to those people,' cried Alfred, really worked up by now. 'A German, a Slav, all kinds of rubbish! They don't have the slightest spark of a sense of honour in their bodies ... A Russian, a barbarian ... All Slavs are false.'

Hugo had to smile and forgot his own desperate situation for a moment.

Pitroff spoke German again. He smiled politely and minimally. Sometimes he blew air through his nose when he couldn't remember a word. People were becoming bored.

'Aha, there they are!' cried Alfred.

At the doors there were a number of similarly clad young people, all in sports shirts and with green hunting hats on their heads.

'Who are they?'

'The Wotan Athletics Club – my friends.'

The newcomers pushed their way into the hall and positioned themselves along the back wall. Suddenly one of them called out loudly: 'Waiter, a beer!'

Pitroff paused; he thought someone had asked him something and stopped speaking.

'A beer, a beer ... two beers!' shouted the gymnasts. They pounded the floor with their sticks, 'Service, service!'

A few people in the audience laughed. A waiter was sent to the new customers. Someone from the Committee had already understood the seriousness of the matter. He used his arm, which was decorated with a red ribbon, to push his way from the front row to the strangers at the back. Another member of the Committee who was sitting on the podium insisted that Pitroff carry on speaking.

'A beer!' roared the Club one after the other and in chorus. The audience burst out laughing again. The Chairman who had finally noticed the disturbance, pleaded with them, 'Gentlemen!' The intruders deliberately misunderstood him and, as if he were the waiter, reproached him. 'Well, is the beer coming soon?' Up on the podium Pitroff leaned over the table and started speaking again although no-one noticed him anymore.

At that moment Alfred Popper bent far forwards over the neighbouring table, supported himself with one hand on a chair and one on the nearest pillar so that he could lift himself high up. From that vantage point he opened his eyes wide and gave a shrill whistle. He waved his hat and shouted, as he let himself fall back, 'Withdraw!'

That was the signal. The gymnasts joined in with 'Withdraw, withdraw Pitroff!' and pushed forward in a group towards the podium. The Chairman was thrown to the floor. Glasses tinkled. Women shrieked in fury. People had jumped up on all the tables and the workers and gymnasts began to fight each other. In vain the Chairman called for order; his calm voice was drowned out by the hurly-burly. Then he picked up his hat and declared the sitting to be at an end. The Committee members left the podium, each of them concerned for their families. The landlord swore loudly and drove his waiters into the fray. Some people paid, but others fled, white with fear. Someone shouted, 'Police!' Two side doors had been opened and through those poured a stream of frightened people, with no interest in any further proceedings. A draught rose up, cold blasts of wind blew in, and the lamps began to flicker and to grow dimmer at the same time, so that it seemed the turmoil had reached the upper regions. In the middle of the hall a wild crowd had gathered around Pitroff who had suddenly become lively and was gesticulating; around Nussbaum whose voice was booming out, and around Alfred who was screaming like a madman and throwing punches. Hats could be seen flying, sticks being brandished

The Public Meeting

and tables overturned. The Parties spat old insults into each other's faces: 'Rogues! You are all corrupt, Jewish peasants, and socialists!' A punch rang out, some people were fighting each other on the floor. The continuous shouting merged into one long noise. Hugo was excited and peered into the turmoil. There was fighting, passion, and it was about politics, not love. He felt good there, at home. He raised his fists. To Irene's rescue! With sudden decisiveness he threw himself into the middle of the fight – head first. He felt a steely resolve in his chest, jumped over the hostile rows, stepped on other peoples' toes, climbed over legs and up and over chairs. He was there. He saw Irene's waving scarf, her hat. Just another step … Irene stood between Dr Taubelis and Nussbaum who with their tall figures, even taller than her, were clearing a path for her. She also towered above the crowd, not least over Hugo who rolled at her feet like a bottle-stopper. She didn't take any notice of him at all. She probably didn't even see him, drawn forward by the two towers at her side. He rolled past between stomachs, waistcoats and jacket buttons in the dark, the noise and the throng. Kneecaps were pressing on his head. Now he understood it. He was too small – just too small! He froze with pain at that realisation and all the strength went out of him. A short while afterwards Irene disappeared with her companions and the crowd closed around Hugo once more.

Olga

Betrayed! Rejected! With the shrill music of the fight still ringing in his head, he made his way through the empty streets to the Castle park. The pond reflected the cold shining moonlight. It was here that he had looked at the white swans with Irene, here that he had felt the greatest happiness. He took a step forward to throw himself into the water, and in that moment thought: 'I'm going in, making an end of everything! That's how it should be.' He ducked under the railing, then straightened up again; he was now standing on the narrow strip of ground behind the railings with his foot tangled up in creepers and grass. Without a farewell letter, without any ceremony. Yes, that was how it should be! Tomorrow people would say: 'He was drunk. For no obvious reason he fell into the water, quite by chance.' He felt flattered by the thought. Only one person would guess the reason, only one, who would be deeply shocked. Oh, yes, she would be deeply shocked. He heard a cry in the distance, perhaps from the swan house, and lost his balance. His foot slipped on a clump of weeds and slid into the water. He quickly grabbed at a sapling, as a terrible

Jewish Women

feeling of fear overcame him. Then he crawled back under the railings and hurried home.

As he walked down to the dark corridor and past the dining-room, the door flew open, and Olga stood there in the light. She had been waiting up for him.

'At last ...'

'You know already ...'

The Baroness had also been at the *Volksversammlung* to support Pitroff. Olga had heard from her about the stormy ending to the meeting, but she had not told Hugo's mother so as not to cause her anxiety. Frau Lucie had already gone to bed. Only Olga waited anxiously. 'Where have you been all this time?'

'It went on for a long time ...' he muttered, 'before I could crawl home.' The light was dazzling him because he had been wandering about in the dark for almost an hour; he had to hold his hat half in front of his face.

'And you look dreadful, Hugo.' She drew him right into the room.

He really was a pitiful sight. His boots were wet and muddy, his trousers splashed to above the knee, his collar ripped open. In the crush his tie had come undone and he hadn't even noticed. His brow was sweaty, one curl sticking damply to it. The rest of his hair stood up in tangled tufts. Then he saw himself in a mirror and was alarmed. His first reaction was to move aside so that the image of a white-faced, shattered-looking young man disappeared. He threw himself into a chair: 'I'm tired.'

Olga looked at him with concern. 'You haven't even had anything to eat yet, have you?'

He shook his head.

Immediately, and without saying another word, she hurried into the hall and quickly came back with a plate on which there were several slices of sausage. He felt hungry then and called out, 'Yes, yes, let me have it.' She quickly ran into the kitchen and brought him some bread as well and put down the salt cellar and a jug of water next to him. 'You are very kind ... Mama's in bed? ... Why are you still up so late?'

'I have some darning to do.' Olga showed him a sock pulled over a piece of wood that looked like a mushroom. 'You wear things out so fast ...'

He did not reply because he was too occupied with eating greedily. Then he swallowed down two glasses of water, one after the other. She didn't disturb him but turned back to her work. Then he suddenly made a face and said, 'My feet are so wet ... it's horrible ... I must go and fetch my slippers ...'

'Wait, I think there's an old pair somewhere here ... I have seen them in a box.' She knelt down.

'But what are you thinking of, you can't wait on me like this.' He jumped down onto the floor next to her.

'Let me be. Just eat up so that we can finish ... here they are!'

'How clever you are!'

She laughed. 'You would have spent a long time looking for them.'

He slipped into the room next door which was dark. Then he pulled off his wet boots and socks. His feet were icy. Only when they had been slid into the slippers did he feel some semblance of comfort again. At the same time it seemed that the whole of his behaviour since his return home was like a swiftly passing dream. Everything went so quickly, so unconsciously – the speaking, the bolting of his food. But how Olga had spoiled him! He saw himself as a spoiled child and he had to laugh at that. A spoiled child – after all the dreadful experiences of that evening. At the same time he felt a sweet emotion rise within him as he went back into the dining room.

'Come on, eat some more,' she said encouragingly.

'I've had enough, Olga,' he said, pushing the plate away, although he felt only half full. 'But you are so kind to me—' He couldn't say any more; something was squeezing his throat shut.

She cleared away, saying 'Like a sparrow, like a sparrow ... what an evening meal that was ... for a grown man.'

She went back and forth. She opened the door with her elbow, and then went through the opening sideways, her arms full of all the crockery. Her shoulders were broad and plumply rounded, her back strong and her shining black hair was put into many braids and wrapped around her head in a thick circle. When she came in again, he noticed that her eyes shone and there were patches of healthy glowing colour on her cheeks. They went right up to her nose and seemed like an outbreak of strength, of inner competence, like a permanent blush. Her bosom, which was already womanly, swelled high and firm under her light pink housecoat, trembling lightly at every step and her happy smile seemed to say that she was proud of that burden while no less modest about it. She brought in a piece of *Pischingertorte*.

'You are spoiling me, Olga. I don't deserve it.' He grasped her hand and pressed it. 'Come and sit down next to me ... why should you sit over there ... there's something I must say to you ... I am so unhappy—'

'But Hugo,' she said in a tone of reproach.

'No, it has to be said. Do I deserve to have you treating me in such a kind way ... it has to be said that it's a shame when

Olga

one has such thoughts.' He couldn't get the words out of his mouth; he had to lean closer to Olga before his voice could come out. 'You don't know how unhappy I am. I was close to killing myself—'

She sprang up in horror, as if about to call for help.

'Wait ... sit down. I wanted to tell you. Isn't it terrible to have such thoughts?'

She stood there, still frozen.

'I regret it already, Olga. But anyway—' He saw that she took his revelation very hard and that comforted him, just as her alarm had comforted him when he confessed to her about his bad school performance, the remedial examination. Then he recalled what had happened on that occasion. Why after that hadn't he turned to Olga much sooner. She understood him so well, was able to sympathise. And it came to him in a flash that there was a connection between her excellent character and her health and her womanliness. She was everything a woman should be, everything that made her so good. Ever ready to console – completely natural. He could depend on her. 'Olga, dear Olga, you are so good, you will forgive me.'

'I don't forgive you for anything,' she finally burst out, completely outraged by his words. 'Do you know what it is ... what you are ... you are a monster, for saying such things. It's a sin in the sight of God – a sin that cries out to God! A young lad ... what's wrong with you? What's up with you? What have you got to be so unhappy about? Fräulein Irene has pulled a long face, and for that reason you obviously have to shoot yourself! There's obviously nothing else for it. Oh, but I thought you were cleverer than that! I'm sorry that I had such a good opinion of you. I will change it from now on, very quickly, I tell you ...'

It did him so much good to hear those reproaches washing over him. He hung his head: 'I quite agree with you.'

'You're not saying another word,' she continued in honest rage. 'I won't speak to you again, any more, you annoy me so much.'

'But I am confessing everything to you ...'

'I know it all. I don't want to know any more.'

The fact that she had already mentioned Irene particularly pleased him – that she had openly gone straight to the heart of the matter. He didn't need to beat about the bush. She understood. 'Look, Olga, when one is so unhappily in love ...'

'In love or not in love ...' She was still raging; but suddenly she became much quieter and he was surprised to realise that during the whole of her angry speech he had not really taken her seriously, not interpreted it as anything to worry about, only as kindness concealed behind cross words. 'Even if you are stupid enough to fall in love then you must still exercise some control over yourself. Or at least that's what I think. If not, then I don't give anything for love at all ... it's not worth as much as that, mark my word.'

'Olga.' He kept calling her by name, as if to hold on to her, out of fear. 'Do you think that one can always control oneself? You don't know all that has happened.'

'*Pfui Teufel*. Now he's whining again! No, I can't tell you how unpleasant it is for me when someone complains so much. You either speak properly with me or—'

He had taken hold of her hand again. He smiled. 'That's just an empty threat. I know it. What were you going to say? That you would go away? I know that you will stay with me, and hear me out to the end, otherwise you won't be able to get a wink of sleep. I know that you are fond of me ... you are my only friend Olga, I know that. I tell you everything. Only sometimes I forget to tell you everything for a while, and then things gets bad. Look, I am going to confess. I think that if one has been so close to suicide, eyeball to eyeball with it ... that can't be put right. It will remain a wound for my whole life—'

'So what actually happened?' Olga hit the table with her hand. 'Speak now!'

He looked at her mischievously. 'No, I'm not going to tell you that.' He had thought in the meantime that he would spare her the details. They could have made a bad impression on her. 'But I will tell you something else ... I don't really think that the wound will remain for life ... that was just a way of speaking.' He noticed something about himself then, that it didn't matter what he told Olga. With everything he said to her he felt relief coursing through his heart.

'So what is it that you want to tell me?' she repeated calmly. 'Not this and not that. I might as well go to sleep.' She felt that she had a duty to carry on showing some firmness.

'Something really special ... something which certainly no-one will ever ask you apart from me!' It pleased him to get her attention and to see that she listened to him so seriously. 'Look, Olga, things are going really badly for me. I am unhappily in love, as I have already said ... no possible future there.' Although he still felt those things deeply and painfully, he could only portray them to Olga in a light tone as though he were already free of them, as if he were already above them. She made him feel so calm, that it seemed to him that she was pouring a lukewarm shower of rain over his dried-out limbs. 'That's my misfortune. I have no luck with women ... and must therefore ask you for advice. How do you manage it?

You have so much luck with men, they all dance around you. It must be similar in the case of women. All hearts fly to you, how do you manage it?'

She didn't understand him. 'What do you mean? What do you want from me?'

He was pleased that she had not understood him. Now what he had said seemed stupid to him. He would have been ashamed if she had realised what it was about. 'I'm just surprised,' he explained, 'that you have so much luck with men. You are always making conquests. Has it always been like that for you? I have only noticed it this year.'

She pulled a 'listening' face, and thought about it, with her brow wrinkled and her eyes raised to the ceiling.

'I have dreadfully bad luck with women,' he whispered to himself, to fill in the pause.

'I really don't know,' said Olga solemnly, 'what kind of compliments you are giving me. I'm not used to getting them from you. What can I say …'

He noticed that she was embarrassed and felt sorry about that. 'We can talk about that another time, if you don't want to any more today.'

'But I would like to.' She was now so deep in thought that she didn't want to let it go. 'It's already very late, but if you really want to know … I don't do anything to make men like me and I can easily prove that. I am friendly to everyone who is friendly to me. That is all. I am not particularly sweet to them. I am not a flirt, am I?' He waved his hand to dismiss the idea. 'If someone makes advances to me, which can happen, then he hears some words that stop him doing the same thing again. I don't let anyone think they are doing me a favour by noticing me. And those men mean nothing to me. I make that clear to everyone. That is the most important thing, Hugo. You must remember that – not to show that you are in love, wrapped up in someone else.'

He noticed to his astonishment that she had previously understood him correctly. She'd just needed time to think conscientiously about it. With great interest he continued, 'But you have it easy, Olga. When you are really not in love with anyone, it's easy to act as if you are not— What are you doing?'

She had jumped up. 'The lamp is smoking ...' She turned down the wick and it became noticeably darker though they quickly became used to it. 'I hope it will last, it isn't completely full.' Then she briefly passed the tip of her tongue over her lips and answered firmly. 'No, it isn't like that. If I were in love with someone, even then I wouldn't tell him. I wouldn't let it show in any way.'

He found the young girl's philosophy of love to be naïve but still wonderfully typical of her. For him it would certainly not work. 'So is that all?' he asked again, not because he thought he would learn anything useful but out of the pure pleasure of telling everything to Olga and becoming closer to her.

'Yes. That is all there is to my way of doing things,' she repeated, almost rejoicing and with no trace of irony. 'That's how I would do it. And what's more, although I am not exactly in love with anyone at the moment – you know that – there is someone to whom I am not entirely indifferent ...' She blushed and colour flooded her face and even reached her ears.

'Herr Klein?'

She nodded silently.

'Yes, but that's something quite different. He loves you

doesn't he? There is a mutual attraction. But if one wants to win someone's heart while appearing to be indifferent – well, I've tried that, but I wasn't successful. It wasn't even noticed; I could wait a long time doing it that way again. That method just doesn't work for me. No, you just don't know what unhappy love is ...'

'Is that what you think?' She looked at him and her dark eyes lost their shine as if they were looking inwards. 'When I was young, a thirteen-year-old girl, in Kolin, we all ran after the farm bailiff, my friends and me as well. But no-one knew how much I loved him. He was a Hungarian, a fiery Magyar. Perhaps I will never love so deeply again. When once he came to visit us, I noticed which chair he sat on and the nail on which he hung his hat and they became sacred places to me. He once spoke to me and I couldn't utter a word in reply. From that time on I didn't run after him. Quite the contrary, I avoided him; I looked at him only from a distance when he was round the corner, so that I could only see the edge of his coat, nothing more.'

'He didn't know anything about it?'

'He had no idea. Then he was transferred. And I didn't want to live any more. I behaved in a strange way. I refused to eat. For three days I ate nothing, until they called the doctor, several times, and then a Professor from Prague who force fed me—'

She had grown in Hugo's eyes. Today Olga seemed really flourishing and voluptuous as she sat next to him. But she too had gone through a painful passion, so she was close to him. He had always thought the best of her, but that evening she surprised him with every word which came out of her red lips, so delicately and with such small nervous twitches – a true daughter of Zion. His hands began to tremble. It was not fair that until then he had always treated her without much consideration – if with the best will in the world – as nothing but an immature and funny girl. But what a *mensch* she was! That pale brow which she lifted before the world, almost like a glacier. He would happily have worshipped at it, that brow, that mouth which continued her tale: 'Nobody knew what was wrong with me. They beat me and called it being naughty and difficult. Then a postcard arrived from the bailiff, addressed to my parents obviously. I secretly took it for myself, folded it up very small and hid it in the courtyard under a stone. Usually Mama saw everything, nothing was safe from her. But there under the stone, that card belonged just to me, although it wasn't addressed to me. "Greetings to the youngster" was written very small on the side. It was the only thing which I had of my beloved. I was so childish then! But, you see, Hugo, I thought my despair would never pass. But it has passed. Everything passes, that's what I'm telling you. After a half, three-quarters of a year, I was thinking less about him, and after a year perhaps not at all. Take that as a lesson, Hugo! Eventually everything in this world passes.'

'It passes? You really believe that?'

'I know it.'

He was trembling so violently he had to stand up to hide it. 'Good so it passes. I believe you. But that still isn't everything, dear Olga, it still isn't the most important thing in my life. I am not talking about the precious time spent in agony which one would have spent more usefully in happiness. No, that's not all.' He swallowed his tears and clenched his fists. 'The fact that it comes back again, *that* is the worst thing. It passes for one love. Good. But then I go onto the next one. I have been

Jewish Women

in love three times – even four, counting Irene – and the latest love is just as unhappy as the previous one! That's what is so embarrassing, Olga. Unhappiness is typical of me, it isn't just an isolated event; the single instance is typical of the whole. I will never have luck with women, I will never be loved as I deserve. It will never be any different until I die. And however I act, whether I flirt or behave modestly, am arrogant or reserved, it's always the same story. At the beginning the girl turns towards me, it goes well for a while and then suddenly, I don't know why, I begin to displease her. That is always my experience. I disappear from her life and others take my place. I even think that women are all naturally fickle, they flirt with everyone a bit, so what does it matter to them if someone takes it to heart as I do? Am I right, Olga?' He walked up and down the room, taking irregular steps in his agitation. 'Perhaps I feel things too much, have a soft heart. And that's in everything I do, not just with women. It's typical of my general bad luck. Everything goes wrong for me. I won't achieve anything in the world – profession, ideals, nothing. It's always ringing in my ears, what someone once said to me: "Hugo, it will go badly for you!" How true that is! I don't know if it's the same for you, but such remarks, which have been made to me in particular situations, have a strong effect on me. They rule my life for years, I relate everything to them, everything. The person who said it probably had no idea how much their words had affected me – for them it was just an aside. "Hugo, it will go badly for you!"' Barely in control of himself, he clung to Olga's chair, and standing behind her he grasped the back of it.

With a sudden movement she turned round to face him while she was still sitting. 'And I tell you – it's good if such remarks have an effect on you! So I'm telling you today, loud and clear: Hugo, things will go very well for you, very well. Do you hear?' She was shaking with indignation at the unknown person who had spoken so unpleasantly to her friend, and was quite convinced that she was telling his true future.

He looked at her face which was glowing. Then he slid down to land at her feet. Suddenly every emotion was unleashed in him. Hot tears sprang from his eyes and he felt new ones welling up behind. His brow was hot and his cheeks trembled. All the sorrow of his life welled up and streamed from his eyes. He had pressed his face into her lap; he did not feel the girl's broad thighs underneath, nor her legs in his hands which were clutching them. He felt only something warm, good, an eternal pain relief, eternal security, better than a grassy meadow, better than silk and feathers; a darkness in which he wandered, cool and warm at the same time, just as he needed it. Not seen by anybody, safe under the ground, where he wandered and rested, moved forward and stayed still again, between mild-smelling fragrances, under slow-moving clouds which didn't press on him or leave him too loose. Most importantly he was at peace without beginning and without end; he didn't feel it as just a cessation of unrest but as an effective blessing from the very beginning, passing straight through his skin and into his heart. And now, as Olga gently stroked his hair, he lifted his head a little. With his tears running together like a very close water mirror in front of his eyes, he cried: 'A sister! I should have had a sister! My brother was taken away from me ... that would have been wonderful, too wonderful ... but a sister, just like you, Olga ... always with me, with me my whole life long ... a sister, yes I have one, you are it, Olga. Isn't that right? You are!' And he lifted his head again and again and then let it fall back into her lap.

'That's what you are, that's what you are!' – while fresh tears came out with each new movement and gathered ready to fall.

She didn't say a word, she didn't cry. She only wanted to calm down his over-excitement. She left him on his knees until he had stopped crying. After a while he got up, grasped her hands and pressed them firmly. 'Thank you, thank you!'

'Hugo – aren't you ashamed?' she said quietly and smiled at him encouragingly.

He denied it with a fierce shake of his head; a stubbornness remained even after the release of crying.

She pulled her hands free and stroked his hair again. 'Everything is nice and peaceful now – isn't it.'

Only then did he take out his handkerchief and dry his face. 'Do you know how long it is since I have cried like that?' For the first time, he returned her smile, after with great difficulty, uttering those words. 'Since I confessed that I had to resit the exam ... at the beginning of the holidays.'

'So always with me, that's nice ...'

'Certainly it's nice, Olga,' he insisted.

'And never with Fräulein Irene?'

'I was too angry with her ... crying requires peace and I only find that with you.'

'But that means you have a much more entertaining time with her than you do with me.' She smiled to show that she was teasing.

'Olga ...' He let the handkerchief fall, gripped her with both hands and looked as though he was about to throw himself at her feet again.

'Hugo! Such a big boy!' She held him up by his arms. 'Sit down there ... and no more complaining. There is something much more important to talk about because you have reminded me of your remedial exam. Do you know everything already, are you properly prepared?'

He was still sobbing and found speaking painful. 'I don't need to tell you ... why I am going to Prague the day after tomorrow ...'

'You still don't know anything then?'

'Oh, yes. I have been learning ... but she disturbs me so much.' With those words a new flood of tears burst from his eyes. Crying came very easily to him, now that he had started. He could cry at the slightest opportunity, and a sweet feeling of peace and satisfaction filled him, because the tears were now within his control. At any moment he could find relief; his head was like a hollow ball warmed by a sea of lukewarm water and with open valves. He cried and poured himself out. He didn't even hold his hands in front of his face, the flowing tears did him so much good.

Olga nodded: 'I thought that was the case ... but do you know what, Hugo ...'

He looked at her, through an opaque veil.

'You will hold out tomorrow, and then the whole story will be at an end. In the morning you won't go to the Manor House, but into the forest or somewhere else. And in the afternoon – there is an excursion to Eichwald, you know. I've been invited. I didn't want to go. But for your sake I will do it. I will not move from your side, I will protect you. Are we agreed?'

'You are so good! Yes, we'll do that.' He swallowed his sobs.

'And then you will go to Prague and study hard and forget that awful girl. She doesn't deserve anything else ...'

He played a drumroll with his fingers on the table-top to

show his agreement and his pleasure. His kept his eyes firmly fixed on Olga. He couldn't speak.

'And will you write to me and tell me if you have passed the examination—'

'Of course, immediately. I will send you a telegram. But Mama mustn't know about it – so Poste Restante?'

'No, I'm not going to do that. Just write to me here, at home. I will catch the postman. Or just change your writing for the address.'

'We can agree upon a secret sign. A word like 'palace' means that I have passed—'

She yawned. 'We can speak about that another time.'

'You are tired!'

She was still yawning as she shook her head, fanned air into her open mouth with her hand and tried to speak, all at the same time. 'No idea.'

'Do you know how late it is?' He looked at the clock which hung on the wall behind Olga.

'One o'clock,' she cried.

'One has already gone, five minutes ago.'

'I know what time it is.' Suddenly she looked sad – drained by tiredness, with moisture standing in her eyes.

He took the candle and the matches which were lying ready on the *Trumeau*.[21] 'I am going now. When do you have to get up in the morning?'

'At six o'clock.'

'That's terrible. So early?'

'At half-past six the milk lady and the butcher come—'

She's just like a servant, he thought and looked at her with sudden sympathy, as he sighed and said, 'Good night then—'

She immediately raised her voice: 'What's wrong with you

now? You are making such a face?'

'No, no.' He made a big effort to cast aside the clouds, which he felt gathering over him again. 'You have comforted me so much. I don't know how to thank you—'

'Don't speak about that. So, good night ... sleep well.'

'I've finished crying!'

Olga laughed: 'Yes, you have ... you get the top mark for that.'

'The next time you want to cry you will come to me, won't you.'

'That's not going to happen.' She wanted to speak in the Berlin dialect, out of pure excitement.

'Well, when the next farm bailiff comes—'

'There isn't one.'

'Don't you ever want to meet one again?'

'Never. Everything is going so well for me! I really lack for nothing.' And she jumped up from her chair and lifted her arms up. 'Don't I look peaceful?' She bent her head down towards him.

'One doesn't hear that said very often. That's wonderful!' He felt very moved. Something in that room was keeping him. 'I must go now,' he said quietly, as if to himself.

There was a splitting sound. Perhaps a string had broken when Olga made a sudden movement or a button had come off her *negligée*. She tried to find out where it was with her hand going upwards over her back and under small fastenings. Her skirt met her pink jacket, worn without a belt and kept in place by knotted fastenings. Hugo only now noticed how short the dark red skirt was – perhaps it was an underskirt.

'You look very funny, you know,' he said as he looked her up and down.

'I could see there was something different about you, but now I know what it is. You've got a different hair style from usual.'

'Yes. For the last couple of days I have been wearing a *Gretl* hairstyle and only now do you notice it.'

'Until now you have been wearing your hair in a *Toupet* style. Why are you suddenly wearing braids?'

She laughed: 'Well, Herr Klein recently said that the *Toupet* suits me very well – and so since then I have been wearing braids.' He laughed with her as much as he could; but in his breast he still felt a painful twinge from time to time which ran right up to his throat. 'So, you're still claiming that you're not a flirt, Olginka.' He was already standing in the doorway and made a friendly warning gesture with his forefinger. She curtseyed to him, holding her skirt with both hands in a graceful courtly bow. He smiled. When he had closed the outer door, he used his raised forefinger to wipe the last tears from his eyelashes.

Little Elsa

Hugo had slept quite well and spent the whole morning in the excellent Teplitz swimming pool.

When he came out of the spa buildings around midday and walked down the street, he felt strangely restored, oblivious to the sun's rays, light and, as it were, inwardly cleansed, as though the water had not only flowed over his surfaces but also through him, and was still flowing. He was happy, ready for anything. He wished that Irene were there, so that he could conquer her. His love for her had reawakened together with his strength, but purer and beautiful now, not tarnished by any of the obstacles that otherwise surrounded them. The world now seemed simple; he loved and hated, clearly and directly. He had confidence again in his power to change everything, in any way he chose and without much ado.

Then he noticed that, while he was walking along the Bahnhofstrasse, Josef Nussbaum and Elsa Weil were going in the same direction. They were arguing. The little girl raised her voice: 'How long will you keep promising me? It's a disgrace that you never have any money. Get some!' Josef craned his neck out of his collar, stretched himself as if to make a particular effort, took some long steps and then in the middle of one of them, buckled like the two halves of a telescope being pushed together. After he had answered quietly, so that Hugo couldn't hear, Elsa cried: 'That's no excuse. Anyone can say that!' A big bow of ribbon hung down behind from the belt of her white dress. This time her hair had been put into a single plait which flew here and there with every defiant movement which she made.

Hugo took a few quick steps and caught up with the pair. He was in a wonderful mood that day, ready to involve himself in anything, to speak to everybody. He greeted them. They both turned round, looking alarmed, as if they had been caught out.

'Ah, Fräulein Elsa – where are you going?'

'We want ...'

'Have you got your water pistol with you? Should I be afraid of you today?'

'We want to go to the station,' replied little Elsa decisively. She waved her fist in the air and gesticulated, with angry nods of her head, to poor Josef who looked around anxiously, hoping to find some peace.

Hugo was astonished and amused: 'To the railway station? What do you want to do there?'

'To go away. Out into the world!'

'And where to?'

'It doesn't matter where to. Just away.' Elsa's dark eyes flashed and her pale cheeks reddened delicately.

Hugo remembered that he had already seen the two of them near the station once before, that they read Karl May together; and after what Irene had said about Elsa the thing began to seem more than just a joke.

'So you want to kidnap Fräulein Elsa, so to speak,' he said smiling and turning to Josef who was barely able to follow the conversation.

Josef stared at him with a paralysed expression and made no response.

'You want to begin a better life with her, somewhere abroad, don't you?' Hugo spoke to him encouragingly and stretched out his hand in a sympathetic way. He was polite to them and aware that his voice was casting a kind of spell. Josef seemed moved by it. He pressed Hugo's hand in response and it was clear that Hugo had found the right tone. Once again he was filled with sympathy for the lad's simple, unspoiled heart. 'That's what you want, isn't it ...'

At first Josef looked around shyly. Elsa nodded to him

'Well?' said Hugo encouragingly.

But Josef remained silent with embarrassment, his gaze fixed upon the ground.

'An adventure,' cried Hugo, in a kindly voice. 'That would be a real adventure ...'

Little Elsa puffed out her chest: 'Is it such a big thing? It has happened hundreds of times. It happens every day. I read about it in the newspapers.' And as if to give more strength to her words, she quickened her pace in the direction of the train station which could already be seen behind the trees. Josef immediately followed her and Hugo had to hurry to keep up. For a moment he was caught up in their joyous excitement; the two of them were striding forward, with all the confidence of youth, not yet disappointed, embarking upon life, both full of hope. The sun shone and the long rows of windows sparkled. The street was full of light. He could make out the green ivy-clad walls of the ground floor of the station, and the semi-circles of red brick over its windows. The trains whistled merrily and blew out steam, and the whole world stood ready to favour the brave.

Elsa stood still and began to laugh.

'What's going on? Are you too late?' cried Hugo caught up in the plan and wanting it to succeed.

'It's nothing,' said Elsa, sounding unconcerned, and strode on even more determinedly. 'We can never be too late!' She pulled out a ball which she had been carrying inside her blouse, threw it into the air and caught it; bounced it off the ground, and caught it again. She capered around the two young men like a baby animal.

'Was it only a joke?' said Hugo to Josef, who was still standing there with a blank look. Elsa played by his side. Hugo was surprised that, even for a moment, he could have taken such an improbable thing seriously. He laughed ruefully at his own foolishness. It seemed to him that that he was floating above everything, wafting between the good or the bad, as though nothing in life really mattered and everything was harmless, unimportant, and funny. But he roused himself from that mood as Josef was still at his side; and it suddenly occurred to him that he had a wonderful opportunity to revenge himself upon Nussbaum, just as on the previous day Alfred had engineered a demonstration against Pitroff. 'Do you need money?'

Josef looked at him mutely.

Hugo pulled out his wallet. He had already received his allowance for September plus extra money for the journey to Prague. So he could riffle the banknotes like the pages of a book. 'You can see that I have something to spare – ten Gulden perhaps.'

Little Elsa

Josef nodded, without reaching out for the money.

Elsa had come up to them. She looked at the money with big, serious eyes and prodded Josef with her elbow.

Hugo was still holding the money in his hand. 'What am I doing?' he thought. 'What madness is this. It isn't clear what these two have in mind to do together. But it isn't anything bad.' And with that thought he reassured himself. He felt so harmless and in the right, without any responsibility, with the strength of the cold pool still at his hips.

'Take it,' whispered Elsa quietly.

Then Josef quickly grabbed the proffered notes from Hugo's hand. 'Thank you very much.'

'So, *Adieu, auf Wiedersehen*,' cheered Elsa and clapped her hands. Her slender body trembled as if in a strong wind. He had never seen her like that before.

'*Adieu*. Where are you going?' shouted Hugo, who suddenly felt heavy-hearted.

The two were now holding hands and ran rather than walked as they went toward the station.

Hugo stood watching them there for a while and then turned around, quite unmoved. And then he left, completely satisfied with himself and with a wicked feeling of joy in his soul, of pure wanton fun.

Eichwald

After a quick midday meal they hurried to the Schulplatz where the Manor House crowd were already waiting for them. He went arm in arm with Olga, who towered over him and matched his stride.

'Aha, so you're also engaged!' cried Lotti Kapper.

Everyone laughed at the joke and pretended to congratulate them.

Then they all climbed into the electric tram. The young girls behaved as though they were intoxicated. They were all excited and merry. The words 'engaged', 'wedding' and 'match' were flying around all the time. They spoke of nothing else. And it was all aimed at Kamilla who was the centre of it. She sat quietly adorned next to Pitroff. He gallantly drew the small curtain across the window to protect her from the sun.

'*Also doch,*' thought Hugo to himself. He too was happy, but in quite a different way. He was seized by a general cheerfulness without any obvious reason. Perhaps it was a reaction after so much depression. He pushed his way through the crowd and when he had climbed aboard found himself sitting right next to Irene. He felt that everything was going well for him that day.

'Where is Alfred?' he asked, out of curiosity, as he looked at the assembled crowd.

'He's already gone.'

'What, no longer in Teplitz?'

'Didn't he even say goodbye to you?' laughed Irene. 'Well, it happened unexpectedly.'

'Like this engagement,' retorted Hugo cunningly, to see if he could discover a connection which he suspected was there.

Irene said, quoting, 'All engagements come as a surprise'.

'Anything like that is an unpleasant surprise,' cried Flora Weil, who sat opposite them. She was wearing a light blue blouse, from which her plump bosom swelled and protruded. 'Isn't that true, Kamilla?' She drawled, intent on teasing her cousin who was in no mood for jokes but played with her new bracelet instead. She opened its tiny gold clasp and then let it quietly snap shut again. They asked her if she knew of any engagement that had recently taken place in Teplitz. Her mouth twitched contemptuously. Pitroff sat staring at her admiringly. But in spite of the inappropriateness of the topic the whole group remained undaunted in their attempts to have fun by making the most of the situation: the tension between the unofficial engagement and the official one, which they all knew was to be announced that evening. There were only close acquaintances sitting in the carriage, no strangers. The conductor, going from one to another with his block of tickets, was the only thing that disturbed them. He finally disappeared and then an uninhibited exuberance at the prospect of their outing took over. Even Frau Popper joined in, saying, 'From now on we must have nothing but surprises,' forcing her usually monotonous voice into a more animated tone.

'Do you know what that is?' said Nussbaum who was sitting on the other side of Irene, and held out his ticket on which he had put the ash from his cigar.

Dr Taubelis, who was sitting in the corner, said in a warning tone, 'That's an old joke ... my grandfather told that joke when I was young, and even then it was antique.'

'Do you give up?' continued Nussbaum, since Irene did not answer. 'It is an *Über-aschung, Überraschung.*'[22]

The Doctor said, 'Ha – ha – hahaha' in an ordinary speaking voice without a hint of merriment in it. That sent Alice into a paroxysm. 'Now, now, calm down!' She had to lean her head on Lotti's shoulder and in turn Lotti found Alice's complete loss of composure so terribly amusing that she couldn't help joining in with the laughter. The two girls filled the carriage with noise all on their own. 'Quiet now,' said the Doctor in a comical tone. That encouraged them even more and the girls couldn't have stopped laughing even if they had wanted to and even though their sides were hurting. And every time they seemed about to stop, the Doctor or Nussbaum knew how to get them going again with a new comment: 'Haven't you finished laughing yet?' or 'Come now, my country wagon,' and they would start off again with their outbursts of giggling and gurgling. A mere wave of the hand was enough to set them off again.

'Do you like this area?' Hugo asked Irene.

She quickly replied, 'An industrial suburb, isn't it?'

'Yes, the journey isn't particularly entertaining.'

'Neither the journey, nor the travellers,' she whispered quietly, and glanced around as she leaned towards him confidentially. Today she was obviously intent on keeping close to him. That gave him pleasure and it seemed to him worthwhile to study her misty grey blue eyes. His gaze kept sliding towards the showy but pretty necklace which she wore around her neck – long rows of steel beads with steel points at their ends like tiny shining daggers hung on a long neck chain. In addition her hat was of the latest fashion – very large and worn low – and whether by chance or design, she sat in such a way that her face was presented to him but obscured from Nussbaum, who tried in vain to overcome the obstacle and to catch her attention.

'What are people saying about yesterday's meeting?' asked Hugo.

'The newspapers have written according to their political views – some criticise and others write positively. Nussbaum hasn't convinced anyone.'

'What do you think?' asked Nussbaum when he heard his name being spoken and with difficulty insinuated his face round the curved brim of Irene's hat.

'That everyone will find his own salvation,' she laughed.

He hesitated. 'That's obvious,' he said and moved his head back again. He didn't understand her.

Hugo was happy even though she didn't say anything further to him. He remembered the meeting of the day before; how he had longed for a word from Irene, and now here she was sitting next to him, wholly accessible and turning away from his rival. What was that all about? He saw himself slipping into the pond, in the moonlight, under the silent trees; and now here he was sitting cheerfully in a rattling electric tram with the same girl and talking to her calmly. Was it possible that a single life could contain so many different scenarios? And Olga? How close he had felt to her the previous evening, and now she was standing outside on the platform with the two Demut brothers, enjoying herself like the other women.

'Are you jealous?' said Irene, who had noticed what he was looking at.

'Of whom?'

'Do I have to tell you? So where are you looking?'

'No idea. Olga is like a sister to me ...'

'But she speaks with such a strong Czech accent, your sister.' And an unusually strong glint of malice showed in Irene's eyes.

'Why are you always finding fault with the poor girl. It just isn't true that she speaks with a strong accent.'

'She comes from Kolin, doesn't she?'

'But she was brought up in Reichenberg.'

'You are a very good defender ... so sincere!'

Hugo was astonished. Could it be that he, who had longed for love during the whole of the holidays, was actually being fought over by two girls on his last day? Olga's behaviour of the previous evening, which he had thought at the time he understood so well, now seemed more opaque. By day the word 'sister' did not sound strictly credible. Struggling to bring some order to his thoughts and to say something sensible, he repeated: 'She would defend me in just the same way if it came to it. We have been friends since childhood, even though I only see her for two months of the year ...'

'You are leaving soon, aren't you?'

'Tomorrow.'

'So soon! We will see each other in Prague, won't we?'

'If you wish it.'

'It's an order.'

Everything was going well today. Irene even promised him, without his asking, to accompany him to the station the next day.

'Olga is really ...'

'Let's not think about her,' Irene interrupted him, with an almost affectionate look. 'Let's concentrate on ourselves. Particularly since you're leaving tomorrow. Anyway, where were you this morning?'

So she had missed him. He began to colour up, in a 'champagne' mood. Irene was enchanting him all over again, with every word, every one of her clever observations.

'I had all kinds of errands to run.'

'Did you speak to Dr Winternitz?' she suddenly asked.

'But I don't know him at all.'

She shook her head: 'You don't know him at all ... and does Olga know him?'

'What makes you think that? Obviously she knows him as little as I do ... but we didn't want to speak about Olga. Look, about Dr Winternitz ... you probably think I'm not interested in him, although it's been on the tip of my tongue a hundred times to ask about him. But I didn't trust myself. You were so proud, so distant ...' He played with the handle of the sunshade she held, and gently brushed her fingers with his. 'You intimidated me so much, Fräulein, frightened me even ... but now you are as before, I dare to ask ... so, now tell me, I am burning with curiosity, what has happened? Have you spoken to him?'

She pulled an angry face: 'Nothing at all has happened.'

'Oh dear! Is something wrong?' he asked anxiously. 'Look, I would gladly have stayed here, always nearby, to protect you. But I really have to go to Prague, I have things to do there.'

Eichwald

He expected to hear a word from her about his examination, but she seemed to have forgotten about it. She has slipped away from me a bit, thought Hugo and looked at her, as one looks at a match stick which is drifting away on the current. But he was self-confident today, and trusted in his ability to charm her back if he had stayed. And yet he was conscious that he was not staying. He could feel his own imminent release and the prospect filled him with relief. Today is the last day here, he said to himself and it belongs to me. I will put it to good use. I have the strength for it – and tomorrow I will be over the hills and far away.

They reached Eichwald. Kamilla took Pitroff's arm, which everyone noticed and good-naturedly smiled at. Firstly they had some light refreshment in Theresienbad, and then visited the elegant terraces and the charming garden. After that Hugo led the group to the church. It had a façade decorated with alternating stripes of red and white marble, and stood on the Marktplatz. It had been begun by the Count after some Italian model, and was in fact an exact copy. Hugo recounted the story that only Italian workers were allowed to work on it and that every individual stone had to be brought over the Alps. In addition, it would never be completely finished. It was not possible to raise so much money. Only Irene listened to him; the cousins chatted among themselves. 'How nice to waste money so pointlessly,' cried Irene. Olga looked at her in astonishment, and then seemed to turn her gaze to Hugo to ask what he thought about it. It was unpleasant for him and he turned back to Irene and said: 'I would do exactly the same.' She gave him with a warm smile and said: 'The little Baron!' as kindly as at the bowling evening.

Then they went along the Landstrasse past the Sanssouci

Inn over which mighty pine trees loomed, and into the forest. A little way in all the ladies felt suddenly tired. Plaid blankets were laid out in a clearing surrounded by blackberry bushes, and they all quickly sat down in a circle. 'Bunte Reihe!'[23] shouted Lotti, in a commanding tone, when she noticed that the two Demuts were sitting next to one another. 'That's not right! Always a gentleman next to a lady.' The guilty parties complied with her wishes.

Alice was enraptured by the forest: 'Oh, the forest ... *Wer hat dich, du schöner Wald...*'[24]

'It's just like in *A Midsummer Night's Dream* here, with Reinhardt,'[25] said Nussbaum, raising his hat.

'Shall we sing something?' suggested Dr Taubelis.

But Flora said: 'Better to have team games, forfeits ...'

They agreed with her: 'But what shall we play?'

Ringeraten and *Sprichwörter* were rejected as too boring. They decided on *Handwerker*.

'No, something else!' cried Irene. 'I know another game; we played it in London – *Grobheiten*'.[26]

'How does that work?'

'One person goes out – the others must all say something rude about the one who is absent to the game leader who writes it down. He then reads it out to the person when they come back, who must confess what has upset him most and then guess who has made the rude remark.'

'That isn't nice,' cried Olga.

Some of the gentlemen agreed, just to please her. Everyone jumped up and argued. Irene calmly stood by her suggestion: 'What's the problem?'

'Why deliberately insult someone?' objected Olga and calmly confronted her. For the first time they looked each other in the eye, the slender one trembling and the strong one with supressed annoyance.

'No-one needs to feel insulted. That is understood beforehand. It's just for fun.'

Nussbaum declared himself ready to be the first to adopt the difficult role and calmly listen to a list of his sins.

Irene collected the comments to show how it should be done. They all had to whisper in her ear so that no-one would know what the others had said. Hugo trembled when he felt himself so close to her downy cheek and shiny golden curls. 'You can come back now.' Herr Nussbaum drew close to the circle with a courtly but at the same time ingratiating bow, as he had on the previous day at the meeting. 'So you are a "confirmed bachelor", "a comedy writer", "ugly", and "conceited". You are "the father of your son" and "a poor imitation of Wilde".'

She read down the list with satisfaction, while Nussbaum made ironic bows to all sides. He was embarrassed but soon regained his composure.

'Now, which of the descriptions has upset you most, honoured Mr Delinquent?'

He thought about it. Then in order to show that nothing had offended him, he asked Irene to read them through again.

She did it mercilessly.

'I think "confirmed bachelor" offends me most,' he said with a friendly and engaging smile.

The ladies nodded approvingly; they liked him. And Nussbaum, who was proud to have turned what had been planned as his downfall into a triumph, joined in the game enthusiastically.

'Now, who do you think contributed the worst insult? You

have three guesses—'

'I guess it was Miss Irene, who is the best at insulting everybody.'

'Wrong,' she retorted coolly.

He made two more wrong guesses then had to sit down.

'So whose turn is it next,' said Irene clapping her hands. 'We can use a counting rhyme ...'

Olga whispered something to Demut who stood up and protested against carrying on with the game, saying it was boring and dangerous. It had already caused nervous tension in the group; everyone was now expecting to be stabbed in the back and thinking about how to defend themselves. They all tried to look unconcerned and congratulated Nussbaum. But Irene would not be put off. She did her counting rhyme and finished with: 'It's Kamilla's turn!'

'I wouldn't dream of it!' growled Kamilla and turned her back. 'Kamilla is exempted today,' Pitroff reminded them, and everyone murmured agreement. Irene counted on with increasing speed. 'So, Fräulein Olga, now it's your turn.'

Some of them called out, 'No – stop it! Stop it!'

'Or are you afraid, perhaps?' taunted Irene.

'Me? Afraid?' Olga had already jumped up, although they tried to hold her back. 'No, I'm going.' She ran off, dark red in the face.

'Someone else can lead now,' said Irene with obvious indifference. 'Herr Nussbaum, you are very efficient ...' And she sat down next to Hugo.

Everyone was in an oppressively good mood. Somebody warbled a song to give them courage. Nussbaum noted down what they said with cheerful formality.

'Ready.'

Olga reappeared with one hand clutched to her breast. She was breathing deeply but from time to time her face swelled up, as if she was holding her breath.

'So, Fräulein, I have been told the most awful things about you.' His put on a pretend sympathetic tone but it differed only slightly from his usual tone. 'I hardly dare read them out to you. Do you want to hear them?'

Olga nodded and went white. Irene's gaze was trained upon her.

'So, first, someone said that you are very beautiful.'

'But that isn't an insult!'

'Wait a moment ...' and here Nussbaum winked to let her know that the remark which he had just read out came from him, 'there is something more to come. That you often know more than you say.'

Olga smiled weakly: 'That's possible.'

'And also – that you run after all the men!'

Nussbaum gave a shout as Olga ripped the paper out of his hand: 'Who said that? Who?'

'But you have to guess that later,' said Nussbaum trying to calm her down.

'No, I want to know who it was!' She had been wounded in the most sensitive part of her womanly pride. She stamped her foot and the blood flooded back to her face which once again had a fiery glow. She flew straight at Irene. The game broke up; people got to their feet and shouted out, all at the same time. Only Irene remained lying on the ground and nodded scornfully; a clear sign that she confessed to making the remark. Olga stood there trembling, tears in her eyes. She stretched out one hand. Hugo was very aware that she was reaching out to him, that he should help her. Irene pulled herself up, hanging onto his arm. Could he suddenly turn on her? But he knew what his duty was, felt the crucial significance of that moment. Olga had only accompanied him today in order to protect him, was here purely for his sake. How, when he should protect her, could he abandon her? She was here alone, among strangers. He looked down. No word passed between the three of them, while all around them were anxious calls for calm.

'Excuse me. I must ... it's time.' Olga turned to face the others, trying to hide her tears. Suddenly she shouted, 'Adieu!' It sounded like a wail. Then she threw back her shoulders in rage and rushed away.

They all hurried after her.
'Where to? Where to?'
'She will go to the station.'
'We will go as well—'
'It's already getting late anyway.'

They saw Olga ahead of them, jumping over ditches and running back to the Landstrasse by the quickest route. They discussed what to do. The good mood had faded and they could not meet each other's eyes. Nobody reproached Irene, but they no longer felt comfortable with each other. They fell quiet. After some hesitation they walked in groups to the electric tram station.

There were loud cries of: 'We shouldn't have let her run away. We should catch up with her.' Some of the men began to run.

But by the time they reached the station Olga had already boarded a tram that was leaving at great speed. They stood together once more, disconsolate now. Someone was heard to say: 'And it began so well.' *Polterabend*[27] whispered Alice behind Kamilla. Hugo bit his lip. Irene calmly looked up at the sky. They waited for the next tram which came from Teplitz.

It soon came, but the group had not recovered from their embarrassing episode when a new and even more shocking one overtook them. A policeman alighted from the vehicle, followed by Frau Weil whose face was covered in sweat and tears. In a frenzy she raged: 'There he is, the murderer, the murderer!' pointing at Nussbaum.

'Are you Herr Nussbaum?' said the armed policeman challenging him immediately.

'Yes, I am.'

'Then, in the name of the law, I require you to accompany me to the police station.'

Everyone cried, 'What has happened?' Frau Popper wanted to run away and drag Irene with her; she thought they were all going to be arrested. Some of the men put on serious faces as if ready to resist when the situation became somewhat clearer. Nussbaum had assumed a mild, saintly expression: 'But gentlemen – ladies.' He swore to everyone that he was being unjustly persecuted. The girls trembled and looked at him in horror as though he were a wild animal. The rattling of a sabre was heard, the unfastening of a belt, firm steps and an unsheathed bayonet glowed sharply in the sun. 'Ah, it's about the meeting,' announced Lotti. 'I am glad that I wasn't there.' 'He's a revolutionary!' shouted someone.

Frau Weil whimpered and cried: 'He has kidnapped her ... Elsa, my daughter ... that idiot, that child kidnapper ... who was it, you ask? It was Josef Nussbaum, they were seen on the station ... she didn't come to lunch, I waited and waited.' She shouted at her daughters Alice and Flora, who were completely stunned and looking after their half-conscious mother. 'You are obviously only concerned with your own pleasure. As far as you are concerned we can all croak ... but I, I ... everything is on my shoulders ... I'm ruined.' She behaved like a mad woman.

At the front Nussbaum was trying to persuade the policeman of his innocence. 'It will all become clear. We just have to take a statement from you,' he was told.

The whole group followed him to the police station with Irene leading them. She couldn't laugh loudly enough at the fun and was the most excited of them all. Hugo had separated himself from her and lagged behind, oppressed by a feeling of guilt on two counts.

On the way they learned the piecemeal story from the raging Frau Weil. There was no trace of the two fugitives. But in her deep anxiety she had got the whole of Teplitz involved, irritated her husband, telegraphed and telephoned the authorities continuously. Fortunately she had remembered that Nussbaum senior was with the outing to Eichwald. He must know something, perhaps he had even participated in the plot; it was definitely his fault.

In the ante-room of the police station they met the telegraph boy. A telegram had just arrived. The senior police officer held it up and smiled — they had already intercepted the pair, in Dux. They were on the way to Teplitz with the next train. Then everything dissolved into farce. Frau Weil collapsed and had to be revived. Until now her anxiety had been suppressed by rushing about but now she broke down in a fit of crying. She sobbed and cried out. 'Elsa! Elsa!' They had to put the telegram in her hand, and read it out again. In the meantime the local residents, and Eichwald spa guests who had followed the entourage, were now gathered in large numbers in front of the police station. They were informed of developments, and depending on their individual characters, participated quietly or with enthusiasm in the event. Meanwhile dreadful rumours of sexually motivated murder, political plots, and railway accidents were spread around among the quiet people who came out to their garden gates to find out what was going on.

Departure

Hugo jumped onto a tram and hurried to Teplitz, feeling racked with guilt. Every jolt of the carriage reminded him. He had indeed bewitched Irene, but to no good effect. Yesterday he had been close to committing suicide and today he had almost been a criminal.

His carefree feeling had disappeared. Suddenly he could see all too clearly what he had done to Olga, Josef and little Elsa.

At the final station, Schulplatz, Councillor Weil ran towards him, saying, 'Where is my wife?'

'I think ... I have arrived before her.'

'Does she know everything?'

'Yes.'

'That the two of them have been caught?'

'Yes. We heard that at the police station.'

'Has she calmed down?'

'To some extent ... '

'Thank God!' said the other man, as he wiped the sweat from his brow. 'All I have to do now is to undo everything my wife has set in motion. Look – she even had it put on posters!' As they walked he pointed out a poster which had recently been put up. Hugo could only make out the boldly printed words – "Reward ... Kidnapping ... 11 year old girl." 'I must obviously have that taken down at once. The scandal must be suppressed. She is so hasty, so temperamental!' He departed sighing and went back to the station to wait for his wife.

Hugo felt relieved that the matter could hopefully end without too much sensation. But it made his heart feel even heavier when he thought of his behaviour towards Olga. He hardly dared to encounter her. Once home, he quickly slipped past the living room and into his room.

He opened the door. Olga was standing there, busily packing his suitcase. She came towards him: 'Hugo ... are you annoyed with me?'

'Me? Annoyed with you!'

'Please forgive me.' She grasped his hand. 'I spoiled your whole afternoon. I am not usually such a wet blanket. But today, all that nonsense really annoyed me. She didn't say anything so very bad ...'

'Oh, but bad enough, I think,' he said, sounding enraged.

'One must expect a bit of fun in a game,' she said.

He was still convinced that her attitude was a pretence. 'Olga, I just don't understand you ... you are too forbearing ... being too good can also be a fault. Instead of reproaching me for being so cruel, for failing to protect you when you were in trouble, so very cruel ...'

She put her hand over his mouth and laughed: 'Shhh ... I wouldn't want to argue with someone who is in love.'

'I'm not in love any more,' he said stamping his feet.

'Don't boast now ... you are head over heels in love ... I

could see it all afternoon. You were so deep in conversation with her. I really didn't have the heart to disturb you. You looked so happy while she was speaking to you ... so let's not talk about that.'

'It was still terrible of me!'

'What strange ideas you have.'

'I must ask you to forgive me ... please Olga.' He grasped her hand and pleaded with her. Then she became angry: 'Hugo ... if you make another scene with me, like you did yesterday evening, I would rather run away.' And when, in shock, he let her go, she said more quietly, 'You see, I have a lot to do for you ... I am only angry with you about one thing. The whole business of today would not have upset me so much if you hadn't said yesterday that I am a flirt. You see, when Irene said today that I run after men – which is a big lie – I remembered your words, and thought that perhaps there was something in it.'

'But Olga—'

'Yes, yes, let's leave it ... now it's too late.'

'But, I didn't mean it like that. We both laughed about it.'

'Good. But you said yourself, sometimes certain words stay with one ... and that's how it was with me.'

He laughed: 'With the best will in the world, I can't feel guilty about that!'

'But so that we can finish with that ... tell me the truth now, look me in the eye – am I a flirt or not? Quickly.' At that moment it was the most important thing in the world to her. Her brow was furrowed with concern.

'Not in the least. You are the best girl in the world. If only all girls were like you ...'

She touched the tip of his nose with her finger: 'Oh dear

'... it's soft ... you are lying.'

'I give you my word,' he cried, becoming heated.

'All right. Let's shake on it.' She pressed his hand firmly with hers. 'And now let's forget it.'

Cheerful once more, she bent over the suitcase again. There was nothing, absolutely nothing, in the world that could make them fight. How she worked, how everything flew under her hands, skilfully and naturally! She darted hither and thither, grace in every movement. He helped her. 'We mustn't forget the most important thing.' He pulled open a drawer in his bedside table and placed his physics textbook and exercise book in the suitcase. The notebook containing his drawings of inventions was contemptuously thrown back. 'That's staying here,' he said, but after a moment reconsidered and put it with the other books.

Olga looked up. 'When I was sitting so angrily in the tram, I realised why Irene Popper was so annoyed with me. This morning, as I came out of the house, someone spoke to me and introduced himself as Dr Winternitz of Prague. He began to ask probing questions about you and Irene. I suddenly realised that he was her former fiancé! Flora Weil told me he is always following her and finding out who she is keeping company with and how – because he is still infatuated with her. He had probably found out that you live here, etcetera and so on. I answered him cautiously. By chance Fräulein Irene came past at that moment. He greeted her. She acknowledged him, but gave me such a look – as if she would have liked to devour me. Probably she thinks that I am a competitor. And so in Eichwald it came to a head. If I had immediately understood the situation, I would certainly not have made anything of it.'

Departure

Hugo also now understood things a lot better now. Hadn't Irene wanted to question him too? He shook his head thoughtfully: 'You girls, you are all the same!'

'You girls!' repeated Olga tensely. He quietly reassured her. 'You are obviously an exception. You are the very model of an exception, Olga.' And before she could stop him he embraced her and gave her a warm kiss, which was aimed at her mouth but landed on her chin.

She wiped her face defiantly with her hand. 'That was our farewell kiss. It means you don't get one tomorrow at the station.'

He laughed. 'That's fine with me ... in front of everyone.'

'You will do as you are told,' she joked and laughed with him.

★★★

The next morning his mother and Olga accompanied Hugo to the station. He was excited to be leaving. His mother suppressed her emotion by talking continually. 'I do hope the porter will be here on time ... so, write often Hugo – but I don't need to tell you that. And we will see each other again at Christmas time ... be sensible, don't spend too much money, but don't deprive yourself of anything. Above all, look after your health ... stand up straight, don't drink when you are overheated and don't study too hard ...' The last warning really moved him, as his mother still did not know about the examination. He had told her that school was beginning fourteen days earlier than usual.

At the station he looked around expectantly. There was no sign of Irene. Had she forgotten?

His mother pressed him to get on board. 'So that you can find a good seat. Reserve it and then you can come out again.' Her tiny figure bustled restlessly backwards and forwards, hither and thither, always busy and full of ideas.

Hugo was continually afraid that Olga or his mother might say: 'Where's your good friend Irene then? She hasn't even come to the station?' He wasn't worried about her absence on his own account – what did he care about her – but the prospect of being shamed in front of these two women, who knew everything, troubled him. Meanwhile they were both too tactful to say anything about it. He thanked them from the bottom of his heart.

He looked briefly into the carriage. He would look around more during the journey, he thought nervously. He went to the window but was crowded out by other people who also wanted to say goodbye to their relatives. So he went along the narrow corridor and opened the carriage door; he stood on the step and looked at his home town again; there was so much to consider; the holidays, his elderly mother whom he was leaving alone.

Then suddenly, just before the train left, Irene rushed on to the platform accompanied by Dr Taubelis.

'The 'moustache trainer' is to blame for everything,' explained the Doctor and Hugo thought it strange that he should use Irene's nickname on himself.

She was happy and not at all overexcited, perhaps on principle, or perhaps because that was her natural self. 'What do you think about Elsa Weil?' she quickly called to Hugo. 'Yesterday night she was still with the police. She's got a future that one, don't you think? She'll drive a lot of men mad—.'

'Probably,' he replied coldly and turned to his mother: 'You will write to me soon, won't you? Write today about what you've done in the afternoon.'

Irene didn't seem to notice anything: 'And have you heard the latest. Nussbaum and his son have disappeared. Just left. Probably he will never come back to Teplitz. His relations will naturally have every reason to use yesterday's fun against him. The morning papers are full of it. Haven't you read any of them? They are making a sensation out of it. They made a terrible noise in the night. And after his big success at the meeting, too. His popularity won't survive it, so he preferred to run away.'

Hugo couldn't help smiling at how wide the ripples were that his ten Guilders had initiated. After all the storms he had endured, he believed he had a right to smile about his own escapade. He was in rather a melancholy mood.

But Irene hadn't yet finished speaking: 'And the very latest news is that Kamilla Popper and Pitroff are saying they're engaged. Aren't you surprised?'

He made no reply. He was not in the mood for jokes. The conductor whose job it was to shut the doors was approaching. 'So, keep well.' He held out a limp hand. 'Goodbye, Mama.' He leaned down to embrace her. He hesitated for a moment. Should he embarrass himself in front of Irene? Then he gave Olga a quick kiss anyway, as had been the custom in the family for years.

The door was shut. A quiet whistle was followed by the small jolt that almost unnoticed starts the train moving, and yet, like the deepest cut, separates the present from the future.

'Goodbye!' they called after him.

He leaned out. Irene waved with big slow movements, similar to those with which she had applauded Nussbaum. Dr

Taubelis waved his hat. Olga ran alongside the train as far as the end of the waiting room. His mother stood there looking very serious. The train turned a bend in the track; black and white smoke blew past the window.

★★★

He moved into his old apartment in Prague with its curved sofa on which one couldn't lie and its uninviting bare dark walls. He studied. He forgot about everything else. He applied himself to his learning with the same heroic enthusiasm with which he had survived worse dangers. And without the hindrances that had troubled him in Teplitz things went very well for him.

The examination was on the fourteenth of September. He passed so well that the Professor gave him a big smile and said: 'Now, Rosenthal. If you had only known an eighth as much before the holidays you would not have failed.'

He went home glowing and then he did something which he had been looking forward to the whole time: he wrote a long and detailed letter to Olga. He thanked her in passionate terms, saying that she had been his only salvation at a dreadful time in his life.

But then after all the excitement he felt completely empty. What now? School would begin in two days' time, but he felt so little interest in it that he preferred not to think about the new year. His enthusiasm for inventing had gone. Theatre? He was short of money – he no longer had the twenty Krone. Should he go to the Hetzinsel? Gretl had not answered any of his many postcards. He was sure he no longer loved her. Although his passion for Irene had now gone, before it left

Departure

it had extinguished his old love for Gretl; he'd decided not to have anything more to do with her. Olga answered his letter. She had become engaged to Herr Klein. And Irene? She had sent him a card from Teplitz, was by now in Prague and had even written to him once. But nothing drew him to her; in fact he felt reluctant to see her, because the fact that he had passed his examinations seemed to him some kind of betrayal, a secession from common misfortune.

Then one morning, as he wandered gloomily through the back streets with his thoughts fixed on Teplitz, someone suddenly clapped him on the shoulder. 'Hello!' Alfred Popper stood in front of him. 'Good morning. How are you?' he said to Hugo who was shaken to the core. 'Things are not going so well with me, but you might at least have congratulated us, you dope—'

'On what?'

'You don't even know! Irene has got engaged!'

'I don't read any newspapers,' Hugo stammered in dismay.

'And you want to be a politician. Oh, you don't—'

'But who is she engaged to, tell me!' He could already see the dreaded name Winternitz on his lips.

'What a question! With Dr Taubelis obviously.'

Hugo was completely astonished: 'Obviously? I can hardly believe it ...'

Alfred took him by the arm: 'He was favourably received right from the start ... and what dear Irene wants, she gets. What's more, you were in the best position to know as she got on so well with you.'

'She didn't say a word to me about it.'

'Sounds just like her! All tricks and secrets! Irene Taubelis, sounds good doesn't it?'

'Are you really such an anti-Semite?' asked Hugo anxiously. He usually held back such comments but in his confusion he let this one slip out.

Alfred ignored the question, perhaps intentionally. 'My consolation is that Irene Popper wasn't much better.'

'How well do they get on together?' Hugo was finding it hard to imagine. Dr Taubelis with his salesman's manners and his earthy roughness. So that pleased Irene then – his robust manliness. Hugo pictured him with his bare chest, standing in the bowling alley in his shirt sleeves. And he had broad shoulders too.

'How well do they get on together? How should I know! How can anyone know with these Jewish women. They are like camp followers, calculating through and through.' He pressed closer to Hugo. 'You see, we men are much too pure-minded, too honest in our idealistic view of life! They enticed me to Teplitz. I must get the two of them together, according to the decision of our family "council". Didn't you see all of that? Don't you ever notice anything? Then you're a real fool! I had to have a small eye inflammation, nothing worth speaking of, treated by Dr Taubelis, so that he would visit us more often. Irene was alone with him, because it was my job to "forget" the occasional appointment. So everything went according to plan, all by itself. To this day the lucky bridegroom has no idea! And once they no longer needed me in Teplitz, I was simply sent home again. "The Moor had done his duty".[28] They were worried that I might disturb the second, Kamilla-Pitroff plan if I stayed.'

'Because of the public meeting,' laughed Hugo.

'That was a laugh wasn't it!' said Alfred, flattered. 'They won't forget me in a hurry! One mustn't let these women get away with everything, these family "councils". That's my guiding principle now. In the end we will triumph with our German *Weltanschauung*.'[29]

Hugo did not feel comfortable with what Alfred was saying, even though he agreed with much of it. But the most important nuance was missing, something tender and melodious which he felt, without being able to express it – something noble and Jewish at the same. He felt it, although he had not experienced it himself.

Finally Alfred invited him to visit them. 'Come with me now!'

Hugo's heart skipped a beat: 'Now? This morning?'

'Just come and pay your respects today. And next time you can stay longer.'

In the end Hugo allowed himself to be persuaded. His feet felt heavy as they approached Stefansgasse. They passed the old church and reached Lindengasse.

'Here we are already,' said Alfred.

'In this house?' Hugo's voice trembled. Although Irene had placed particular emphasis on describing where she lived, until now he had imagined a completely different house whenever he thought about it. But from the moment Alfred had shown him the right house, Hugo could no longer remember the one which he had pictured to himself.

They went in and were met with a strong smell, cool, cleansing and yet somehow unpleasant.

'What's that?' asked Hugo.

'Ah, you mean the liqueur! I've already got used to that. There's a spirits business in the house. I hardly notice it anymore.'

Strange, thought Hugo, that Irene hadn't told him about

Jewish Women

such an important aspect. It fundamentally changed his mental picture of her. Not for the good, nor for the bad. Nevertheless it brought her down a bit, that she had to live in such a house – brought her nearer to his level.

While Alfred was ringing the bell, Hugo took a few steps back from the door. 'Coming?' asked Alfred, and looked over his shoulder for him as he went in.

They entered a dark hall.

'Come in here!' Alfred led the way into a small room off the courtyard. There were crossed swords on the wall under a barred fencing mask. Nearby hung Dürer's self-portrait, in colour, and some reproductions from the 'Kunstwart Folders'.[30] Medical texts lay strewn over the bed. 'I have to take my viva soon,' explained Alfred and called to the next room: 'Irene, I have a visitor for you!'

She appeared in the doorway in a yellowish dressing gown, the same as when Hugo had visited her when she was ill: 'Herr Hugo!'

He blushed: 'I must apologise—'

'No. Please don't.' She laughed and came towards him in a lively manner. 'Come back, all is forgiven ... now you are here with us, and it looks like a pigsty.'

She led him through a living room to the drawing room. The light bourgeois elegance of that room compared very favourably with Alfred's spartan apartment. As they walked she spoke to Hugo in a very friendly way. 'So how are things with you ... I have been expecting you every day. We have been in Prague for four days already.'

'I had a lot to do – problems.'

'You always have problems,' she laughed gaily, and clapped her hands near to his face, while making a noise which

Departure

sounded like 'pshh', as one makes when shooing away a bird. 'But now you must sit down nicely next to me.' She pulled a chair up to the sofa.

'First let me congratulate you! I have only heard today, from Herr Alfred, and that's why I came straightaway ... I was truly very pleased—'

She beamed and took his hands in hers: 'It was a surprise, wasn't it!'

'I wish you all the happiness you can imagine,' he said warmly, pleasantly moved by her warmth.

'I know that you are a good friend to me. And you will remain so. Now tell me, how are things with you?'

She was actually asking about what was happening with him! Astonished, he hesitantly told her that he had passed his examination and would therefore go up to the Seventh grade. Yes, he too was to be congratulated! For a moment he thought of continuing with the comparison – saying that they could both now leave their secret unhappiness behind. But then it seemed to him that it would be tactless to refer again to the sad past, and he suppressed the observation. 'When will the wedding take place?' he asked.

'We are getting married in November,' Irene told him eagerly. 'Then we will travel to Paris and from there to London. We both know Italy already and it seems too ordinary for a honeymoon. I will show my husband London, and he will show me Paris. He actually studied there. You see, he views ophthalmology from a completely different standpoint from our local doctors. He wants to set up an Institute here following the French model, and he has already explained their methods to me.' She chattered on happily. Hugo stared and stared at the changes that had come over her. She looked ten years younger. The lines under her eyes had disappeared and also the sullen downturn at the corners of her mouth, so that her cheeks looked fuller. Her figure, which was admittedly somewhat concealed by the dressing gown, seemed fuller too.

'So this is your home,' he said, as he finally turned his glance away from her pretty face. 'Here you have lived your life ...'

'We will be living in Niklasstrasse,' she continued. 'It will look nicer than this place. Only modern furniture, modelled on the Viennese style. Chic, chicer and chicest.' She was as happy as a child. 'I will take only my childhood bedroom furniture with me, my fiancé would like that. Just imagine, Hugo! He is so interested in everything about me and what I have experienced.' In response to a questioning look from Hugo she said, 'Obviously I have told him everything ... You should also know, that Dr Winternitz has moved to Vienna – so that nightmare is over for ever.' She ran quickly to the next room and pushed the door open. 'Come in here.'

Her childhood bedroom, which she had spoken about so much, disappointed him a little. It turned out to be a single-windowed white affair, decorated with flowery wallpaper. The most noticeable thing about it was a mirrored wardrobe. 'Very nice,' said Hugo, somewhat embarrassed.

She didn't notice anything, but showed him a pair of pictures. A book on ophthalmology lay on the bookshelf. 'I borrowed it from Alfred,' she explained. 'I want to surprise my fiancé.' Then she pointed at a big framed photograph standing on her writing desk. 'That's Frieda Schwarz whom I told you so much about. We became reconciled again the day before yesterday.'

So everything is coming right, Hugo said to himself.

Departure

And he experienced a substantial feeling of relief that Irene looked in such good form and so happy. Until today he had felt himself under a certain obligation to her, as if he had to look after her. Now he was relieved of that task, and instead of perhaps feeling jealous of Taubelis, felt honestly grateful to him and wished him every success in his plans and for his future with Irene. And she had managed it all by herself! Now that the unpleasantness had gone, happiness brought out all her best features. She kindly offered him a plate of pastries: 'All home-made! I am now attending cookery classes. It's a lot of fun.'

They chatted for a long time. They spoke of their memories of their first meeting. He asked her with concern, whether she still sometimes suffered from her anxiety attacks. No sign of them in the last week! Then she took a small book from her pocket. 'I bought this for myself today ... Kant's *Prolegomena*. Apparently it's the easiest thing he wrote. And also very short.' He leafed through it in front of her. 'If one can have all his wisdom together in a few pages, that's certainly very attractive.' She took back the book and looked through it, but did not remember the agreement she had made in Teplitz. He asked about acquaintances. Pitroff was still in Teplitz. He was so in love that he couldn't make up his mind to go home, although the wedding wouldn't take place until next year. And Nussbaum? 'Were you really in love with him?' Hugo ventured to ask. Irene laughed at him. 'That old comedian. He didn't interest me in the least.' 'And what about at the public meeting!' 'That was a joke. I was very excited, because from what Alfred had said, I guessed that there would be a demonstration against him. All I could think of was – when is it going to happen?'

Mr and Mrs Popper appeared, back from a walk. They greeted him in a very friendly manner.

When he made motions to leave – he had seen the preparations for lunch set out in a neighbouring room – Irene called: 'But you can't do that. Obviously you will stay with us, you are our guest!' He put up some resistance, but a place at the table had already been set for him. 'Please, see for yourself, six places. My fiancé also eats here, it will be very pleasant.' Having seen what had been laid out, he couldn't put up any further resistance.

A note of harmless smugness, which he had not previously noticed, permeated all Irene's conversation. Was it due to the influence of her sweetheart, to whom she had so quickly and cleverly adapted, or was it her natural self, which had been suppressed by the trials to which she had been subjected? Now she fitted charmingly into this family, which was a bit rowdy but basically good-hearted. '*Herrgott*, I'm starving,' called the father, 'does no one have any consideration for an exhausted businessman! Just a joke, just a joke,' he said turning to Hugo as he tucked in his serviette.

The doorbell rang. Irene hurried out and came back cuddling up close to Dr Taubelis. 'Excuse him,' she said, 'he had a lot to do.' Dr Taubelis nodded. Then she pointed to Hugo, who had stood up – 'An old friend of the family.'

The engaged couple were madly in love with each other. They had to be reminded from time to time to eat something. Alfred suggested telegraphing the fire brigade as they were glowing so hotly. The doctor kissed Irene's finger tips; she stroked his hands.

'I think perhaps you are short-sighted,' she turned to Hugo and said when he did not recognise a certain vegetable.

Departure

'Can you read that business sign?' She pointed through the window to the house opposite. 'You should soon have yourself examined by my fiancé!'

'I call that advertising,' cried her father, laughing.

Taubelis seemed blissfully happy. 'I can see that my wife will support me in word and deed ... Irene?' He was anxious, because she had stood up next to him.

'I'm coming back ... I'm just seeing to the coffee.'

When she came back, Hugo gripped his wineglass and raised it. 'To the betrothed couple!' It seemed like a dream that he could participate in so much happiness.

As evening came on, he was finally released from the joyful entertainment and he hurried to the Graben. His heart felt free and transformed. He was gripped by a sudden nostalgia for his school, a burning curiosity, or perhaps the desire to be busy. He looked for school friends and found them. Suddenly he felt closer to them, a boy among boys. 'Which teachers are we getting this year?' They mentioned some names. He interrupted with comments like: 'Oh no, that one likes to give a B – that one is clever – that one is a mean examiner!' They talked about the setting up of a *Kommerskassa*[31] for the banquet which would take place in two years' time, after the *Matura*. They wanted to set up a *Kneipe*[32] here and there during that year. Naturally some of them were enthusiastic about wearing fraternity colours. Hugo bought exercise books and pens, wandered through the side streets with friends, listened to what they had done during their holidays and talked about his. Then he made his way to bookshops and antiquarians, ordered whole cargos of textbooks, took out what he found suitable immediately and impatiently leafed through them as he walked around. He paused excitedly to think about mysterious lines – how that would all be made clear. 'See you tomorrow at school,' he called. 'Where will you be sitting? I will be sitting in the third row, that's the best – one is in front, looks hardworking, but can cheat better than in the first or second.'

'I will sit next to you.'

'If the Professor doesn't separate us.'

He was so tired that once in bed he fell into a deep, refreshing sleep.

And now, sleep my boy, little Hugo. Good night, my dear! Rest, just as you are doing, and become mature and strong. Grow up a little, before you venture into life. Stay a child for a little longer, that is my advice to you. Leave your inventions for now and instead learn your physics diligently. Leave the girls alone until you are older, and then they won't run away. What you have been doing up to now was too early. Premature, as you said yourself; passing infatuations. No searching for fruit before the blossom – that is the universal rule which you must accept, my eager young friend! First learn, then invent. First look around carefully, take your time, and then you will find the right girl, the great shining love, who will make you happy. All in all, I think that you will become something decent and worthwhile, my dear young man. And even if ministers don't wait in your entrance lobby, as you once boasted they would, you will do something significant and useful – I am sure of that. In any case, *you* should be convinced of it. Strive, fight on, as your noble heart dictates. Forwards! And now, one last thing – good luck!

Notes

[1] First published in Berlin by Axel Juncker in 1911, Brod's *Jüdinnen* was reprinted in Leipzig by Kurt Wolff in 1915. Wallstein Verlag issued a new edition in 2013 as part of a series edited by Hans-Gerd Koch and Hans Dieter Zimmermann. The Brod Estate, awarded in 2016 to the National Library of Israel after a controversial series of trials in Israeli courts, includes the Max Brod-Axel Juncker correspondence.

[2] See Gaëlle Vassogne, *Max Brod in Prag. Identität und Vermittlung*, 2009, and Mark H. Gelber, 'Max Brod's Zionist Writings', *Yearbook of the Leo Baeck Institute* 23 (1988), pp. 437-48. For an account of Brod's encounter with Buber, see his autobiography *Streitbares Leben*, Kindler Verlag, 1960, p. 79.

[3] Quoted in Hans Dieter Zimmermann, afterword to Max Brod, *Jüdinnen. Roman und andere Prosa aus den Jahren 1906–1916*, Wallstein Verlag, 2013 [my translation].

[4] *The Diaries of Franz Kafka*, edited by Max Brod, Schocken, 1988, pp. 45-46. Kafka scholar Hartmut Binder suggests that in this passage Kafka was writing

under the influence of a highly critical review of Brod's novel by Hugo Herrmann, secretary of the Zionist Organization of Bohemia, chairman of the Bar Kochba Association (a Zionist society in Prague), and editor of *Selbstwehr* (Self-Defense), Prague's Zionist political and literary weekly. Herrmann argued that *Jüdinnen* could not qualify as a 'Jewish' novel, nor even as a 'novel'; it was instead a 'Darstellung' (representation or depiction) of the most ordinary Jews. Using a fictive prosecutor and advocate, Herrmann puts *Jüdinnen* on trial, and judges that Brod could have lent justification to the Zionist cause had he written into the novel an antagonistic non-Jewish presence (*Selbstwehr*, May 19, 1911, p. 3; and see Brod's rebuttal in *Selbstwehr*, May 26, 1911, p. 1).

5 Nadine Gordimer, 'Letter from His Father', *The Threepenny Review*, Summer 1984, p. 4.

6 For more on Brod's view of Jewish women, see his essay 'Jüdinnen', *Neue jüdische Monatshefte* (July 25, 1918).

7 Selbstwehr, June 25-30, 1913, p. 4.

8 Weininger published his infamous book *Geschlecht und Charakter* (Sex and Character) in 1903, eight years before Brod published *Jewish Women*. The Austrian scholar Gerald Steig called it 'the psychological-metaphysical prelude for National Socialism'. For an accessible English translation, see *Sex and Character*, translated from the German by Ladislaus Lob, Indiana University Press, 2005.

9 *Gymnasium* – a secondary school emphasizing academic learning.

10 *Realgymnasium* – a gymnasium focussing on modern languages.

Notes

[11] *Grossstadt* – the big city.

[12] *Antiefen* – go into deeply.

[13] A *Couleur* student was one who showed his membership of a particular student society by wearing their colours e.g. ribbons on a cap.

[14] A reference to the threefold principle of weight/balance/support in Greek classical architecture.

[15] Biedermeier architecture (developed in Europe between 1815 and 1845) is marked by simplicity and elegance.

[16] Schwabing was famous as Munich's bohemian quarter.

[17] Lit. – 'Too much or too little is the same thing.'

[18] A Henrystutzen is a fictional gun probably based on the Henry repeater rifle.

[19] A marble bust at the corner of Lipova Steet, commemorates the German Romantic poet and writer, Johann Gottfried Seume (1763-1810) who lived in Teplice for the last two years of his life.

[20] *Amor praematurus* – immature love.

[21] A Trumeau was a mirror originally designed in France in the 18th century.

[22] *Über-aschung* (lit. over-ashing) *Überraschung* (surprise).

[23] 'Bunte Reihe' means placing persons at a table or in company so that there is always a gentleman sitting next to a lady.

[24] From *Der Jäger Abschied* by Felix Mendelssohn.

[25] Max Reinhardt (born Goldmann in 1873 in Baden, near Vienna) was a very successful theatrical director.

[26] *Grobheiten* – lit. rude remarks.

[27] *Polterabend* is a German wedding custom in which on the night before the wedding the guests break porcelain to bring luck to the couple's marriage.

28 'The Moor has done his duty. The Moor can go.' From Friedrich Schiller's play 'Fiesco'.
29 *Weltanschauung* – world view, philosophy of life.
30 *Der Kunstwart* (The Guardian of Art) was a magazine founded in Dresden in 1887 by Ferdinand Avenarius.
31 *Kommers* is a traditional academic feast taking place at universities in most Central and Northern European countries.
32 *Kneipe* – a celebratory drinking evening for those having taken the *Matura* (final leaving exam).